FORTY-EIGHT HOURS
OF
DEATH

TERROR IN THE HEARTLAND

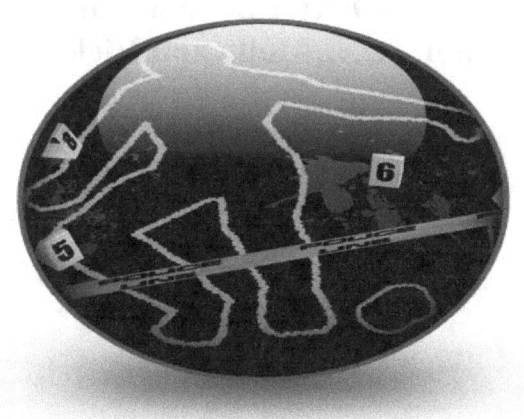

Author

Patrick Pritchard

DEDICATION

**This book is dedicated to the two women
who are the light of my life and inspire me
to be a better person than I
am………Molly and Vicki.**

Forty-Eight Hours of Death

Terror in the Heartland

PRELUDE

Greg Tenant was puzzled. Normally, the auditing of a non-profit organization was fairly mundane. That was not true in this case. Greg was a CPA with the Norris and Finch, Inc. Financial Services Group on assignment to audit the books of the Citizens Group Foundation, a nonprofit organization in Wheaton, Kansas. The foundation mission was to monitor and lobby against governmental tax increases at the state and local level. While reviewing the organization's computerized ledger of expenditures Greg had come across several entries that were unusually large outlays. The recipient of the expended funds was something called SADIL-110601. When Greg brought the entries up to the chief accountant at the exit meeting he was told that the issue would be researched and the information forwarded to him in a couple of days. Greg thought that to be somewhat odd, since the outlays totaled over seven million dollars. Most Chief Accountants would know the precise details of such outlays. Greg made a notation in his preliminary report to follow up on the entries. As was his practice he emailed his preliminary report to his own email address at work in case something happened to the hard copy.

Greg was late getting on the road, because he had to check out of the hotel and gas up. It was a blustery cold December evening as he headed north on I-35 anxious to get home to his wife, two girls, and warm bed.

The sky was steel gray, and the wind was sweeping across the Flint Hills which made driving all the more challenging than usual on the Interstate. Greg wished that he was driving his own car, but instead he had a company issued car which was unfamiliar to him. Unknown to Greg he was being followed.

While Greg was checking out of the motel a secret meeting was being held outside of Wheaton in a remote location known as 'The Barn'.

"Alright who gave Tenant the wrong computer printout to review? Is someone deliberately trying to expose us?"

"I believe that to be the case," answered Dan Sexton, Chief of Security.

"We have a mole in the organization. Whoever ran the print out used my access number, and I know for damn sure it wasn't me. At the time and date the print out was ran I was in a meeting with the bank president. I have a good idea who it might be, and I'll handle the matter. We need to get our hands on that preliminary report and destroy it, before someone starts asking some hard questions."

"I think Mr. Tenant will need to have an unfortunate accident. Make the arrangements immediately."

"Arrangements have already been made," said Sexton.

Lester Davis was a highly skilled professional driver who hired out his talents to the highest bidder. A former formula three race driver he knew how to handle a car under all kinds of conditions. Lester had a rather unique skill of creating situations that caused other folks to have accidents....usually fatal accidents. It was not necessary to ram the other vehicle or even bump it. Lester's skill was in forcing the other driver to panic and over compensate. The result most often was a one car fatal accident. Lester had honed these skills on the race track when pitted against professional drivers. It was much easier to effect with the ordinary everyday driver.

As Greg Tenant began to negotiate an S curve in the road, the car behind him had moved up almost bumper to bumper and hit his high beam head lights.

"What the hell is that fool trying to do," questioned Greg. "The bastard is tailgating me with his high beams on"

As Greg reached up to adjust his rear view mirror to compensate for the bright lights, the fool swerved around him. It looked to Greg like he was going to side swipe him, thus Greg swerved to avoid a collision with one hand on the wheel. His hand was sweaty and slipped off the steering wheel causing Greg to lose control at the S curve.

The last thing that Greg remembered on this earth was the scenery swirling around him, and then a crash and everything went black.

Lester pulled over to the side of the road jumped out of his car and sprinted toward the wrecked vehicle. Immediately he saw that Greg Tenant's neck was broken and a piece of jagged metal had penetrated his juggler vein. Lester quickly found and retrieved the preliminary report in Tenant's brief case. Several cars had parked on the side of the road and Lester shouted to them to call 911. After helping others to secure the area, Davis walked back to his car and made his phone call.

All he said was, "Mission Accomplished."

CHAPTER 1

DISCOVERY

The night moves in like a spreading ink blot masked by dark, swirling cloud cover. Lightning flashes and the thunder rumbles like a monstrous bass drum reverberating across the countryside sending ripples through the body. A bolt of lightning acting like a strobe light flickers across the partially clothed bone-white body lying in a brownish muck of a ditch a few feet from the black-top asphalt road.

Cars speed by…. snapshots of the strobe lightening….. heading for anywhere unaware that a life had been snuffed, quick and clean, barely at their momentary door step. A thumb tack size hole behind the ear, barely noticeable underneath a thatch of blonde hair, had rendered a body perpetually in motion…motionless. A life has been ended. Someone that had meant something to souls touched, flesh caressed, thoughts of a child, then a woman who had occupied space and other people's lives, until the cold, calculated hole had been carved behind the ear. Someone's grown child was silent, forever.

The night storm passed, the air was sweet and washed clean with the morning of new promise and passion.

The rising amber morning sun dissolved the remnants of the rain drenched soil and the trees whispered with the help of the cool, gentle breeze "dust to dust, ashes to ashes…another soul breaks the bonds of earth".

I kept my steady pace along the asphalt path, my breathing unlabored at the three mile mark. I gathered my thoughts for the day sorting through what had to be done.…a great American need for daily planning passed down from generation to generation…like a sort of mental smallpox. I never had a problem with this simple process; but sometimes I preferred to let events unfold without thought or preamble.

Why I had a tendency sometimes to land into the middle of other folk's problems was a great mystery of my life. Like I didn't have enough problems of my own. Take my name for instances. Needless to say, not many have a name that transcends history. Every time I had to pronounce my name, it evoked stunned disbelief and a refrain of "What did you say your name was?"

"My name is Abe Lincoln."

"What? What's your name? You're kidding me, right? No one would name their kid Abe Lincoln. Honest Abe? Come on, you're putting me on!"

My parents should have thought ahead to the consequences of their actions before giving me a name like Abraham. I envied those with a name like Bob, or Bill or Jim.

The folks had a real sense of humor, but it never seemed too funny to me. You can imagine the torment that I experienced all through school. I learned to fight at an early age. I always thought that it would be great to be able to pick your own name anyway. Maybe, the bureaucrats could issue you a temporary name until you were able to decide.

I enjoyed running after a morning rain. Everything smelled fresh and new. The leaves on the trees glistened with rain drops. The earth seemed to have been reborn in primeval clay with life and promise for a new day.

I could still sense the electricity in the air from the previous night's storm...but my senses told me that something was not right......something was out of sync and didn't fit. Caught in the corner of my eye was the sight of a mangy coyote emerging from the murky ditch a few feet to the right of the roadway with something that looked like a piece of raw meat in its jaws...then scurry away beneath the scrub brush into a grove of dogwood trees.

I stopped in my tracks, walked to where the coyote had emerged. I gazed down into the dirty brown mire of the ditch. Before me was the dead body of a blond female, partially clothed, and missing two fingers on the left hand. I was startled by the beauty of the women even in death. Her sky blue eyes stare fixed and straight ahead.

I quickly recovered and ran back to my truck to call the local sheriff's office on my cell phone.

I didn't want the coyote to come back and reclaim his prize; therefore I removed my windbreaker in order to cover the body to keep any predators away until I could return. Most critters shied away from fresh human scent for a while.

On the way back to the truck I wondered how the poor soul had died in that ditch beside the road. She hadn't looked more than 25-30 years old, in fairly good shape and obviously a beauty in life. No doubt it was some kind of foul play...a jealous lover or drug related. None of my business. Let the sheriff figure it out, although Fremont County hadn't had more than one homicide in three years.

Probably someone had killed her elsewhere and decided to dump the body in this remote area. But why in a ditch beside a fairly busy roadway, unless the person or person(s) had panicked, or maybe they didn't know that the road was well traveled. Go figure. Had to be an urbanite, no local person would be that dumb.

I reached the truck that was parked on the shoulder of the road within a few minutes, hopped in, called 911, revved the engine, and went back to the site where the body lay undisturbed.

The dispatcher had promised to send a deputy. I tried not to trample too much in the immediate area for fear of contaminating the crime scene, but I wanted to search the perimeter for possible clues.

I found no clues.

Most probably the victim had been dumped into the ditch without the person or person(s) committing the crime ever leaving the vehicle.

I wondered about the young lady's family. Were they searching for her? How had she gotten herself into this situation? What chain of events had conspired to bring her to a death bed in a cold mucky ditch beside a road? Maybe she had been kidnapped, although there didn't seem to be and signs of a struggle or of her being bound or gagged. Would some mother or father, or husband be pacing the floor waiting to hear from her?

These were the times that I was thankful for still being single. The agony of a learning your child had been lying dead in a ditch would be horrific. I'd seen more than enough misery in my thirty-five years.

The sheriff's car approached from the west at a rapid pace. He parked his vehicle on the shoulder of the road opposite the ditch, and Deputy Jess Davis eased his 290 pound frame from under the steering column. Jess stood 6'7" and was intimidating just sitting in the car. He was an easy going bear of a man who was noted for his gentle nature and slowness to anger…but when he was riled look out. He cleaned out a whole bar of ranch hands one night that had gotten into a brawl.

They made the mistake of not taking Jess seriously when he told them to cool it. In fact they had taunted him by calling him the Pillsbury Dough Boy…big mistake.

"Hi, Abe. What we got here?"

"Hi, Jess. Looks like someone was anxious to get rid of a body. I was out for my usual morning jog along the road and spotted a coyote climbing out of the ditch with what looked like a piece of meat in its' jaws. When I reached this side of the ditch I discovered the body. Looks like she's been here most of the night. I looked around the perimeter, but found nothing. Whoever it was tossed the body into the ditch and drove on."

"Well, I've got a call in for the coroner and the crime scene investigators, so I'll just secure the area. " Jess stated. "I can take a statement from you now, or you can come down to the office later, Abe. Your choice."

"Might as well do it now. Looks like my morning jog will get cut short…no big deal."

"Let me take a look around then get the paperwork…be back in a minute", said Jess.

"Need any help?"

"Naw, just stay put, Abe. Sheriff don't like no civilians involved in these things. Too many legal complications these days", said Jess.

Jess lumbered down into the ditch to take a closer look at the body to determine if he could find the cause of death. He had to make sure not to move the body until the coroner could do his business.

Man, she sure was a looker, no question about that...even in death she looked almost angelic. Jess did notice that she was partially clothed in some sort of business suit which made her seem out of place in these surroundings.

Looking closer he noted a trickle of dried blood in the temple area...and what looked to be a bruise or powder burn behind the ear. Jess had been around crime scenes long enough to know about execution type killings...and this had the look of one. Most of the time this type of killing was related to a drug deal gone bad, but all that would be pure speculation until the crime scene boys and the coroner completed their reports. Problem was she didn't look the type.

Jess checked the area around the body but saw nothing that could pass as a clue or evidence...particularly since the ditch still was muddy from the storm of the previous night. He moved out of the ditch and searched in a circular arc the ground and bushes closest to the ditch but found nothing of any significance. Perhaps, Abe was right after all...maybe whoever did this just dumped the body and drove on...like it was nothing but worrisome human trash.

Maybe the crime scene crew will come up with hair or fiber evidence which could lead to DNA. Not that it will help a great deal without a suspect.

Jess hated this kind of scene...no clues, no evidence, unless they found something on or under the body...and more than likely another unsolvable killing. If it wasn't a crime of passion like a jealous boyfriend, husband or relative, then chances of solving it were slim. Unless she could be tied into the drug scene and there were eyewitnesses, forget it.

To complicate matters, it was fast becoming obvious that this wasn't the killing ground...which means it could have happened almost anywhere within at the minimum a hundred mile radius. If it was an execution style killing, forget the crime of passion angle in most cases...unless the person was totally deranged. So much for speculation...better get the paperwork started.

"Hey, Abe!" said Jess. "I'll be there in a sec...sorry to keep you waiting".

"Well, did you find anything?"

Jess came over with clipboard in hand.

"Naw, just that she's a very pretty lady, and no one left any obvious clues", said Jess.

"Looks like she was dressed for a business conference...now this is just speculation between friends...but it looks as though she may have been shot execution style. I'd have to agree with you that it looks like someone just dumped her by the road and moved on.

Guess we better leave things in the hands of the crime scene boys for now," said Jess. "We aren't going to solve this one standing here jawing."

I gave Jess the essential information needed for his statement and by the time we were finished, the crime scene investigators and coroner were busy doing their work. It was quickly established that the young woman had been shot behind the right ear with the bullet proceeding at an angle into the brain. No exit wound was evident which meant a small caliber bullet.

Death was instantaneous, and the killing did have the markings of an execution. There were no appearances of a struggle or any restraints. More than likely the assault came without warning. Perhaps she had a split second to realize her fate, and then the life spilled out of her quickly with little time for anguish.

***

I pondered the whole scene as I jumped into my truck. Although I knew not much happened in this relatively quiet rural area, the world was becoming a very strange place indeed. 9-11, the Unabomber, Oklahoma City, Waco and Littleton, Colorado were changing the character of this country, and I was wary of the trend in increased mass violence.

It seemed as though people were becoming more unpredictable, short tempered and prone to resort to violence to solve their frustrations and anger. For all of the new technology and electronic means for people to communicate, it appeared that people were more isolated than ever.

As I headed down the road, the more I thought about the seemingly senseless killing the angrier I got.

Whatever the woman had done, I doubted that she had deserved to die in that fashion...like a meaningless piece of garbage on a deserted road...being gnawed in death by a coyote...just one more piece of meat on the food chain. My understanding of people grew less and less each year.

It was my sometimes belief that humanity was entering into another era of barbarianism...with random acts of violence becoming the norm, and the unprotected huddling behind their security alarm systems...traveling in twos and threes...and staying away from certain sectors or staked out territories in the city or even the countryside after dark. People were buying security patrols, guns, and dogs and their own arsenal of weaponry with a siege mentality.

The barbarians of the twenty-first century would be far more lethal and deadly than in the past with the advent of technology and instant knowledge of weaponry through the Internet....mass transportation, mass communication, mass hysteria equals mass catastrophe.

It was not like humanity had any real time to prepare or counter this phenomenon, because it was here in real time …in every village and city and country of the globe…just turn on the idiot tube and it was unfolding before your eyes…or being instantly replayed like some macabre sporting event.

Sometimes I thought about packing up and moving to some isolated spot that was too barren for anyone to care about or notice and let it all blow over or up for that matter. But then again there weren't too many of those places left…and it really didn't seem to matter where you lived anymore. The barbarians would find you.

I pulled into the driveway of The Lodge. As I unfolded from the front seat, I wished that I could regain that certainty about life that came with youth, but too many dark events had conspired over the years to believe otherwise. Jane Doe will be just another statistic on the human misery indicator. Nobody saw anything; a story that's becoming all too frequent these days.

Later this one really began to eat on me. She didn't appear to be a druggie…or someone who might be mixed up in that trade. There weren't any of the telltale signs of a user at least. But then, things aren't always as they seem and people are just simply harder to read these days.

People do strange things for material gain….Tis sadly a twice told tale.....too often repeated. I have been continually surprised by what people will do for a buck.

I didn't like the idea that people thought that they could come around here dumping bodies in my neighborhood thinking that no one gives a damn. End of story. Just once I would like to see someone brought to justice to prove that some people still care about solving these heinous crimes. I had a strange feeling that there was more to this murder than was evident.

I had been known to get involved in situations from time to time. I called them projects. Call me a sort of half-ass adventurer...in some ways a private detective without portfolio or license. Occasionally, friends or an acquaintance of a friend would ask me to find things or fix problems when all else had failed using the official law or the private for-hire law.

Maybe in a sense I felt responsible, since I found the body. Most folks just don't want to get involved anymore...to busy living the American dream, while the society around then erodes. I'm not built that way. When things went wrong or something didn't add up, I wanted to straighten it out, fix it.

More often than not it got me into some real tight spots, but it made my life interesting and gave me a sense of purpose and direction. Sometimes you just gotta draw a line and say enough is enough.

CHAPTER 2

MARI'S STORY

Mari Denton was a co-host of a local morning radio show, "The Mari and Dave Morning Show". She had wanted to be in radio for as long as she could remember...certainly since age 9. Mari loved music and had a natural curiosity about people. Since high school she had worked at the local station doing odd jobs, running errands and observing the local talent.

She didn't have any formal, professional training, thus she had to take what she could get in the way of real experience. Mari had a smooth radio voice and was generally at ease in public. She and Dave Brewster began working in high school as DJs for afternoon and evening teen music shows and were able to build a business as DJs for local dances, weddings, birthdays and similar events.

Dave and Mari had built a good on-air rapport with each other and after high school were offered a morning slot to play country music, report the news and weather and promote special events and features. The rest is history. Their show became the top morning show in the area.

It was evident that they loved what they did. Dave and Mari had always been good friends. Their on air chemistry didn't carry over to their personal lives which probably helped them keep their on-air relationship going without the dangers that a personal relationship might have produced.

Dave was married with a child on the way, and Mari had begun to explore greener pastures.

Mari had taken a break that evening from taping a segment for the show and dropped by the local watering hole for a beer.

She was sitting at the bar listening to Elaine Myers, the evening bartender and owner, who was talking about her latest flame when her attention was captured by a certain gentleman sitting in the back of the room….dark wavy $25 styled hair cut with an expensive looking polo shirt and slacks….a casual, sensual looking man who looked out of place in this setting.

He might have frequented up-scale bars in high class hotels…but not a local bar she thought. He was well tanned and had boyish good looks with soft brown eyes, a square jaw line, with a trim body that one could get only from regular fitness workouts.

In short, he was a hunk…but what was he doing here…in this place?

What was more remarkable was that he had totally focused his attention on her …hardly taking his eyes off of her. She had felt his eyes riveted to her.

Mari felt flush and hot by his attention. Mari made up her mind that she would work her way back to his table. She had boldness about her when it came to meeting new people. Did she know him? She didn't think so.

***

Martin Parrish was bored to tears. Three days in another strange city auditing the books of another civic organization that was a client of Norris and Finch, Inc. Make no mistake about it Martin loved his work and the expense account provided to make these trips. Since Martin was single, he really had no reason to dislike travel. At the age of 26 he was comfortable in his bachelor life and saw no reason to change his status.

Earlier he had his curiosity perked about the Citizens Group Foundation which was the non-profit civic group that was under audit. He had asked the Director about a notation that had been made by the previous auditor regarding an entry called SADIL-110601 which included a sizable outlay.

The previous auditor, Greg Tenant, had been killed in a one car accident, but had emailed his preliminary report of the audit with a notation about an item titled SADIL – 110601. The Director had seemed confused about the entry and told Martin that he could discuss the entry in more detail tomorrow when his chief accountant would be available and could answer specific questions. Martin had made a note in his address book to follow-up the next morning.

The problem with civic organizations was that rarely did they employ people who had sampled the night life of their own community. Most were family types consumed by school, church and related activity and not given to bar hopping. Martin had wandered into this local bar while taking a leisurely walk not far from the motel.

Martin had not noticed her when he came in. Then he noticed nothing else.

She was gorgeous....absolutely beautiful....with soft blonde hair and smooth textured skin thought Martin. She had an absolutely perfectly formed body, and big beautiful sky blue eyes that suggested innocence.

She was talking to the female bartender and had glanced his way for an instant or so he thought.

***

Elaine Myers had an endless supply of bawdy jokes to make Mari laugh. If there was anything that Mari needed in life it was a good laugh now and again. God knows her life was full of tragedy.

Her mother and father died in a terrible car accident when Mari was twelve. She, her brother and sister went to live with an Aunt and Uncle that were more interested in tax deductions and foster parent payments that raising three kids.

Conditions in that household were unbearable at times, particularly when her Uncle Max continually hit on her from age thirteen until she left at seventeen.

If it hadn't been for the protection of her older brother Billy, she could have easily been another statistic of sexual abuse.

Her younger sister Eva had left that household at age 15 and ran away only to be shot to death in a drive-by gang related shooting in Des Moines, Iowa of all places. Mari had lived with her brother in a two bedroom apartment until she was 18 and started making a livable wage at the station.

Billy joined the Army and was killed two years later in a helicopter crash at Fort Hood, Texas. As far as Mari was concerned, she had no family other than a few close friends at the station.

Mari was into drugs pretty heavy after Billy died, until she realized they were destroying her life. She swore off drugs for good and made an effort to discourage others from getting hooked.

Mari had been through two serious relationships that had ended when she refused to give up her job for married life. She was twenty-four years old and ready to make a move to a bigger media market. Her Mari Fund was in a healthy state due to some wise investments and ready to support her for a period of five years, if she was careful. If she didn't make it in that period of time, she never would.

If it didn't work out, she was still young enough to go back to school, finish her education and teach communication or journalism. Mari vowed to continue to work in the communications field. She loved it too much to give it up.

Mari knew enough about herself and the business to know that she had to make the break now, or she never would. It was her time.

She had discussed her plans with her co-host Dave Brewster, and he had been very supportive. Dave hated like hell to lose her and told her so. But he knew that he couldn't hold her back. She had too much potential.

***

Martin's eyes locked on Mari as she moved toward him, then she abruptly sat down with two older gents' two tables away from him.

Must be steady customers Martin thought. Surely she couldn't be attracted to either of those guys. Suppose it could be a sugar daddy deal. Now, why the hell do you care Martin? You don't even know the woman. What she does or who she sits with is certainly none of your damn business. Quit acting like a teenager. How vain and arrogant can you be to think that you have the animal magnetism to draw this beauty to your table? Get a life. You certainly didn't come in here looking to start a relationship for cryin' out loud.

One minute Mari was talking to Red Francis and Randy Miller….and the next minute she was standing at Martin's table asking if she could join him.

Her sudden appearance startled Martin and caught him off guard. He had just relegated the rest of the evening to observing. He hadn't realized Mari was standing there until she spoke…and she spoke so softly, he wasn't sure that he understood her.

Mari said, "Hi....my name is Mari....Mari Denton. I didn't mean to startle you, but you looked kind of lonely. If you're waiting for someone or I'm interrupting something let me know and I'll go away. I can't stay long anyway. I'm in the middle of taping my radio show."

Martin just starred at her for what seemed like minutes…..then said, "No, you aren't interrupting anything. Please sit down. Uh...my name is Martin Parrish. I'm just trying to unwind from a long day in a strange town. Can I get you something to drink?"

"No, thanks", answered Mari. "I try to stick to one beer while taping."

Mari smiled. She had an infectious smile.

"Are you new in town, just here on business, or just passing through?"

"I'm an auditor…here for a few days to audit a civic organization. Just stopped in here for a night cap."

"Mmmmmmm…an auditor, you're not with the IRS are you? You don't look the type."

"Not guilty!" Martin laughed. "I do not work for the IRS. I mostly audit civic and charitable organizations to keep them straight and out of trouble."

Mari thought for a moment, then said "…..uh..well, listen, I have to get going. Are you going to be around for a while? I have to finish taping…should be half an hour to forty-five minutes, I'll come back if you want some company. If not…well, good luck with your audit."

"I really don't have any plans for the rest of the evening", Martin answered. "I can hang til midnight."

Mari smiled, "That's fine….what time is it? Oh, well…it is only 7:30….I should be back here in about 45 minutes. The station is right across the street. How's that?"

"Works for me. I heard your show on the way down. Enjoyed it. I mean how often does one get to talk to a radio personality?"

Mari laughed, "Oh my God! What have I started here. Okay! In the meantime you ought to chat with Elaine, the bartender. She can give you a low down on everyone in this town."

"I just might do that," said Martin with a big grin.

It was exactly 45 minutes from the time Mari left until her return. Martin was sitting at the bar listening to Elaine's repertoire of jokes and guzzling his fourth draw of the evening. Not only had he gained admiration of Elaine's ability and skill at telling a joke, but he had gotten a short bio on the virtues and talents of one Mari Denton.

According to Elaine, Mari was destined for stardom as a media celeb...perhaps the next Katie Couric. She was that good. Mari had won numerous awards for her reporting and as co-host of the morning show and had an audition in a few days for a morning TV show in Chicago. Although Mari, according to Elaine, had primarily worked in radio, she had done some stringer reporting for television in Topeka and Kansas City and gotten great reviews. She was sure that Mari was on her way to the big time.

Martin could tell that Elaine had nothing but admiration for the way Mari had overcome some real personal barriers to get a foothold on life and was now beginning to reap some reward for her struggles.

"Let me tell you something about that little gal", Elaine said. "She is a fighter. First her parents die, then she has to fend off an uncle, then her brother and sister die tragically...it is more than most people could deal with. But not, Mari. She beat personal loss and drugs to get where she is....and she is determined to get her shot at the big time. She may never reach the top, but she'll give it one hell of a run. That woman has earned the respect of everyone who knows her."

You make her sound bigger than life," said Martin. "I'm duly impressed and maybe a little intimidated. There is a certain amount of self-confidence about her that I sensed when I met her. She does have a way of putting people at ease. That's a real gift in her line of work."

"You guys talking about me behind my back," announced Mari as she approached the bar.

"God, I can imagine what garbage Elaine has been dishing out. You weren't giving him your "She's the next Katie Couric!" routine again….. Elaine?"

"Heaven forbid," said Elaine.

"I'm glad you returned," said Martin. "Here I thought you were just feeding me a line to make me feel good. Be nice to the stranger in town, etc. etc. I now have 101 bawdy jokes for all occasions, thanks to Elaine. Thank you, Elaine.

You should really consider hiring Elaine as your publicist. Not only does she do an excellent job of building your image, but she has impeccable timing for a punch line. Dynamic combination."

"That she does, and I never feed lines. I'm but a simple local country girl trying to promote harmony wherever I go. As for Elaine, she just wants me to leave town so she can have all the eligible bachelors….all two of them.

"Okay, you two knock off the crap or I'll go find two shovels," said Elaine. "Now, Mari you are three behind Martin and I. What'll it be?

"Hit me with a big red and go light on the tomato juice," replied Mari. "Looks like this place has been deserted. Give me some quarters for the juke box Elaine…let's show this stranger that we know music.

Elaine has all the great tunes from the 60s, 70s and 80s! Unless of course that isn't your type of music?"

"Hey…you're talkin to a real rock n' roll buff here. Got any Bob Seger?"

"Alright, I knew there was something about you that I liked. Bob Seger it is!"

In her best radio voice Mari said, "Here he is straight from the juke box at the Downtowner Bar and Grill…..Bob Seger and the Silver Bullet Band."

"Hmmm….is that your radio persona coming through?" laughed Martin. "Can't resist a performance, huh?"

"It gives me a real high," remarked Mari. "It's better than any drug that I've unfortunately tried in my past."

"I've been down that road as well. My experience was more from curiosity than anything. A couple nights of not knowing where I had been or what I had done cured me fast. I guess that I'm too much of a control freak to handle a steady diet of that life."

CHAPTER 3

ENTER JACOB GRANT

I decided to check in with Sheriff Miles, but no one had reported a missing person or inquired about the woman in the ditch. The local newspaper ran an article regarding the missing body which was picked up by area newspapers but still no response. Abe had an acquaintance in the Kansas City, Kansas Police Department Detective Bureau he contacted. Another dead end.

Three weeks had past and no new evidence, no inquires, nothing, zilch, nada. I was frustrated. I had some time to scuffle around the area looking for a thread to unravel the mystery of the unclaimed blonde.

Deputy Davis had told me that the lab work came back. Apparently their Jane Doe had been heavily sedated prior to the bullet to the brain. The bullet was most likely from a .22.

She must have been unconscious when the fatal shot was fired. Very strange. It was almost as if the killer or killers had acted out of compassion, although their compassionate behavior just bought them a charge of premeditated murder punishable by a death sentence. Go figure.

Whoever heard of a compassionate hit job? This was no drug related hit job. The motive had to be something other than that kind of cold calculated act. Drug hits were a form of business communication.

If anything, they were totally devoid of any personal element. Nothing personal Jack, but business is business, or perhaps it's a regulatory device to keep the soldiers in line. Additional lab work indicated that she had not engaged in sexual intercourse within 24 hours of her death.

According to her stomach contents, she had eaten a good meal within that same 24 hour period. Great. Woman gets wined, dined, drugged and then shot to death and thrown into a ditch on a lonely country road within a 24 hour period. I wonder if the person or person(s) gave her flowers. The meager facts were beginning to point to a romance gone badly or the actions of an emerging ritualistic killer.

Law enforcement in the area had combed their files for similarities from other cases without any luck. Rather than bringing clarity to this case, the evidence was adding confusion to the whole process.

I was sitting at the kitchen table in The Lodge trying to make some sense of the meager evidence gathered thus far. I had built The Lodge as a business venture several years ago from trust funds left to me by my parents. It was used by hunters and fishermen from time to time as a base camp and departure point for their activities. The Lodge had always operated in the black and turned a modest profit. I had hired a manager/cook to keep the place presentable and run the day to day operations.

Nothing fits. We have a Jane Doe with a bullet in the brain, unconscious from drugs, well dressed, no visible marks of a struggle, no idea where or when the murder took place, no suspect, no evidence except that the murder weapon was a small caliber .22, and absolutely no clues. Where is she from, who does she belong to, why was she killed and dumped in a ditch in the middle of nowhere? Why is no one inquiring about her? There had to be a loose thread somewhere!

I had adopted a new project. I decided that this is one of those times when it was necessary to get some professional help. The satisfaction would be in the solving of this crime and maybe bringing someone to justice. The question was where to start. I had no idea where this lady had lived. Apparently, for reasons unknown no one who knows her wants to admit that she's missing.

Someone planned this murder very carefully and made sure that it would be an enigma that couldn't be easily unraveled.

Had it been a spur-of-the-moment emotionally-charged act of passion, it would have been a hell of a lot messier with all kinds of loose ends to track down. Someone knew the victim well enough to know that they wouldn't be missed and was careful not to leave any incriminating clues. What puzzles me is the choice of a ditch by the road to dump the body.

Why not hide it deep in the woods somewhere and let the trail grow cold before discovery? It is almost as if someone is taunting law enforcement, knowing that they don't have the resources for a prolonged investigation.

As long as the body remains unidentified, there is no one to push the investigation....to keeping it alive. It will become just another folder in the cold case file.

Unfortunately, that scenario is all too real. I decided that it was time to pay a little visit to my good friend Jacob Grant and see if he has any ideas on how to move this thing along. I have a strong feeling that there are some messy details just beneath the surface of this case. I've got nothing but time to spare and whoever or whatever the lady was, she has paid the ultimate price for some justice.

***

Jacob Grant was a retired detective and an exceptional cop most of his working life. Jacob was still on retainer with the local law enforcement agencies and received calls from time to time on troubling cases.

Abe had become friends with Jacob when Abe was helping a friend get untangled from an extortion scam several years ago.

At first Jacob wasn't too friendly when he heard a freelancer without even a private license was meddling in police business, but when Abe came up with critical evidence to arrest the perpetrator, Jacob quickly changed his mind.

Jacob and Abe had crossed paths several times since then and had built a long term trust in each other.

If anyone would have a clue about where to start on the case of the Jane Doe found in the ditch, it would be Jacob. The local sheriff and his staff had hit a dead end on the case and didn't have the time or resources to go any further.

I called Jacob from The Lodge early the next morning. No answer. This worried me. Jacob had been responsible for populating the prisons with some very nasty characters that seemed to keep getting recycled through the justice system. The prisons of today allowed inmates the use of the gym every day, seven days a week until paroled. The first few years after Jacob left the force he had kept up his routine of jogging five to ten miles early in the morning three days a week and going to the gym two days a week to keep in shape.

However, since Beth had died of cancer about a year ago, I had heard through friends that Jacob had ignored his routine and had developed a slight midriff bulge. His reflexes had paid the price. Jacob was spending more and more of his time in a local bar playing pool and drinking beer which compounded his weight problem.

Jacob seemed to have lost interest in those things that he used to care about like solving crimes. He groaned and covered his ears with a pillow when the phone rang. Who the hell would be calling him at this hour? Probably some damn salesperson, or charity wanting to hassle him. To hell with them.

The Department had called upon him less and less as the old timers moved into retirement and crime detection became another victim of the new technology. The young guns of today had computer models for everything imaginable and left little room for gut feelings or hunches.

Jacob didn't give a shit. Let em' rot with their computer games. He'd had his fill of crime and the revolving door of justice. His passion for the good fight had died with his wife.

Through his morning haze Jacob could hear the phone continue to ring. He cursed himself for not investing in an answering machine. Fuck it. Let it ring. It could be his former partner Ryerson trying to fix him up with another damn date. Damit why didn't they just leave him alone? Let him drink his beer and play pool in peace. Hell, he had earned it after 30 years of dealing with hustlers and pimps, drug scum, thieves and murderers.

"Give me a break, you sons of bitches, I'm retired!" he yelled at the phone. Miraculously the phone stopped ringing.

Jacobs's head felt three sizes too big and made him walk to the bathroom very carefully. He had to take a piss real bad. God, he must have really tied one on last night.

He didn't even remember walking home. Not good. Former cop out for a stroll after midnight. Even though it was only three blocks, he'd have been a sitting duck for some disgruntled former collar. The truth was that Jacob really didn't care that much. The sooner, the better.

Maybe he would be reunited with Beth, and they could pick up where they left off before she got the Big C. Jacob slowly raised his head to the mirror and saw rivulets of water running down his cheeks.

"GOD DAMNIT!"

Not another spell of self-pity. Beth would kick my ass, if she saw me standing here like this. It's just so hard…everyday it gets harder and harder to go on without her…knowing that when I come home….I'll be suffocated with loneliness…no one to share my day with…no one to share my life with…..no one to share my heart and soul with…..just memories, too vivid to forget…too painful to remember.

Jacob knew that he told himself a lie every day when he headed to Mick's Place. He wasn't going for the company, the telling of old war stories, or the pool.

He was going to get drunk…to forget…to numb himself from the truth and the pain of Beth…no longer there to touch, to feel next to him, to sooth his emptiness.

His true purpose in life had never been about fighting crime, or anything related to the job. His true purpose was being there for Beth…being there with Beth to share his life…to take care of each other. All the rest was just a means to an end, some crazy damn circus that kept revolving around them but was never a true part of them.

Perhaps it would've been different, if they would've had children. But they didn't. Beth couldn't. That made having each other all the more important. Too bad Jacob couldn't see all this, realize it, before Beth died. Not that it would have made losing her any easier. But at least he could have told her as much. Let her know how deeply he loved her. But then in his heart he knew that Beth knew. It was in her look and the way she squeezed his hand in those last days. And in her final words of comfort when she told him that she would always be a part of him and that no disease could kill that.

All their hopes and dreams had dissolved in that cold antiseptic hospital room that had become their prison.

CHAPTER 4

A NAME FOR THE BODY

I was perplexed that Jacob hadn't called for several months. Although I hadn't seen Jacob since his wife's funeral, I couldn't imagine him ignoring old friends. It was a thirty-minute ride via the Interstate. I'd know soon enough. I thought Jacob would have some ideas about what direction to go with the investigation. He may have encountered a similar case in his thirty years that would give them a fresh approach. There had to be something that Abe had overlooked.

I got off the Interstate at California and headed south to 37th Street. I made a left on 37th and counted three houses down on the left. At least Jacob's vehicle was there as was an ambulance and two police cars. Oh, shit! What the hell was going on?

The shot had missed Jacob by a half inch when it came through the window. Had he not bent to the sink to splash water in his face, he would be a corpse. Jacob had dove to the floor...some habits don't die...and crawled to the bedroom and retrieved his S&W 9mm. He moved slowly in a crouch position toward the front door.

Luckily, the assailant was stupid enough to charge the front door anxious to complete the job, and Jacob dropped him as he entered the doorway with a shot right between the eyes. Jacob cursed himself again for forgetting to lock the door last night.

Jacob waited a minute to be sure, then with his weapon trained on the man turned him over with his foot. Dead for sure, but no one that Jacob recognized. Blond, fair complexion, no visible scars, about 5'10" and 190, stocky build. Jacob searched him and found absolutely no identification on him. Certainly didn't look like anyone Jacob had put away. After thirty years who could tell. Maybe, someone hired him to take Jacob out.

What a way to start the day. Whoever paid for this fiasco must be low budget. Obviously the intruder was new at this game. Well paid hit men don't take risky chances. Charging the door was not a bright move.

Jacob called the station and reported the shooting, although he knew there would be no leads to follow on this one.

While waiting for the detail to arrive, he walked outside to see if he could find a vehicle not familiar to the neighborhood. Nothing. Nada. Zip. He must have had a driver and a prearranged pick up.

Okay, Jacob this is a wakeup call. Time to get back in shape, lay off the booze. A razor inch of luck is nothing to count on the next time. Time to find out who is out and about recently. It has to be someone that I put away Jacob thought. My pool skills sure as hell haven't infuriated anyone. I haven't been chasin' anyone's wife or girlfriend. My pension is no fortune. That rules out three prime motives for killing someone: jealously, sex and money, which left revenge.

Two rookie patrolmen were first on the scene, followed quickly by the paramedics. Jacob didn't know any of them. Brad Miller and Tyson Bruce from the detective squad arrived, and Jacob told his story as it had unfolded. No, he didn't have any idea who the perp was….never seen him before.

Yes, there were probably a number of ex-cons who would like to see him dead, but no one in particular. No threats or strange calls or warnings had been received. Just then Abe walked through the door.

"Jezz, Jacob! What the hell is going on? Are you alright?"

"Well, I'll be damned!" said Jacob, "Look who shows up when the action gets hot. Another razor inch, my friend and you would be staring at a body bag and asking these two gentlemen questions."

"No wonder I couldn't get you on the phone. You were too busy dodging bullets. Looks like you haven't lost your touch."

"Yea," replied Jacob, "The damn fool rushed the house after the first shot. He musta been a rookie. Any pro would have known better than to take that kind of a risk. Musta been some dumb cowboy lookin to make a few bucks."

"We're going to look around the area and file our report", remarked Detective Bruce. "I'll be in touch if we come up with any leads. If you happen to think of anything, give me a call. We're going to have a patrol car cruise this area on a regular basis for a while if you don't mind."

"No, that's fine", said Jacob. "I appreciate the concern, but I doubt if whoever planned this will try again around here. Course, the person may not be too bright considering the yo yo that he hired for this attempt."

Bruce and Miller left and the medics loaded up the body bag and took off. The media had been and gone after Jacob refused to talk to them. He hated the media and wouldn't give them the time of day now that he was in retirement. Let them find their news elsewhere. The neighbors had drifted back to their homes after they told the media what little they knew. Jacob and Abe adjourned to the kitchen for a beer.

"Got any ideas?", Abe asked.

"Not a damn one til I find out who was released recently", replied Jacob. "It has to be someone that I sent up. I can't think of any other reason someone would want to take a pot shot at me. Unless, someone was offended by my poor skills with the pool stick. I haven't been doing anything but eating, sleeping and playing pool at Mick's."

"Well, whoever it was knew your routine", I replied. "Someone was watching your movements and tried to catch you at a vulnerable time. The guy may have been a yo yo, but less than inch with you in the upright position, and he would have been somebody's hero."

"No kidding. By the way what brings you over to this neck of the woods? I haven't seen you since the funeral my friend", said Jacob.

"Well, what I came for doesn't seem all that important right now. I have a real mystery on my hands, but you seem to have a more urgent one."

"Nonsense," said Jacob, "let's hear the story."

I related the facts of the Jane Doe as accurately as I could remember leaving nothing to chance. Jacob listened intently. I was amazed that Jacob could lock out what he had just been through and concentrate. But that's why Jacob was one hell of a detective.

"Yep, you got a hell of mystery," said Jacob. "Apparently, the woman has no close living relatives and isn't married, or someone would have been making noise, unless they did the deed of course. Sounds like someone wanted her found, yet unidentifiable, to confound the homicide investigation. It looks like they've succeeded. Let me get cleaned up and let's go visit the sheriff and have a look at the evidence. Is this one of your projects?"

"As a matter of fact it is."

"Any monetary angle?"

"This is on the house."

"Sounds like the kind of thing that I need to get me out of the rut that I've been in. That is if you don't mind. Maybe, we could team up again like old times and have a go at it."

"I hoped that you'd say that. But what about the action here? Someone wants you iced."

"That'll have to wait," laughed Jacob. "If they want me, they'll have to come find me."

CHAPTER 5

48 HOURS OF DEATH

Mari was in a daze. Her whole body tingled. Seldom had a man had this kind of effect on her. She felt like an unattached observer, yet totally absorbed as Mark caressed her lips and her neck.

All she could think about was how good it felt as her body filled with desire. She wanted this man more than she had ever wanted anyone in her life. Mari started to respond, then suddenly pushed him away.

"Uh… I think we need to slow down. It's not that I don't find you attractive and desirable, but I have certain unalterable rules about first dates."

Martin gave her a shy smile.

"Thanks for being level headed. You're right, we barely know each other."

Just a few moments ago they were sitting in his car on a little used country road gazing out upon the glittering lights of the city. In fact they were laughing and telling stories of teen-age days making out in the back seat of a car during their youth and listening to Bob Seger's "Night Moves". They had suddenly stopped talking, stared into each other's eyes and embraced.

Martin said, "I'm not usually a spontaneous type person. But you looked so incredibly beautiful. One moment we are laughing about our exploits in the back seat of a car. The next minute we're reliving it. I hope you don't think that this was planned. I've never been a one-night stand type guy. I wanted this to be the beginning not an ending to a relationship."

A small tear welled up in Mari's eyes, and Martin folded her into his arms.

"Don't cry, please. I didn't mean to make you cry."

"Oh, Martin, you didn't make me cry. It is just that so many terrible things have happened to me in my life. It seems like all at once I had met someone who was honest, and funny, and kind. I don't want things to end here either. There was something that drew me to you when I first saw you watching me. Don't ask me to explain it. I can't. I just knew that I didn't want you to leave the bar before I had a chance to get to know you. I can't believe this is happening to me now. "

"Well, since we're confessing, I tried to will you to my table and was actually jealous when you stopped to talk to those two gents. Isn't that crazy? I know that things are kinda crazy for you right now with the audition and all. No matter where you go, I'd like to keep in touch. Are you busy tomorrow night?"

"I have to drive to Chicago for my audition in the morning, and you'll be gone when I return. I'd still like to keep in touch."

"Then it's agreed. Give me your number, and I'll call you when you get back."

"Sounds like a plan."

Martin kissed Mari again and drove her to her car and headed for his motel. He collapsed into bed at 3am.

***

Mari started to pull out of the parking lot, but a figure loomed ahead of her......looked familiar.....she rolled down the window.

"What on earth are you doing out at this late....."".

That was all the further she got. The dart hit her in the arm, and she was out like a light. The form moved forward, opened the driver's side door, pushed Mari over to the passenger seat, got in and drove away.

The drug was good for several hours, but death would come first. She would never know what hit her, no pain, just darkness. Such a waste. She was really hot. But it had to be done. Mari, her companion of the evening and the bartender had to be eliminated.

The companion had seen something that he wasn't supposed to see, and the Council didn't know if he had realized the significance of what he saw that day and told the girl and the bartender. But the Council was playing it safe, and the Council was always cautious.

He hated this kind of work. He didn't mind if the person was a real ass or had double crossed the organization, or was a snitch; but to take out a totally innocent person who really hadn't a clue was depressing. Besides he knew this person and respected her. But, it was what he signed on for, and the Council's needs had to come first. He really didn't have a choice. He would have to do her and dump her in another location as far away from Wheaton as possible.

He would hide the body and head north in the morning to find a good location and dump her after nightfall. A member of the movement would be waiting in Kansas City to take possession of the car and find a place to strip the parts and burn it out.

He pulled into an alley behind a bar, fitted the silencer to the barrel and shot her behind the left ear. He hated that part.

Somewhere in the deep reaches of his mind a steady bzzzzz…..ing sound awakened him. Martin tried to lift his head from the pillow to no avail. It felt like a lead weight. When will I ever learn to control the booze consumption while on the job.

He tried to focus his eyes on the alarm clock. Holy Shit! It's almost 8:30 am and I'm supposed to meet the Director at 9 am. I'll never make it. Martin rushed around, took a quick shower, shaved, dressed and was out the door in 15 minutes. He shouldn't have bothered. When he turned the ignition key, the car blew up in his face. He never felt a thing in the mil-second before death.

The bartender would be tricky, because they would have to wait for the opportune moment and hit when there were no witnesses around. The opportune moment came a few nights later. Mission accomplished.

***

Jacob and I paid a visit to Sheriff Vern Miles. The sheriff, wasn't available, but Jess was there. He called Sheriff Miles who was more than willing to share what they had in evidence with Jacob. The Sheriff was as perplexed by this case as anyone and was glad that his ol" buddy Jacob was interested. Sheriff Miles and Jacob had worked a number of cases together over the years.

I placed a phone call to a newspaper reporter in Wichita who had stayed at The Lodge on a number of occasions. He had been helpful in the past when I needed information. I didn't know if he'd have anything, but it was one area of the State that I hadn't explored because of the distance. While I was on the phone, Jacob sifted through the evidence including the autopsy report.

"Mmmmmm"....said Jacob. "Now I see what you mean by skimpy information. Not a whole lot to go on, but maybe drugs are involved in some fashion.

The murder was execution style and the fact that she was drugged prior to the killing points in that direction. There's no evidence of her as a user, but nothing yet that would rule out dealing drugs. Can't let her mode of dress or persona fool you, cause anyone is capable of dealing if they need fast cash. The fact that the women was killed elsewhere and dumped in a rural area is typical for a drug killing in this part of the country.

If she wasn't directly involved, she could have known someone who was or simply been in the wrong place at the wrong time. You'd be surprised how many innocent folks get mixed up in these deals and wind up on a slab in a morgue.

If this were a murder of passion, I doubt that the perp would have dumped her by the road. Usually, they try to hide or bury the body hoping that it will never be found. If it were a serial killer, they would want the body to be found in some conspicuous place or left some ritual clue, not by a roadside without any clues. No, this one smells like drugs."

"I just talked to Jeb Bouchner, crime reporter for the Beacon, and he tells me a radio talk show personality from the Wheaton area has been reported missing this week. Her name is Mari Denton. It seems Ms. Denton had an audition for a TV job in Chicago. She never showed up for the audition.

Ms. Denton was a blonde and very good looking. She matches the description of our Jane Doe. Bouchner is faxing me a picture. We may have a break. Bouchner has no information regarding her involvement in drugs and doubts that Ms. Denton would be directly involved. She was known for her strong convictions against the use of drugs and was very active in the community's anti-drug campaign.

Apparently she was last seen at the Downtowner Bar and Grill in the company of a man by the name of Martin Parrish and the bartender and owner of the Downtowner Elaine Myers. Mr. Parrish was the victim of a mysterious car bombing, and Elaine Myers died in a hit and run accident the next day. Parrish was an auditor from a CPA firm in Topeka in town to do an audit for a nonprofit group."

"Well, well maybe we need to check out the background on Mr. Parrish and Ms. Myers," said Jacob. "Drug dealers have been known to use car bombs and hit and runs from time to time."
In the next few days the police matched Ms. Denton's dental work to our Jane Doe.

I told Jacob that I had decided to pay a visit to my crime reporter friend in Wichita and then head over to Wheaton to poke around and see what I could stir up.

Jacob decided to pick up a few things from his house and move into The Lodge until he could figure out who was taking pot shots at him.

He wanted to touch base with some of his contacts in the KBI to see if they had a line on any heavy drug activity in the Wheaton area, and if they had any background information on Ms. Denton, Martin Parrish or Elaine Myers.

CHAPTER 6

BATTER UP

I packed a bag and headed down the turnpike to Wichita to meet with my reporter friend Jeb. I didn't know if he had any additional information, but I had to start somewhere. I checked into the Holiday Inn Express and met Jeb at Denny's.

Jeb scooted into the booth and ordered a cheeseburger and fries and a coffee. I had coffee and a piece of coconut cream pie.

"Don't have much more to report," said Jeb. "Mari met a Martin Parrish in a downtown bar and they spent the evening together. That was the last time that she was seen. The bartender was a good friend of hers and was bartending the night that the two met. Mr. Parrish apparently did return to his motel room that night alone according to the motel manager who saw him pull in and get out of his car and go to his room.

As you know the next morning he got in his car, turned the key and 'Boom".

The police are mum about any details pending a full investigation. The bartender, Elaine Myers, was killed in a hit and run the next evening."

"Sounds like someone wanted to eliminate all three," replied Abe.

"Yep, three suspicious deaths in as many days is remarkable for Wheaton. Apparently Mr. Parrish was in town to audit the books on a local non-profit group and was to have a meeting with the Chief Accountant that morning. The organization was the 'Citizens Group Foundation' who support efforts to improve the efficiency of government. "

"You got anything on the group? Like maybe they were pushing more than good government on the side, or maybe a front for some other nefarious purpose."

"Nada. They look legit as far as I can tell. Director is a local bank President by the name of David Peterson. Chamber member, KU alumni, and church deacon are a few of his credits, and he's being considered for a spot on the State Corporation Commission."

"Maybe I'll just poke around and see what surfaces. Does the Wheaton Police have all of Mr. Parrish's effects and can you get me access to peruse them?

"I have a few contacts over there that may be able to help. Play nice if you're going over there. You know how the local cops are about third party investigators, particularly when they're unlicensed. I can give you a bona fide as a contract reporter for the paper as long as you don't piss anyone off, okay?"

"I'll play by the rules and suck up if that's what it takes to get access. If I find anything of real interest, I'll share it with you. Have the police given any indication that they think there is a link between Ms. Denton's disappearance and murder, the car bombing, and the hit and run on the bartender?"

"The police haven't mentioned any connection. They're keeping things quite. Their Chief of Detectives runs a tight ship and refuses to speculate on anything."

"I'd say he's pretty smart."

"It's a she and don't piss her off. I'll guarantee you'll regret it."

"A real ball buster huh!"

"You best believe it. My advice is to be careful. The methods used to kill Parrish, Denton and the bartender smack of professionals, and I'm sure that whoever it is would think nothing of offing a Hunting Lodge owner. You've been lucky in the past, but one of these days that luck may run out ol' boy."

"Yeah, I remember the last case that we worked. I believe it was the Tolan murder. I got shot in the butt and couldn't sit down for a few weeks. On second thought I think I'll try the old insurance investigator ruse. I still have my Mutual Benefit Equity business cards under the name of T.J. Bonham with The Lodge phone number.

Maybe you better identify me under that guise to your contact. I'll have Jacob man the phones in case someone wants to confirm bona fides."

"Okay. Is that old cuss still around? He was one hell of a detective."

"He's still kickin' and is working with me on this one. Someone had a contract on him and missed, so he's staying at The Lodge for now until he can get a line on who wants him dead."

"God knows he made enough enemies during his years on the force. Well, good luck. By the way I did a check on the bartender and Mr. Parrish. Neither have any criminal records or known connections to drug activity in the area. The bartender, Elaine Myers, had a DUI. She had no drug record."

"Thanks Jeb, I'll be in touch."

I called Jacob with the updated information on Martin Parrish and Elaine Myers.

"It looks to me like all of those folks were targeted for elimination. I don't believe in that kind of coincidence. Someone thought they knew something of importance."

"Well.....well"... said Jacob, "What in the hell have we gotten a hold of here? Hit-and-runs, car bombings, disappearances? Someone was out to silence some folks."

"Listen if you get a phone call at The Lodge from someone trying to verify my identity as T.J. Bonham, insurance investigator for Mutual Benefit Equity, confirm it. You might also alert Miriam. She knows that I use that as a cover sometimes. Okay?"

"Let me know what you find out and watch your back. Whoever is behind this plays damn rough."

"Tell me. I'll let you know when I have something. Later."

I headed down State Highway 96 to Wheaton after Jeb made a call to the Deputy Chief of Detectives who was his contact in Wheaton. Evan Miles was a tall lanky gent with a slow draw and manner.

"Mr. Abe Lincoln is it? That's an unusual name. Your folks must have had a hell of a sense of humor."

"You could say that. Guess the folks wanted something for me to live up to. You know 'Honest Abe'. So, I assume Jeb told you what I wanted to see?"

"Sure did. Back this way to the evidence room. Not much was left. His briefcase, laptop and most of his papers were destroyed in the blast. Searched the room but didn't find anything of note. You can check the clothes that he had hanging and his toiletries. About the only things that he left behind. Police in Topeka are checking his apartment for any possible clues."

I checked his clothing and toiletries and found his address book among them. I noticed a strange notation on the inside cover of the address book. "Ask – SADIL-110601" had to mean something. I slipped the book into my pocket.

"So does anyone have a theory about the bombing?"

"Don't have much to go on. Standard type bomb was used and wired to the ignition. Probably got the instructions for construction on the damn Internet.

Doesn't appear that he had any enemies of note. As far as we know he wasn't involved in drugs or gambling. Current thinking is that it must have something to do with Mari Denton and Elaine Myers but the basic problem is that we can't find a motive or a real connection. We're pretty sure neither Mari nor Elaine were involved in any illegal activity."

"So where does that leave the investigation?"

"Right now we're in the process of questioning friends and relatives of the victims to see if we can develop any leads. Chief of Detectives Hamel still believes the deaths are somehow connected to drugs. Maybe the victims saw or heard something that they shouldn't have. It happens."

"That it does. Well, I'll be pushing off. Thanks for allowing me to view Mr. Parrish's effects. Would it be alright if I took a look at the motel room?"

"Sure no problem. I'll call the motel manager."

"By the way has anyone talked to the group that Mr. Parrish was auditing? What was that all about?"

"The Chief talked to Mr. Peterson, and apparently it was a routine annual audit. The Citizens Group Foundation have been around for 15 years. Mr. Peterson is the Director and has been bank President of the 4th National Bank for 25 years. Nothing out of line there."

"Okay, thanks. I've got what I need for now. I may look around the motel room and the Downtowner before I leave. Take it easy."

"You, too and tell Jeb he owes me a dinner."

"Will do."

I exited the police station and headed to the Hampton Inn. The motel manager was cordial and told me that Room 237 was still unavailable to the public. It had been thoroughly searched by the police, but I was welcome to look around.

I searched through the room and found nothing of value. I decided that it was time to visit the Downtowner and maybe have a short chat with Mr. Peterson.

The Downtowner was a cozy tavern that served both food and drink. A mahogany bar was located to your left as you passed through the entrance and ran the length of the wall.

Behind the bar was a full length mirror that ran from ceiling to floor. Tables and booths were off to the right. The booths and chairs were covered with imitation leather that gave them a rich and comfortable look. The tables were made of some type of imitation knotty pine. The room had a cedar smell to it.

The bartender was a tall, slightly overweight but sturdy built gentleman with a bald head that glistened. He wore wire frame glasses that gave him an air of intelligence. I ambled over to the bar and struck up a conversation.

"Hi, T.J. Bonham, insurance investigator with Mutual Benefit Equity, and I was wondering if I could ask you a few routine questions about a client of ours, Mr. Martin Parrish. I understand that he visited the Downtowner while in town and became acquainted with the former owner Elaine Myers and a patron by the name of Mari Denton. He was killed in that car bombing several weeks ago."

"The name is Maury. Nice to meet you. I'd like to help, but I'm afraid I can't. I just moved back to town a few weeks ago. Don't know much about the whole situation just what I've read in the papers and heard from the patrons. I know that Elaine was well liked by everyone. No one believes that her accident was an accident. Likewise with Mari everyone thought highly of her and was pulling for her to succeed in Chicago.

Of course no one knew much of anything about Mr. Parrish. Rumor is that maybe he was into drugs or something similar and that his death was a hit job. Maybe Mari and Elaine were silenced for fear that he told them something that night about his dealings. It's the only thing that seems to make any sense.

You might want to talk to a couple of regular patrons, Red Francis and Randy Miller. They usually come in 'bout 7 pm every night for a few drinks. Mari was a good friend of theirs."

"I might do that. I appreciate the information. I agree the whole thing doesn't make much sense.

We've thoroughly investigated Mr. Parrish's past and can find nothing out-of-the-ordinary. If he was dabbling in crime, he kept it well hidden. How do I find the 4th National Bank?"

"It's just three blocks south of here on the corner of 5th and Main. Can't miss it. It's the tallest building in town."

"Thanks, Maury. Maybe I'll see you later this evening."

"You bet. Anytime. Sorry I couldn't be of more help."

"By the way who took over management of the Downtowner when Ms. Myers died?"

"The bank took it over. They hold the note on the place. Elaine had no living relatives. Mr. Peterson, the bank president, appointed his assistant, Harvey Bacon, to manage the day to day operations."

"Is he around?"

"No, but he should be in this evening. I'll tell him that you were here and would like to talk with him. I'm sure that he won't mind. I'm told that he was kind of sweet on Mari."

"Thanks I appreciate that."

"No problem."

Maury made me feel uncomfortable. I've had that feeling before and circumstances proved me right. His speculation about Mr. Parrish involvement in drugs or related crime almost seemed too practiced. Given my previous experience in feeling out people, something seemed to be out of kilter with him. He just didn't fit the mold of your average bartender.

Maybe I was being overly suspicious. I had a feeling that he was trying to guide the conversation. I'd been exposed to a variety of bartenders over the years, and Maury looked somewhat out of place behind the bar. He didn't have the smooth movements of a practiced bartender. My gut feeling was that he hadn't been a bartender very long.

I found the 4th National Bank and was ushered into Mr. Peterson's office complete with comfortable furniture, a sofa and wet bar as well as a very elaborate mahogany desk with softly cushion chair.

Peterson was short and overweight with a close cropped hair cut and vacant eyes with a double chin. He had the smile of a Cheshire cat.

"How may I help you…… Mr. Bonham, is it?"

"I'm an insurance investigator with Mutual Benefit Equity looking into the death of Mr. Martin Parrish. I understand that he was auditing the books on the Citizens Group Foundation of which you are the Director. Mr. Parrish carried life insurance with us, and I was sent down here to look into the circumstances surrounding his death. Could you enlighten me on the nature of the audit that he was conducting?"

"Sure. No problem. It was a routine annual audit that we conduct to satisfy the requirements of state law in order to keep our tax exempt status. To my knowledge Mr. Parrish had just completed the second day of a three day audit. Normally we don't know the results of the audit until the wrap up on the third day. That's really the extent of my knowledge about the matter.

I had a brief preliminary discussion with Mr. Parrish, and then he began the process. I had never met Mr. Parrish before.

Greg Tennant from the same firm use to conduct our audits, however I believe that he was killed in an auto accident last month near Emporia."

"I see. So I assume that Mr. Parrish didn't provide any summary about the audit to anyone in your organization?"

"That would be a correct assumption."

"I take it that Mr. Parrish didn't appear to be unusually tense or nervous or preoccupied during your conversation with him? Did you notice anything unusual about his behavior?"

"On the contrary he seemed to be quite relaxed and confident. He was a pleasant man and seemed to be very knowledgeable about the audit process. I noticed nothing out of the ordinary about him."

"Did you know Ms. Denton and Ms. Myers very well?"

"Well I stop by the Downtowner on occasion for a brew. Elaine Myers was the best story teller in town and genuinely liked by everyone. If there was something going on she knew about it. Mari was a jewel. Everyone that I know use to listen to her and Dave's program. Although we hated to lose her, we were pulling for her on the move to Chicago.

We were very saddened to hear of her death. It was like losing a family member or an old friend. Why do you ask?"

"Apparently, Martin Parrish was in the company of Mari and Elaine at the Downtowner the evening prior to his untimely death. Speculation among local folks is that Mr. Parrish was into some unsavory dealings and Mari and Elaine were unwitting victims of a deal gone bad. You heard anything about that?"

"No, I hadn't. I suppose that would explain some things, but I find it hard to believe. Mr. Parrish came highly recommended, and I doubt very much that Mari would be associated with someone of that nature knowing her background. I know that Elaine wouldn't tolerate anything unsavory in her establishment."

"I understand that the bank has taken over management of the Downtowner."

"That is correct. We hold the note on the property. Elaine had no living relatives or a spouse and was the sole proprietor. My assistant, Mr. Bacon, is handling the day to day operations until we can sell the property to a prospective buyer."

"You know the bartender by the name of Maury? I had a brief chat with him earlier."

"I believe that is the person Mr. Bacon hired a few weeks ago. Mr. Bacon knew him from his college days. I understand that he just moved back here from Texas and was looking for employment. Why do you ask?"

"Just curious. Seemed to be a friendly sort."

"I hate to rush out on you but I am due for a bank meeting in five minutes. Is there anything else you need to ask of me?"

"No, not really. You've been most helpful. Thanks for your time."

"No problem. If you need me for anything else just call my Secretary and set up an appointment. Have a good day."

"You have a good day too, Mr. Peterson. Oh, before I forget. I was going over some notes in Mr. Parrish's address book. This may not have anything to do with you or the audit but does the term 'Ask – SADIL110601" mean anything to you?"

I noticed just a slight expression of concern in Mr. Peterson's vacant eyes at the mention of the term.

"No, I have no idea what it would mean. You say that it wasn't in his audit notes?"

"No, it was in his address book."

"I haven't a clue. Must have something to do with his personal business or maybe another audit. I can ask around if you feel it's important."

"That would be helpful, good day sir."

"Uh, yes good day Mr. Bonham."

It was obvious to me that the term 'Ask –
SADIL110601' came as a surprise to our Mr.
Peterson. The look on his face was unmistakable.
The question remained as to what the significance
was. Unfortunately I couldn't ask Parrish.

My plan was to continue to poke around and
maybe stir something to the surface. I found a
local drug store and purchased a plain brown
manila envelope; placed the address book inside;
and sealed it. I found the local post office and
mailed the envelope to myself at The Lodge. It was
the only real clue I had.

It was getting toward evening, but I didn't want to
hit the Downtowner again until around 7 pm in
hopes of cornering Mari's friends and Mr. Bacon.
I found a steak joint and had a steak well done,
baked potato and a couple of scotches.
I lingered over my meal and drinks as long as
possible then drove downtown and parked in front
of the Downtowner. It was 7:15 pm.

Before I could enter the bar Maury came out the
entrance and motioned for me to follow him down
the street. He stopped at the corner lit a cigarette
and waited for me.

"What's up?" I asked.

"Mari's friends, Red Francis and Randy Miller,
want you to go to this address to meet with them.
They think that they may have some vital
information for you, but they don't want to be
seen talking to you in the bar. I can't say anymore,
I gotta get back to the bar."

He gave me the folded note and walked briskly back to the Downtowner.

I shouted to him, "What about Mr. Bacon?"

"He ain't here tonight. He'll be in tomorrow morning around 9 am", he said over his shoulder.

I unfolded the note. The address was Easy Ed's Bar and Grill at 17th and North Lorraine. I proceeded north on Main Street and turned right on 17th to Lorraine. It didn't look like Easy Ed was still in business as the bar looked deserted and no cars were parked in the lot. I parked in front of the bar. A short stocky man came from around back of the building and motioned for me to follow him. What the hell was all this intrigue about?

Apparently these jokers thought their lives were at stake based on the information they had. The man started trotting down an alley and I followed him. He stopped turned around, and suddenly I became aware that somewhere along the way he had picked up a baseball bat. Then my whole world went black as someone clobbered me from behind.

"For Christ sake, is he dead? This is supposed to be a warning you idiots!"

"Calm down. He's still breathing. We'll put in a call to 911 when we're done searching him and his car. Relax."

"We don't need another killing right now to get people stirred up."

The two men search through Abe's clothing and the car and could find nothing.

"Well, it ain't here. He either stashed it somewhere or gave it to someone. Now what do we do? The man ain't gonna be happy."

"Not much else we can do. I never thought it was that critical anyway. Without Parrish around this guy won't have a clue what the code means. Better call the man and tell him."

"Shit! Now I'll have to listen to him rant and rave for an hour."

He proceeded to give Abe another kick in the ribs for good measure to take out his frustration.

CHAPTER 7

LISA WITH THE GREEN EYES

She was a green-eyed strawberry blonde…and through the haze of my vision she looked like a true angel of mercy. As my blurred vision began to focus, I could just make out her face …. hmmm very angelic. My head pounded and my body felt like someone had tried to tenderize my whole being…..I barely made out her faint smile or was it a grimace…before I passed out again.

When I awoke again, it appeared to be late evening through the window by my bed. I could see the glare of the street lights against the window pane and a soft pelting of rain drops glistening and running like little rivulets to the sill. I heard a rustling and turned to see my green-eyed angel adjusting her position in a chair.

"Welcome to the world of the living", she said. "We were getting a little worried that you didn't want our company."

"Oh!, my head hurts like hell", I said. "It feels like my neck is attached to a watermelon. Please don't whisper so loud."

She replied, "You're very fortunate. Whoever worked you over could have very easily split your skull wide open. Some friends you have there?"

"Ouch! Oww! I don't think they were exactly friends…more like messengers with a very physical and demonstrative message to deliver."

Lisa suddenly felt Abe's piercing pale blue eyes staring at her and a certain electric tingle ran through her body….just momentarily….enough to give her goose bumps. It was as though they had made a connection.

Abe had felt it too…but mistakenly associated it with his present condition….which was one gihughic ache from head to toe. He had been in a number of fights and brawls in his day, but never had he felt so totally consumed by pain even with the medication.

Lisa could only imagine how it felt and had empathy for this lean rawboned stranger.

"Well, you may be in here a few days to make sure that your concussion heals properly and that there are no other internal complications from the beating," she remarked.

"How long have I been here?"

"It's been three days since they brought you in."

"Oh, great…bed pans and sponge baths…and hobbling up and down the halls like a ninety year old man…and slimy lime Jell-O for dessert….just the right combination for a sunny disposition. Look, I really would like to stay and play compliant patient for the staff….no offense, but I really do have places to go and people to see…and messages to convey. Know what I mean."

Lisa felt a twinge of desire within her to know more about this disarming patient with his self-mocking sense of humor. It said something about his character and resilience.

"Mr. Lincoln, I really don't believe any sane doctor would agree to release you in your present condition….and in all honesty it will undoubtedly be a few days until you can navigate to the john…much less dress and go find your tormentors. I suggest that you just relax and allow your body to mend before slaying any future dragons. You were in very critical condition when you came in here.

By the way, I am not a nurse. My name is Lisa Hamel and I'm the Chief of Detectives with the Wheaton Police Dept."

Oh, great the ball buster. I tried to rise up and the whole room swayed and shimmed before me like a room of mirrors in a fun house. I eased back into the pillows.

"Maybe I will wait a day or two, just until the room quits moving from underneath me. Could I have some of that slimy lime Jell-O?"

Lisa smiled and said, "I'll see what I can do, but I think that it's vanilla ice cream and ginger snaps this week."

Yes, she really did like the give and take with this man......... something she hadn't felt in a long, long time. Don't get carried away, woman....he probably has a girlfriend or wife and ten kids or both. The interesting ones are always taken or turn out to be gay, psychotic or not what they seem. You don't need disappointment in your life right now.

"Is there anyone you want notified, your wife, etc. in the next couple of days?" said Lisa.

"Not unless you know something I don't know," Abe stated.

"There is no Mrs. unless something happened while I was unconscious...in which case it isn't legal. I do need to get a hold of a friend. Could you get a hold of a Jacob Grant at 785-865-2397 and let him know my whereabouts and status? Also tell him that there is a package on the way to The Lodge and to hold it for me."

Lisa silently sighed with relief and told Abe that she would convey his message. Abe closed his eyes and started to drift off to sleep as she adjusted his covers before leaving.

"By the way, Ms. Lisa , you have a very angelic presence. Are you sure I'm still alive?"

"I assure you that I'm human," said Lisa. "You're indeed very much alive. I'll need a statement as soon as you feel up to it."

"Mmmmmmm...good"...I murmured as I drifted off to sleep.

It wasn't until four days after my first encounter with Lisa that I was able to leave the hospital, and I was still taking meds for my headache. I was lucky that my skull wasn't fractured. After a few days I did remember the incident that brought me to the hospital. It seems as though I was chasing a man who was reluctant to answer a few questions surrounding the murders of Parrish, Denton, and Myers. I had followed either Red Francis or Randy Miller into an alley and suddenly found myself facing three thugs wielding baseball bats. Before I could even react, a fourth man clobbered me on the head from behind. The other three took turns fracturing three ribs, one wrist, a forearm and creating multiple contusions and bruises to the body and face.

Oh, yes….there was the matter of a broken nose. Actually, the nose looked better after it was broken….better than the last time that it had been broken two years ago. I conveyed all this information to Lisa, not that it would help find the thugs.

I did manage to trade sketchy accounts of my life history with Lisa during my convalescence, and I offered to take her to dinner after I'd fully recovered. She was thirty-four years old and divorced with no children.

After the beating that I took for trying to ask a few simple questions, I had elevated this search for the killer or killers from strong interest to dogged determination to catch the sons-of-a-bitchs, preferably with a baseball bat in hand. Revenge is sometimes a great motivator, particularly when you were caught from behind.

Lisa drove me to get a rental car for the trip back to The Lodge, then I followed her to her townhouse before we went out to eat.

I took Lisa, well actually she took me to a quaint little Italian restaurant off the beaten path in Wheaton which in fact had excellent food and a better than average wine choice.

She wore a beige summer dress which subtly displayed some cleavage and a very nice mature womanly figure. Her makeup and perfume were likewise subtle but very effective. Her presence made my palms sweaty.

"We found your car stripped and burned in a field north of town," said Lisa.

"We also found the bodies of two men in the woods near your car. The two were friends of Mari's by the names of Red Francis and Randy Miller. They had been killed execution style with a .22 caliber bullet behind the ear. They had been there for a couple of weeks at least. We've interviewed family and friends of Red and Randy, but they were in shock and had no idea why the killings occurred.

The killer or killers left no clues. Also the bartender, Maury, has disappeared. He never showed for work the day after you were beaten."

"It appears that anyone that might have any information regarding the death of Mari and Martin are a target for execution. Someone is hell bent on keeping a secret about something vital to their interests. Wonder what that could be? Did anyone talk to Mr. Bacon?"

"Yes, and he seemed to be just as puzzled as everyone else. He said that Maury just showed up one day looking for a job. Bacon needed a bartender at the Downtowner, and since he knew Maury from college Bacon hired him. End of story."

"Well, it appears to me that Maury and his friends are trying to hide something, and they got me mad."

"There was some confusion about your identity. Mr. Peterson claims that you were posing as an insurance investigator by the name of T.J. Bonham. Of course you are Abe Lincoln owner and operator of The Lodge.

We were able to establish that you have a fairly good rapport with the Topeka Police Department and have been responsible for helping them to solve some rather puzzling homicides in the past.

Now the law does frown upon a person posing as an insurance investigator for a non-existent Insurance Company, but at least you didn't try to monetarily defraud the public. There could be a question of interfering with an ongoing investigation, and we don't allow outside interference in the conduct of any ongoing homicide investigation unless we specifically contract with someone for consulting services.

It would have been nice if you would have at least attempted to work through us at the onset. It might have saved you from taking a beating. What is your real interest here?"

"I'm the person who found Mari Denton's body while jogging. It was my initial interference in this case that helped get the body identified. I took a personal interest, because it appeared to me that Mari deserved to have her killer or killers found. Based on my past experience these type of cases usually wind up in a cold case file for lack of evidence. I'm not faulting the police mind you, because I know that when the evidence is meager and doesn't point to a specific list of the usually suspects your resources are limited.

I was warned about not getting crosswise with you, and I apologize for not checking in with the Wheaton Police Department beforehand; but at the time it seemed wiser to do some snooping on my own. I didn't realize that I was going to be invited to local version of batting practice.

I should've known that the trip to Easy Ed's was a set up. If you'll allow me, I really can be of help. I'll promise to behave and work through your department."

"I've already discussed your involvement with the Police Chief, and he thinks it useful to have your assistance providing that you run everything through me before you start poking around for more information. I mean everything. I guess that he feels it would be better to have you inside his tent so to speak. By the way the Chief talked to Jacob Grant who happens to be an old drinking buddy of his which helped your cause immensely. The Chief told Jacob that he wants him involved as well."

"And how do you feel about having us involved?"

"Normally, I'd be against it, but in this case I can see the logic. I'll have fewer sleepless nights at least knowing what you two are up to."

"Now there's a backhanded compliment."

Lisa smiled.

"It might be best for you to lay low for a few days to give whoever is behind all this the impression that you've been scared off the case. I agree that there appears to be something going on here that someone feels strongly about keeping secret.

We need to work harder on finding the connection between all these killings and why the Downtowner appears to be at the center of things."

I agreed to lay low for a few days. Lisa was intelligent and blessed with a great deal of common sense. She had a subtle sense of humor yet knew when to be all business. She had made it clear who was in charge. I couldn't believe that she apparently had no fiancée or boyfriend at the present, but sensed a certain trace of sadness.

She was by far the most complex and interesting woman that I had encountered in a long time. Not many women achieve the rank of Chief of Detectives in a city the size of Wheaton. I wanted to know her better.

I drove her to her townhouse on the west side of town after dinner. She invited me in for a brandy. As we sat on her couch I gazed into her beautiful green eyes that reflected maturity yet a certain flirtatiousness.

"Well, Abe Lincoln off the record if you don't mind me asking, why have you never married?"

"I don't really know. Guess I just haven't found the right person who'd put up with me or compel me to want to spend the rest of my life with them. I don't mean that in a conceited way, just trying to be honest. Maybe I've gotten use to just depending on myself for everything. I've nothing against marriage, but maybe it's not for everyone. And yourself?"

"I tried it once. Didn't work out. I wanted to be treated as an equal and his nature wouldn't allow that.

He was a nice man, but he wanted a stay at home wife whose whole life could be consumed and satisfied with children and home decoration and that simply is not me. Our emotions and passion took us to the alter.

He was a great kisser and love maker, but a lousy partner. When I wouldn't bend to his image of a wife, he went elsewhere for his passion. Since I will share many things but not a husband, I divorced him. I never regretted it, and have become very content with my life. I've had several lovers, but none that ever compelled me to go down the aisle again. And you?"

"You mean what do I do to relieve the sexual tension?"

"You're very astute!"

"I try. Sometimes it is difficult to read a woman's subliminal thoughts, but to answer your question I have casual affairs with unmarried women that are always brief but pleasing to both parties. They seem to drift away when they find out that there will be no champagne and wedding cake."

"Never been tempted with a married woman?"

"Tempted yes, but involved no. Too many complications that I don't need and too often too many people get hurt in the process, especially if there are children involved."

"Very thoughtful answer."

"I know that its old fashion in this day and age, but I do maintain a few standards. Part of the name that I bear."

The next thing I knew I felt a strong compulsion to kiss her and I did. It was a long lingering kiss, and her lips were soft pliable and extremely delicious.

"Does this mean what I think it means?," she murmured softly between kisses.

"I think it does," I replied.

She stood, took my hand and led me to her bedroom. Lisa turned down the comforter and top sheet turned on a soft light by the bed.

She turned to me and ever so slowly unzipped her dress in the back and let it fall to the floor. She unhooked her bra, caressed her ample breasts, then slid her brief panties off and dropped them to floor.

I stood there transfixed and unable to move. She was definitely a full figured woman in the classic sense and very sensual. She quickly moved to me and proceeded to undress me item by item as we engaged in some very intimate exploration using lips, tongues and hands. Needless to say I had totally forgotten my aches and pains of the past few days and was lost in her soft and velvety breasts.

I murmured to her between urgent kisses, "Don't you want me to use some protection?"

Between the probing of our tongues she sighed, "Do you have any?"

After a particularly lengthy kiss I replied, "Of course not. That would have been kind of premeditated of me, wouldn't it?"

As her kisses moved further down my body she whispered, "Yes it would. Not to worry I'm on the pill."

As we fell onto the bed she straddled me and our sensual exploration continued at a fever pitch until I could hold back no longer and exploded within her. After one more encore we spent the remainder of the evening in each other's arms.

In the morning there were no expressions of regret or promises made about the future. It was obvious that the attraction between us was very strong, but both of us were smart enough to accept things as they are and not force any talk of commitment. The conversation was light as we both prepared a breakfast of ham and eggs, toast and coffee. After we ate I dressed and Lisa walked me to the door.

"Have a safe journey and try not to get yourself into situations that render you unconscious. I like my lovers conscious and alert."

"I'll remember that. After last night I certainly wouldn't want to miss out on anything. You take care and I'll be in touch."

"You better be. I'm your local contact person mister."

With that she gave me a soft and lingering kiss then shoved me out the door less she had to call in sick for the day. As I walked away from her townhouse I knew one thing for certain. I definitely want to see her again, perhaps under better circumstances.

CHAPTER 8

A PLOT FOR REVENGE

Jacob Grant had packed his bags and moved into The Lodge after locking up his house and getting his mail forwarded. He had acquired a list with about fifteen names of folks that he had sent to prison and who had recently been released. None appeared to be very good candidates for the shooting episode, but he knew that he would methodically check them out.

His efforts proved fruitless as ten had no visible financial means to hire a shooter. The other five had moved out-of-state prior to the shooting incident. That did not rule out the possibility that one of those five folks hadn't taken out a contract killing on him, however the possibility seemed remote.

The shooter had been identified through fingerprints as a two time loser who had served time for armed robbery. Jacob had not been involved in his arrest or conviction. As an assassin he was a rank amateur.

Frankly he was more concerned that he hadn't heard from Abe in almost a week. Certainly he had learned something in Wichita or Wheaton by now? In that instant the phone rang.

"This is The Lodge, Jacob Grant speaking."

"Mr. Grant, this is a voice from your past Chief of the Wheaton Police Department Ron Kessler calling to advise you that your friend Abe Lincoln has been hospitalized in the Wheaton Memorial Hospital after receiving a rather sever beating at the hands of persons unknown.

Apparently he asked the wrong people too many questions about the death of Mari Denton. He wanted me to notify you of his situation and that he should be on his way back to The Lodge in a few days."

"Well, I can't say that I didn't try to tell Abe to go slow, but then Abe doesn't take advice very well. Glad to hear he's on the mend. I appreciate the call. By the way you still owe me a case of beer from the last KU-K-State football game, Kessler."

"Damn, I was hoping you forgot about that. Anyway you need to get your butt down here and help us out on this one if you aren't too busy being retired.

"I'd be happy to help in any way I can. I guess that I must have done something right on the force, cause people are still taking pot shots at me. Probably good that you hired Abe on. If he took a beating he won't stop until he gets to the bottom and finds out who was responsible for Mari's death. Whoever they are, all they've accomplished is to get Abe damn mad at them."

"I reached that same conclusion. Normally we don't bring someone in from the outside, however given Mr. Lincoln's past track record and his association with you we've made an exception in this case. As you say Abe would have continued to pursue the case anyway. Abe will bring you up to speed when he returns to the Lodge. Hope to see you in a few days. Your beer will be waiting for you."

"In that case I'll be there. Later."

***

Bobbi Ann Henry awoke with a start and rushed to the front door of her duplex to get the newspaper. Before she reached the door she stopped, because she remembered that she was wearing a sheer negligee. She ran back to the bedroom to retrieve her robe and hastily threw it around her and ran back to the front door. She opened the door grabbed the paper and quickly shut the door and locked it.

Her hands were shaking and she could feel beads of sweat break out on her forehead. Clam down girl she tried to tell herself. It had been five long grueling years since Bobbi Ann had first decided to undertake her mission to right a grievous wrong.

Bobbi had worked her butt off first as a waitress then a bartender at the Matador Lounge in the Holiday Inn.

Bobbi Ann needed the funds to support herself until she accomplished the task that would even the score for her family. Once that was done Bobbi Ann would be free to quit that lousy job and go back and complete her education in nursing. All Bobbi Ann really wanted was a normal life.

Life had begun normal enough for her. When she was a child her mom and dad had given her all the love and support a child could want along with a sense of self-worth and a dose of good discipline. Her Dad was her hero. Although he was a truck driver and was on the road a lot, he would spend a great deal of time with her when he was home. She followed him everywhere when she was a toddler. Her Dad could fix anything. He was good to her mom and would bring her flowers when he came home from the road. He was honest and blessed with good common sense.

All it took was one day for her ideal world to fall apart. Bobbi Ann remembered as if it were yesterday. She was sitting in her afternoon seventh grade social studies class when she was summoned to the office. When Bobbi arrived her mother was there and in tears. Bobbi Ann became frightened and ran crying to her mother. It was then that she noticed a policewoman standing next to her mother. Her mother and the policewoman took Bobbi home. The policewoman was a Social Worker and very kind. She tried to explain that her father had been arrested and taken to jail.

"What for?" Bobbi asked in tears.

"We have reason to believe that you father was part of a plan to rob a bank", the policewoman had said.

"No!, no!, no!.........my father would never do anything like that. He's an honest man. He wouldn't do that. You can ask anyone. Tell them Mom. Tell them they're wrong"

Her mother grabbed her and held her close and whispered, "I know sweetie. I know. I don't believe it either. I don't care how many witnesses they say they have or what evidence they have, I know that Wayne wouldn't do that. Your daddy would not do that. We'll get a lawyer. We will prove them wrong and bring Daddy home."

"I'll help mommy. I have $125 saved that we can use to get a lawyer."

Her mother mortgaged the house to hire a good lawyer, but to no avail. Her Daddy never came home. Despite the pleas of the attorney that it was a set up and the evidence was planted, her Daddy was convicted and sent to prison. A week after he arrived at the prison he was killed by a crazed inmate in a dispute over a pack of cigarettes.

Bobbi Ann's mother was devastated and began drinking heavily and taking up with abusive men. She sold their house and moved them into a trailer.

When Bobbi Ann was sixteen one of the men raped her in front of her mother. Her mother was too drunk to protest. He was an off duty policeman and threatened to kill mother and daughter if they reported it. The next day her mother hung herself.

Bobbi Ann had to move in with an aunt and uncle whom she despised. They kept telling Bobbi Ann that what had happened to her and her parents was God's will. Bobbi Ann reasoned to herself that no just God would allow the things that had happened to her family. If that was God's will, she wanted no part of religion.

It was during this time that Bobbi Ann learned that her father had indeed been innocent of the charges. The witness who had testified against her father admitted to a drinking buddy that he had lied and planted the evidence on her father. He was a truck driver who had a long running grudge against her father. Bobbi Ann lost all faith in the judicial system and the law.

Bobbi Ann turned to drugs and wild parties to kill her pain.

The next year she dropped out of school and moved in with her boyfriend who was dealing drugs on the side.

Bobbi Ann worked two or three part time jobs as a waitress until she finally went to work at the Matador. Eventually, her boyfriend was arrested for possession with intent to sell and was sent to prison for five to ten years.

Bobbi Ann began dating a guy who was one of the regulars at the Matador. After a few dates she moved in with him and told him about her past. It was then that Bobbi Ann hatched her plot to administer her own justice and kill the men that had helped to convict her father. In bed her boyfriend told her that he could do the job. At first she thought that he was just trying to impress her, but he persisted with stories of previous successful hits and finally she relented.

A month ago Bobbi learned that the judge in her father's case had died the previous year of a heart attack. The prosecuting attorney had been killed in a plane crash about two years ago . The arresting officers were Stan Hurd and Jacob Grant. Hurd had dropped dead last week with a heart attack. Jacob Grant was retired from the force and the only remaining member of the law enforcement and judicial team that had sent her Dad to prison.

Bobbi gave her boyfriend $2,000 in cash of the $71,500 that she had left from her father's wrongful death benefit with the remaining $3,000 to be paid upon completion of the job. He was to kill Grant.

Once the deed was done, Bobbi Ann planned to use the rest of the money to move to Colorado and start a new life.

Her boyfriend was to have done the job yesterday morning after several weeks of shadowing Grant to learn his daily patterns. He would then drive to Kansas City and lay low for a few weeks. He told her to watch the newspaper for any news. Once she had confirmed that the job was done, she was to text his cell phone and leave a message 'Activity Confirmed'. He would pick up the additional $3,000 in cash when he returned.

On page three of the newspaper Bobbi Ann found that her boyfriend had botched the job. He had been killed by Jacob Grant after an attempt on Grant's life. Obviously her boyfriend had lied about his skills as a hit man. It was just another lousy disappointment to cope with.

That's alright she told herself. I'll do the job myself and damn the consequences.

She would right the wrong that had been done to her mother and father and to her family. She would get the job done. She had lived with enough of life's disappointments. It was time for revenge.

A few days later the police questioned her regarding her boyfriend. She told them that she and her boyfriend had a fight a few days ago, and she hadn't seen him since the fight. She had no knowledge of his plans to kill Mr. Grant.

CHAPTER 9

THE RED BARN

As a yellowish dusk settled over the landscape they came in twos and threes to the old red barn. The barn was located on fifty acres of farmland outside Wheaton. Although a sturdy structure, the barn had been standing for over thirty years. Outside it looked weathered, but inside it had been totally renovated. The walls were reinforced concrete. The floors and the stage had been covered in oak hardwood. A second floor had been installed and the inside walls had been covered in freshly painted wallboard. Part of the building was divided into rooms for offices, a break room, and a room devoted to security and operations. There was a state of the art audio visual and communication equipment room at the back of the building. Security cameras and body heat sensors were placed around the building and security monitors screened the visitors as they entered.

A podium and video screen had been installed and behind the podium hung a large red, white and blue banner that read "Sons and Daughters in Liberty!" Below the lettering was the motto: "It is only through revolution that freedom and liberty will survive."

The Sons and Daughters in Liberty had chapters in Kansas, Missouri, and Oklahoma with additional chapters scattered throughout other states. Actually the Sons and Daughters was an organization within an organization.

The front or public persona was of a benevolent nonprofit organization dedicated to the preservation of democracy and liberty through non-violent action. The organization that the public knew had a website and held public rallies with noted conservative speakers. State and Local law enforcement agencies had no knowledge of an inner organization. The inner organization's purpose was to incite revolution using terror and violence.

The inner organization was composed of a carefully screened permanent membership dedicated to its purpose. The Sons and Daughters inner organization had been in existence for ten years and was the creation of two men and a woman.

These three individuals had taken over a rather benign ultra conservative movement and molded it to their agenda. To say the organization was anti-government would be putting it mildly.

Blair Logan was the Director of the visible Sons and Daughters organization. She was a no nonsense business woman who owned a string of beauty salons and day spas throughout the Midwest. She was well respected in the business community. Blair had entered the beauty salon business when she was nineteen after completing beauty school. She was talented and acquired a steady clientele in the small community of Great Bend, Kansas.

When Blair was twenty-three she seduced a local banker and became his mistress. She was able to secure a low interest loan to start her first salon called Angel Hair.

Within three years she had salons in five Kansas communities in the Central Kansas region. Blair sought out the most talented stylists through her connections with beauty schools and offered profit sharing plans and benefits that could not be equaled by others. Blair's benefits package was underwritten through her intimate relationship with the local banker.

Blair had no desire to marry. She came from a very dysfunctional family and as a youth had lived in fear of her often unemployed, drunk and verbally abusive father. Blair's mother had to hold down two jobs just to keep the family in shelter, food, and clothing. Finally her father succumbed to his drinking when she was sixteen to the relief of her and her mother. Blair respected her mother and sent money to support her until her death when Blair was twenty-five. Blair's stylists became her family and a few became her lovers.

She preferred women to men; however Blair coldly used her sexual favors and some of her stylists who wanted to earn some extra money to seduce certain powerful men as a means to expand and enrich her business ventures. She invested wisely in a few profitable real estate deals and at thirty-five owned forty beauty salons, fitness centers and spas throughout the region. Blair had reached the multi-millionaire plateau.

Blair quickly became bored after achieving her status of wealth. Although she had only a high school education, she was a vociferous reader. Her reading list was diverse; however she became particularly interested in politically conservative movements and the inner workings of radical groups throughout history. Blair had always been mistrustful of government and the exorbitant way in which it taxed the wealthy.

She had enough business and personal experience with the local politicians and government officials to know firsthand of their ineptitude and personal weaknesses. Blair learned quickly that most vain and powerful men were easily corrupted.

Her banker friend was a strong John Birch Society supporter, and Blair attended several meeting with him. She felt that some national conservative commentators like Rush Limbaugh were nothing more than cheap hustlers who would say anything to get attention.

Blair contributed heavily to Ronald Reagan's presidential campaign and attended his inaugural only to become quickly disenchanted with his policies which she believed to be too moderate. It was through these activities that she became acquainted with Maury Williams.

Maury Williams was not a bartender. Maury was the tiller head of the Sons and Daughters inner organization. Maury was a professional radical and had been since his early college days. He was a disciple of the Hayden's, Rubin's and Cleaver's of the sixties. He had studied their styles and techniques and practiced his craft in their movements.

He knew that the money was in the conservative movement and Maury had always been interested in money and what it could do. He was obsessed with the idea of how money translated to power.

Maury had toyed with the idea of anarchy in high school. He read everything that he could get his hands on dealing with the idea of permanent revolution. Maury came to believe that a revolt was like a cleansing operation to the established order of things.

To Maury it was every man or woman for themselves anyway so why the pretense with governmental rules. Why not created a Darwinian world which truly reflected the survival of the fittest? Rules didn't mean a damn, because most of the time people sought the means to circumvent the rules in order to get ahead.

Maury came from a relative middle class family. His father was a bank officer in Peoria, Illinois and his mother worked as a dental assistant.

Maury was an only child. His home life was very orderly with prescribed routines for home work, chores, and play activity which were closely monitored by his father and mother. The family went to church every Sunday and to worship services during the week. Maury's attendance was mandatory. Maury quickly learned to hate rules and structure.

Maury was rather small in stature and uncoordinated; therefore he didn't participate in sports. He opted for school plays and debate where he honed his communication skills with a great deal of success. His success on the debate team earned him State honors and scholarship to the University of Kansas in Lawrence. It was here that Maury became enthralled by radicalism and began his tutelage in its uses.

He managed to lose his scholarship and quit school to engage the current radical movements in California and elsewhere. His parents totally cut him off from any financial support. Maury drifted from one movement to another learning all he could and was a willing victim in the gassing and clubbing at the Democratic National Convention in Chicago in 1968.

After that experience Maury decided to put his skills to use in the conservative movement. He went home and apologized to his parents. He did a complete makeover returned to school and finished with a degree in business and accounting. While completing his degree he met Harvey Bacon from Wheaton, Kansas.

Harvey was a mover and shaker with the Young Republicans and an avowed conservative who had idolized Senator Barry Goldwater when he was a kid. Maury decided that Harvey would be an ideal conduit into the conservative movement.

Harvey Bacon was the inner organizations Director of Operations. His parents had been lifelong supporters of the conservative movements like the Birch Society and the conservative wing of the Republican Party in Kansas. Harvey's parents had been born into wealth. His paternal grandfather had made his fortune in cattle, gas, and oil. His maternal grandfather had accumulated his wealth in publishing and communications. Harvey would never have to worry about where his next meal was coming from.

Harvey had majored in banking at the University of Kansas and eventually was given a relatively high level position through his father's connections at the 4th National Bank in Wheaton upon graduation.

While Harvey was in college he met and became fast friends with Maury Williams, a fraternity brother. The studied, drank and bedded women together. What fascinated Harvey about Maury was his self-assurance and charisma. Harvey tended to be more subdued and reserved. Maury wasn't cocky or a braggart. He simply had the quiet ability to persuade others in cold logical terms to agree to his ideas.

In an informal setting Maury would make each person feel that they were the most important person in the room. He was never disagreeable nor rarely did he argue with others. He would simply state his case, provide his reasoning and facts and let others decide for themselves whether he was right. Maury would frustrate the more liberal elements on campus, because in most cases he would turn their arguments against them with cold calculating logic, particularly the more emotional liberal advocates.

Harvey and Maury would have long conversations well into the early morning hours about the inadequacies of government, political parties, and the lack of courageous leadership in government and business. Maury slowly and carefully spoon fed Harvey bits and pieces of his radicalism. He would interject not only the failures of liberal factions and thinking but the failures of conservatives as well and the corruption and ineptitude that ensued.

By their senior year he had Harvey convinced that society would be better served by a very minimalist national government whose major role was a national defense against foreign enemies; while state and local government should focus its efforts to protect society against the most vial criminal elements and maintain the infrastructures to support business.

Government by and of itself was an infringement on individual liberty. Government didn't grant freedom and liberty, it impeded it. Ronald Reagan only had it half right. Government wasn't only the problem. It was the enemy.

Blair and Maury Williams met at a Reagan rally in Kansas City in the spring of 1980. They were seated at the same table and had forked over $5000 a piece to attend.

It began with small talk and evolved into a lengthy discussion about the proper role of government in society. The conversation continued through dinner at an exclusive downtown private club and ended with Blair bedding Maury in her hotel room.

Maury was different. He was vibrant and exciting. He was strong and intelligent. Their verbal intercourse had stirred a heated desire in her that demanded a physical release.

She couldn't seem to get enough of him. By morning they were totally exhausted and slept until well into the afternoon. They ordered in and afterward spent another three hours of intense lovemaking.

When they parted the next day they vowed to meet at least once a month at some mutual location to continue their relationship. It was during this time that Maury began sharing his plans with Blair about organizing a conservative movement more radical than any organization in existence. Blair became intrigued and excited about his ideas.

She had discovered the purpose in life that she had been seeking. They had reached the same conclusion. The only way to bring about true and lasting change in this society and government was through violent means. Their blueprint was to incite a national revolution to overthrow the current corrupt national socialistic government.

Together and with the help of Harvey Bacon they developed the organizational structure for the inner Sons and Daughters in Liberty. They would use the front organization to camouflage their real plans. Those members who were selected for service into the inner organization would have to take a vow of silence and understand the penalty for breaking that vow was immediate death.

Those who were chosen had to have proven skills and talents useful to the movement and demonstrate a willingness to perform. Each member had to commit to forfeiting 15% of their monthly income to assist in funding the inner structure. New members went through a two week indoctrination process. There were no exceptions no matter the person's station in life.

The indoctrination process consisted of lectures in doctrine and testing of knowledge. Each person was required to perform tasks that demonstrated their useful skills and talents. Everyone received tactical combat training.

Those individuals who had signed on for the Security Enforcement function were required to demonstrate their proficiency by eliminating those who failed to successfully complete the indoctrination process or those who betrayed their oath of silence.

Individuals who broke the oath of silence were executed in front of the membership assembled for a special meeting. The bodies were then dismembered, burned, and buried in undisclosed remote locations. Word of the executions quickly spread to the other members nationwide to serve as an example. From time to time when there were no training failures or oath breakers, the Security Enforcement trainees would be allowed to hone their skills on homeless vagrants in a nearby city. Homeless vagrants were considered to be worthless and nothing but a drain on society. Their disappearance would not be noticed.

Blair, Maury and Harvey hired Dan Sexton as their Chief of Security. Dan had served as an Army Ranger in Iraq and Afghanistan running a black ops squad. After leaving the service he joined the local Madison County Sheriff's Department and managed to earn a degree in Business and Criminal Justice.

He left the Sheriff's Department and started his own Security Consulting firm. Sexton had joined the Sons and Daughters organization and his abilities were quickly noted by Blair and Harvey. Dan was a strong advocate of the inner organization's purpose.

Blair's connections to the banking community over the years, and her files on the sexual preferences of a number of its members aided their efforts. The banker who had secured a loan for Blair to start her chain of beauty salons was the CEO of the 4th National Bank in Wheaton.

It was through him and his non-profit civic organization Citizens Group Foundation that she and Harvey managed to transfer funds to their operational arm. The CEO was not a member of the Sons and Daughters in Liberty (SADIL) inner movement and knew nothing of its hidden doctrine or mission. Harvey Bacon, as the assistant to the CEO, had primary control of the Citizens Group account.

Blair had numerous photos and videos of the 4th National Bank CEO in very compromising positions with selected employees of her salons and documentation of questionable loans issued by him. If the photos and documentation ever surfaced to the public, the CEO would wind up penniless. He rarely asked any questions about the Citizens Group account.

As time passed several executions were required because some individuals had inadvertently learned of secretive information about the organization's true purpose. More recently these victims included Greg Tenant, Mari Denton, Martin Parrish, and Elaine Myers. Mari and Elaine were killed because of their contact with Martin Parrish who had inadvertently stumbled across information that could have exposed the inner organization.

All members of the Sons and Daughters In Liberty inner movement below Council status were considered associates. There was no hierarchical rank. The Council of Three deliberated on project recommendations of the associates after proposed projects were presented to the Council. Many times these projects were spoon fed to the associates. The Council's final decision on all matters prevailed.

Each associate was assigned certain tasks to perform. Leaders were selected by the Council for working group assignments on a temporary basis until the task or project was successfully completed. The Council assigned group members based on their accomplished skills and talents.

The meeting this evening at The Barn was to announce progress in implementing the next phase of the movement's operation. Maury felt that it was time to make a visual and profound statement to an unsuspecting public. It was time to stir general unrest and bring real fear into the minds of the public.

The meeting was called to order with one hundred and fifty associates in attendance. Maury approached the podium and began his remarks to the group.

"My fellow associates the time for action has come. The time for rhetoric has past. It is decision of the Council to proceed with our plan to attack the very suppressors of our liberty. It is time for the goal that we have all embraced to become reality.

The Federal Government as we know it shall fall. I am not at liberty to divulge the specifics of our plan for surprise must be our ultimate strategic weapon. Suffice to say that our actions will be historical and monumental and the message that we send will be unmistakable. It will become evident within the next twenty days the nature and scope of our attack.

Prior to these attacks you will be given instruction via the usual process on your individual assignments. It is vital to our plan that you act quickly in order to sow the seeds of dissent and fear into the mind set of your friends and neighbors.

There are plans for additional follow-up action to build on your activities and to sap the authority of the Federal Government. We intend to create chaos. It is our belief that within a matter of months our actions will result in bringing the Federal Government to its knees.

Only then can a true effort to restructure the federal role in our lives be undertaken. If our efforts are successful, we will all be the benefactors of considerably less federal infringement on our God given rights to liberty.

It is imperative that each of us do our part to the best of our abilities. The Council has spoken."

An hour and half documentary followed on how the federal government usurps liberty and was narrated by a well-known right wing radio commentator.

Following the video was a social hour and catered dinner. Speculation abounded as to what the plans for action involved and of the upheaval to come. The air was electric with excitement. All the prior training and discussion would finally come to fruition. The sentiment was that the revolution was upon us. It made one feel as though they were a true patriot much like the patriots of the first revolution about to undertake the task of overthrowing and ridding their country of an oppressive despot.....their own Federal Government.

Ever so quietly a lone figure slipped out of the back of The Barn cut across a field and made his way toward his Honda Civic that had been parked along a little used road. He had been planted into the organization as an undercover agent by the FBI for the past several months. He never made it to his car. He was intercepted by three rather burly men in dark clothing wearing Halloween masks. One of the men held him while another slit his throat. The loaded him into the back of their van. His body would be dismembered and burned beyond recognition.

"Arc Angel One this is Arc Angel Two come in!"

"This is Arc Angel One, what say you?"

"The bird has been silenced. I repeat the bird has been silenced."

"Roger that. Good work. Make sure you get pictures."

CHAPTER 10

JUST THE FACTS

As Abe sped north on I-35 to Salina and then east on I-70 on his way back to The Lodge he had no new ideas on how to proceed with this case. Anyone who had any knowledge about events that led up to the murder of Mari and the others had either disappeared or were dead. Abe was lucky to be alive. That held some significance. Why didn't they just off him when they had the chance? He needed to talk with Jacob. Something had been overlooked.

The remaining key players were Harvey Bacon, the bank president David Peterson, and the disappearing bartender Maury. They fit into the equation somehow, but how? At least Lisa had been able to get them permanently assigned to investigate which was a minor miracle.

Lisa, now there was some fascinating woman. She had looks, brains and a terrific sense of humor. She was probably intimidating to most men, but not Abe. He was intrigued. Her ability to overcome the adversity of the gender issue and work herself into a very responsible position on the police force attested to her innate ability and fortitude. Abe knew that he was strongly attracted to her and needed to be very careful and not let the attraction distract from his focus on this case.

As Abe sped east on I-70 he hit the speed dial on his cell phone for The Lodge. His housekeeper Miriam answered.

"You didn't tell me we would be having a guest, Abe. Nor did you let me know that you were laid up in the hospital." said Miriam.

"Sorry Miriam. I figured that Jacob would let everyone know about the hospital. My mind was pretty foggy at the time."

"I should think so. You need to be more careful. You're not getting any younger you know. Running around the countryside sticking your nose into other people's business. What kind of life is that? Never mind you won't listen anyway. You want me to get Jacob?"

"Sure Miriam, and I promise to be more careful. It's good to hear your voice. Is Jacob behaving himself?"

"Well, at least he seems to have enough sense to stay out of dark alleys. When he gets cleaned up he's a rather handsome man. Just a minute and I'll get him."

"Okay, Miriam I get the point."

Wonder what is going on there? Miriam wasn't one to make such observations about men that she just met. In fact she had totally resisted the idea of male companionship, at least since she had come to work at The Lodge.

Miriam had migrated to the U.S. from Israel in 1990 after her husband and son died in bombing attack by a Muslim terrorist in a shopping center. Miriam had been a member of the Israel army and trained for combat. She couldn't bear to remain in Israel. There were just too many memories in too many familiar places that she and her husband and son had shared together.

All Miriam wanted was a roof over her head and a job that wouldn't require a great deal of thinking or any heavy burden of responsibility. She had enough of that in her past to last her a lifetime. She simply wanted solitude.

The Lodge was an ideal fit for her. Her only responsibility was to manage the facility and insure that the lodge was kept clean. She cooked for Abe and any guests that utilized the lodge facilities during hunting and fishing seasons. There were twelve cabin units to maintain that were never more than three quarters full at any time during the year which was manageable by her standards.

Abe was a good boss and let her set her own pace. Miriam was an excellent cook and rarely did anyone complain about her preparation of food. Most visitors to The Lodge would agree that Miriam actually ran the place. Abe just paid the bills and hired the guides during the season.

Miriam had received numerous offers from businessmen who visited the lodge for similar employment at a much higher salary. Miriam had her own cabin and felt sufficiently paid.

She had no desire to look elsewhere for better employment. As far as Miriam was concerned she had the ideal job and the ideal boss.

The Lodge turned a modest profit each year, although it really wasn't the main source of Abe's income. Abe had inherited a considerable sum of money upon his parent's untimely death in an automobile accident. Abe had never revealed to anyone but his accountant his total wealth. Many acquaintances speculated that it ran into the multi-millions, but no one really knew his total value. Abe's father had been a very successful trial lawyer whose services had been in demand throughout the country. He had invested his money wisely and had amassed a considerable fortune.

"Abe, this is Jacob. What's up? I understand that you ran into a buzz saw of sorts. I thought you knew better than to wander into a dark alley without a weapon or backup?"

"Okay, okay I admit I screwed up. Everybody wants to be a critic. We need to talk when I get back. Anyone who may have any information on this case are either dead, disappeared or don't want to talk about it. The two remaining connections to the case are a banker and his assistant. I have a strange feeling that they aren't telling us everything that they know. We need to figure out what our next move is. I have a hunch that there's something that we're missing, but I'm not sure what."

"Whatever is going on must be highly sensitive, otherwise why go to the trouble of killing everyone that had direct contact with Parrish. My hunch is that they didn't kill you because whatever is going on will surface real soon, and they didn't want the additional scrutiny. When are you due in here?"

"I should be there in a couple of hours. Have Miriam put some coffee on and make some of her delicious cinnamon rolls. I'm starved."

"Okay, I tell her. You got quite a deal here. You never told me that you had a good looking housekeeper. I get the impression that she rules the roost around here and very efficiently I might add. See ya later."

"Alright, my advice is to keep your hands to yourself she's ex-Israel army. Bye."

"Really!"

Abe wondered what might be brewing. Maybe Miriam would be just the person to get Jacob out of his depressed funk. Likewise, maybe Jacob would help Miriam realize that it's time to move on with her life. Whatever was happening, it could only be positive.

Abe arrived at the lodge around 6:30 pm. He was greeted by Miriam who reminded him that since he hadn't stayed in touch there were numerous decisions to be made regarding the operation of The Lodge. Abe set aside time later in the evening to sit down with Miriam and discuss those issues. Abe ventured into the den to find Jacob.

Jacob was sitting at a desk going through the mail that had been forwarded to him.

"Anything interesting in there?" asked Abe.

"Just bills and flyers. Welcome back my friend. It's good to see that you've mended. Maybe next time you'll remember not to chase bad guys into dark alleys without a backup or a decent weapon."

"Yeah, so you mentioned on the phone. It was a very painful lesson. I should have known it was a set up. I was too fixated on getting a lead on what the hell was going on with this case. Let's get some coffee and rolls. We need to see if we can make some sense of this mess."

Jacob and Abe carried their coffee and rolls into the den and settled into two comfortable leather recliners.

"Okay what do we know and what can we deduce from what we know?," declared Jacob.

"Mari, Martin, and Elaine were executed after spending an evening together. Mari and Martin were killed in the early morning hours after they met and Elaine's death followed the next day.

Red Francis and Randy Miller were in the bar the night Mari and Martin met and were executed the same day that you ventured into the Downtowner asking questions.

We can surmise that they were all killed because of something that they knew or were suspected of knowing. It's the only premise that seems to make any sense. We know sex, drugs, jealousy and money don't seem to be motivators in these deaths, even though the perps tried to make four of the murders look like drug executions.

We have the banker David Peterson and his associate, Harvey Bacon, and a missing bartender named Maury who may or may not know more than they're willing to admit. The only real clue that we have is a note left by Martin that alludes to something called SADIL-110601 that was found in his address book. We assume that the note referred to an audit that he was conducting on the Citizens Group Foundation."

Jacob said, "Maybe we need to concentrate on the audit. Martin's only reason for being in town in the first place was the audit. If Mari or Elaine knew something that was damaging to someone else why would they share that information with a relative stranger who has no connection whatsoever to the community. Martin on the other hand would have a reason to share information with Mari and Elaine. He would know that they were connected to the community and might be a source of information or at least the clarification of information.

It seems to me that someone was deeply concerned about the audit. What does SADIL-110601 mean? Is it a budgeted line item of a questionable nature? Some secret organization? A person? A formula? What?"

"All well and good, Jacob, but the problem remains that the original copy of the audit review has been rendered confetti by the bomb blast. There is nothing left to examine. Mr. Peterson, the director of the Citizens Group Foundation, claims no knowledge of SADIL-110601 as it related to the audit or his organization. We'd need a search warrant to look at his books which requires probable cause that a crime was committed. I doubt a warrant would be granted on such flimsy evidence. "

"Well there's always breaking and entering but any evidence found would be inadmissible. Not to mention that breaking into a bank is no easy task. But on the upside it might give us a clue as to what the hell is going on here. Unless you want to believe that there is a serial killer running loose picking the victims at random. The black hole in this whole case is the motive. Why did someone go to a lot of trouble to make this look like a series of drug killings?"

"I agree Jacob, but I'm not sure getting a hold of the books is going to be of much benefit. If SADIL – 110601 is some kind of coded entry, I doubt that a ledger is going to provide a key to that code. The arrangement of those numbers could almost be a calendar date, but I haven't a clue what SADIL means. I can't believe that I just heard an ex-cop suggest breaking and entering."

"Well normally seeking out a judge for a search warrant is the accepted practice, but when the evidence is almost nonexistent we ex-cops tend to resort to creative methods practiced by our adversaries.

No, you're right. We probably wouldn't find much that way. I have another idea. Let's put a tail on the banker Peterson and his assistant Bacon for a few days and see what develops. I have a gut feeling that those two are connected in some way to this whole mess. Maybe we can find a way to make Peterson let us view the Citizens Group Account or interview the Chief Accountant."

"Good idea. I'm going to contact Martin's former employer to see if they know anything about the notation. Then I'm going to do a little research via the Internet on 110601.

I'm thinking those are dates and are either November 6, 2001 or June 11, 2001. I want to see if anything significant occurred on those dates particularly in the vicinity of Wheaton."

"Sounds like a plan. I'll pack a bag and head down to Wheaton and set up a tail on the banker and his assistant. Since you're known, it would be better if I did it. I've got a few retired cop pals around there who would like nothing better than to get in on some action. Don't worry I'll clear everything with Lisa. I don't want to sour that arrangement."

"Lisa will appreciate that. Let's keep in touch daily in case I come up with something. I think something major is brewing. Someone made a mistake and panicked for some reason. There's been too many killings in a short span of time which means to me that time is of the essence."

"I'll buy that. I'll call you when I have everything set up. Call me if you find something."

"Will do."

Jacob finished off his coffee and rolls and headed to his room to pack. Abe located Miriam to have a sit down and go over the decisions that were needed to keep The Lodge running.

CHAPTER 11

EVERYONE HAS A PLAN

Blair Logan was worried. She and Maury had their first real argument. Blair felt the killing of Red Francis and Randy Miller was an excessive action. Both men were loyal to the cause and really had no intention of sharing any information with authorities about Mari's death. Likewise she felt it was a mistake to attack the insurance investigator who as it turned out was none other than Abe Lincoln. Blair was aware of his reputation. Big mistake. It served no useful purpose, and more than likely would only increase his interest in the case. It would have been better to have killed him and made it look like a mugging gone bad.

Everything was in place to implement the plan, and it was imperative that nothing happen that would deter or postpone their efforts. The associates were keyed up to act and any delay could cause loss of control and the exposure of the inner organization's intent. She felt in her gut that Maury had panicked when Abe Lincoln appeared on the scene.

The fact of the matter was that Blair just plain didn't trust men. Maury over time had become too arrogant and self-assured. Come to think of it he had been far too easy to seduce. She would have to watch him carefully.

If he showed any more signs of panic, she would enlist Bacon in an effort to liquidate him. No one person was bigger than the plan, and the plan had to succeed.

***

Bobbi Ann Henry's plan was simple. She would track down Jacob Grant, stalk him, and when an opportunity presented itself she would kill him. Bobbi had decided that she wouldn't strike until she was sure that she could get away undetected. After the deed was done she would flee to Colorado, assume a new identity and start a new life.

She had searched the Internet and found the necessary information on how to create a new identity. Bobbi had packed away most of her belongings that she would take with her in the garage and withdrawn all her savings.

Bobbi Ann quit her job at the Matador the next day and began the process of tracking down Jacob Grant. She had learned through a friend at work that Grant had taken up residence at a place called The Lodge as a guest of Abe Lincoln. Bobbi had heard Abe Lincoln's name mentioned on numerous occasions and learned of some of his exploits while working at the Matador. She knew that he was not one to mess with.

She would have to hit Grant when he was away from The Lodge. She didn't think that anyone would make a connection between her and Grant especially since her ex-boyfriend was dead. She would never be a suspect in Grant's demise.

The question was where and how to confront him? She couldn't just walk into The Lodge and shoot him. She had made some inquiries and learned that The Lodge was located in a remote rural area near Gove Lake off of County Road S1000 and only had two access roads.

Bobbi Ann decided to get a job as a waitress in a town called Maple Grove not far from The Lodge and wait for the right opportunity. She could spend her evenings driving around and learning the roads near The Lodge and refining her plan of attack. She set a time limit of thirty days maximum to complete the job and make her escape.

Jacob Grant's cop sense told him that someone ambitious enough to hire an assassin would not give up easily on accomplishing his demise. Police had identified his assailant as Lenny Brunner a twenty-five year old two time loser who had served time for armed robbery and was on probation. Lenny apparently bragged while serving time in prison about connections to organized crime and his prowess as a hit man. Obviously his skills left a great deal to be desired.

Since he had never heard of Lenny prior to the police identification of him, common sense told him someone or some group contracted a hit on him. But who? And why now after he had retired? Groups like organized crime didn't hit folks who had taken themselves out of the game unless there was a very personal grudge, and Jacob could think of no personal vendetta that he would have inspired. It had to be an individual. Here the possibilities were limitless.

It could be anyone of several thousand people that he had arrested in his years on the force or their relatives for that matter. In all his years on the force he remembered only one case that had really troubled him. The guy was a truck driver and as it turned out had been framed for an armed robbery of a bank. Jacob had been one of the arresting officers and had testified at the trial.

Before everything could be sorted out, the truck driver was killed in prison by some idiot over a pack of cigarettes.

He had heard that the wife eventually took to drink and hung herself. There was a daughter, but he had no knowledge of what had happened to her. Now he remembered that the truck driver's name was Henry. Wayne Henry.

He remembered that the daughter had been very close to her Dad and had attended most of the trial with her mother. She had to have been devastated by what had happened.

When the mother hung herself the daughter no doubt held a high degree of contempt for the whole judicial system. The daughter had accused a policeman of raping her at age sixteen in front of her mother; although that was never proven. If he were in her shoes he would probably have a tremendous amount of pent up anger toward the law.

Taking things a step further the most visible representatives of the legal system were the cops, specifically in this case the arresting officers. Stan Hurd had passed away several years ago, so that left Jacob as the sole target. Although plausible, it was still a long shot.

It was a possibility to explore. No one had offered any better theories on who had tried to off him. As he was packing for his trip to Wheaton he called his friend Larry Sutton who was an ex-cop and sometimes private investigator in Topeka to ask him to run a check on the Henry girl. Bobbie ....something was her first name he believed.

***

The plan was simple. Blow up five Federal Buildings throughout the East, Midwest, Southwest, Mountain West and West Coast. Strike fear into the hearts of every American. Create chaos and panic. It was only through chaos and panic that any real change could take place. If people believed that their country couldn't protect them, they would begin to look elsewhere to find that protection.

The plan called for five three person teams who would carry out the primary mission. The fifteen participants had been carefully screened based on their dedication to the cause over the past several years and their particular skills related to transportation, surveillance, and explosives.

Five large vans had been purchased from different areas of the country that fit the specifications of vehicles used by UPS. The vans were painted and detailed accordingly. The floors of the vans had been reinforced to hold the weight of the explosives. Five nondescript black 2006 Chevy Cobalt's had been purchased and would be parked in strategic locations as getaway vehicles.

One member of the team would be responsible for driving and parking the UPS van in a strategic location close enough to the Federal building to cause maximum damage then locating and driving the getaway vehicle. The second member of the team would act as the spotter and be located near the Federal building in question to ensure that law enforcement was not monitoring their activities. They would be aided by a mobile police scanner. The third team member would act as the explosives expert and would be responsible for loading the van with explosives according to specifications provided, troubleshoot if problems occurred with the explosive device and detonating the device at the precise designated time.

The designated time was scheduled to be April 19, 2012 at precisely 11:02 am CST. The date was the anniversary date of the Oklahoma City bombing.

The contents of the explosive device were an updated version of the Oklahoma City bomb complete with a remote detonator that would function within a two mile radius of the parked van. Each van was packed with 5,500 pounds of ammonium nitrate, which had been purchased from numerous Coops throughout the Midwest; 1,500 pounds of liquid nitro methane; 400 pounds of To vex; twenty bags of ANFO; spools of shock tube; and electric blasting caps.

The mixed ingredients of the bomb were contained in fifteen barrels arranged for maximum impact. Major Federal buildings had been examined in five cities for possible targets. Targets had been chosen based on their proximity to highly populated areas of the city and included Kansas City, Missouri; Austin, Texas; Seattle, Washington; Denver, Colorado; and Philadelphia, Pennsylvania.

Three additional two person teams in each city had been charged with the secondary mission to call in reports of potential sightings of the bombers at various locations in the city at precisely the moment right after the major bombs were detonated. The teams would then set off small mobile explosive devices modeled after the IEDs used in Iraq. These devices will be installed inside of well-populated shopping malls and public gathering places the previous evening. The events would increase additional chaos and fear in the general population who would come to believe that they were under attack by foreign terrorists.

The plan called for additional strikes at new geographic locations every three months until the people demanded a form of government that could protect them. Citizens Militia formed by core members of Sons and Daughters in Liberty would come to the forefront to assist the impacted communities. Of course their presence would deter any further attacks and be requested by other communities not yet affected.

The militia would build trust among the citizens and turn over to the police bogus individuals who would be framed as possible terrorists engaged in the bombing activity. The plan was highly detailed in the method of selection, planting of evidence and arrest of suspects. The suspects themselves would be foreign nationals suspected of criminal activity. Planted evidence in the form of alleged statements and bomb making paraphernalia would be uncovered.

Elements of the plan were in place and implementation would occur in twenty short days. Harvey Bacon was responsible for giving the "Go" signal to the mission teams via a special secure satellite link on April 18, the evening prior to the attack. The voice message would simply announce "It is time for a renewal of liberty."

Blair Logan decided to call a meeting of the Council in her apartment at the Hilton in Wichita. The purpose of the meeting was to review the status of the plan, although Blair had acquired some additional information that would require a decision.

Maury Williams had dropped out of sight after the incident with Abe Lincoln and was staying at The Barn. Harvey Bacon picked up Maury and drove to the Hilton.

"We are at minus twenty days and counting, are we sure everything is in place?" asked Blair.

"The teams are on their way to the staging areas and should be on site at minus five days. The vans are loaded and parked at the staging areas. The secondary teams will assemble their explosive devices at minus two days," responded Harvey.

"I have been giving this whole operation a great deal of thought Blair, and I think that we ought to postpone for an additional three months to allow things to cool down", said Maury. "I have a feeling that our investigator friend will be back soon and could cause untold complications for us in carrying out this mission. Surely, you and Harvey can see the wisdom in my thinking?"

"The only thing that I see is your cowardice. You're all talk and no walk Maury. You always have been," said Blair. "You're married to your own image of yourself as the great thinker, a man of wisdom and vision when in reality you're nothing but a con man. You're nothing but a used car salesman who can't close the deal. It took me some time to see beyond the rhetoric, but what I see is a million little flaws about to crack."

Blair moved up to within a foot of Maury and continued.

"You conned Harvey and me into believing in a worthy cause which in the final analysis you have no faith in. You bungled the job with the investigator; needlessly killed five people and have come very close to exposing our whole mission. You are a liar and a theft, and you have betrayed the cause. For that you must pay the ultimate price."

Before Maury could reply, Blair displayed her weapon of choice, a 9 mm Walther PPK/S with silencer hidden in her jacket and shot Maury in the forehead at point blank range. Maury tumbled to the floor like a rag doll with a look of astonishment on his face. Harvey was stunned. He could not believe what he just witnessed. It was absolutely surreal.

His body began to shake as he stammered, "Wha....What the hell did you do that for?"

"He was a traitor to the cause. I should have opposed him when he ordered the deaths of Mari Denton, Elaine and that Parrish fellow. They knew nothing of any importance. That decision has brought law enforcement and a very good private investigator into the equation and that should never have happened. He exposed us at the very moment that this operation was in the implementation phase and has made our task much more difficult.

Maury was simply using you to gain acceptance and creditability with your conservative movement friends. He wanted to further his efforts to gain complete power over the more radical members. Granted he was far more articulate than most of us in terms of his rhetoric, but second rate when it came to implementing operational plans.

Harvey, it was you and I who put this plan together down to the last detail and Maury screwed it up. Think about it. It was unnecessary for those people to die including Red and Randy. None of them knew enough to harm us in the slightest, yet Maury wanted to demonstrate to all the members that he had the power and the balls to use it. Foolishly, we went along and sanctioned the killings without thinking it through.

It brought none other than the infamous Abe Lincoln into the game. Do you know who he is? Once you get past the name you realize that he is the most successful unlicensed investigator in the country. He's relentless in his efforts to solve cases that he takes on.

I've done a little research since Maury decided to discourage him instead of kill him, and the only way to stop Mr. Lincoln is with a bullet. Hell, Maury didn't even know who the investigator was. If Maury wanted to clean up his mistakes he should have had Abe killed. He didn't and we may yet pay for that mistake. Any postponement of this mission as proposed by Maury would only give Mr. Lincoln more time to uncover our plan.

I've had Maury under surveillance by Dan Sexton and discovered that he was planning to flee the area. He had managed to stash away over five million dollars from our treasury into a secret bank account in the Cayman Islands and had booked a flight to Brazil for tomorrow. Maury thought that we were doomed and was running sacred. Need I explain further or are you going to help me get on with implementing our plan? We don't need Maury. We can always find a spokesperson with rhetorical skills. They're a dime a dozen."

"Okay, okay....you're right of course. I didn't know any of that. I didn't want those people killed. After all Mari and Elaine were friends of mine, but Maury insisted that it was necessary to silence them in order to carry out our plans.

He pointed out that many times innocent lives are lost to further a noble cause. Frankly, I didn't take the time to think through the possible repercussions."

After witnessing what just happened, Harvey was sacred shitless. What if Blair decided that he was the next one to be eliminated? Talk about a cold blooded woman, she didn't even give him a warning. His best chance for survival was to keep on her good side until he could sort things out. He wasn't about to cross her or even argue with her at this juncture.

"Call Dan Sexton and have a crew clean up this mess and dispose of the body," said Blair. "I want the hands and feet cut off and burned and all the teeth pulled and thrown away. I want the body cremated. I don't want anyone to be able to identify the body. When the time is appropriate we will announce Maury's treachery and his elimination. Agreed?"

"Yes, yes of course," Harvey stated nervously. "What next?"

"We'll go forward with the plan. You will assume Maury's responsibilities. We will meet again here in five days to reassess the progress of the mission. In the meantime please keep a low profile."

"You don't have to worry about that. For all intense and purposes I am on vacation at my cabin in Idaho. See you in five days."

"Be careful Harvey, I need you to be strong for us."

"Not a problem Blair."

Harvey let himself out of her apartment. He had some thinking to do before the five days were up.

Blair was not worried about Harvey. She had enough dirt on him to send him to prison for a lifetime, marital discretions notwithstanding. She was certain that her little drama with Maury had sacred him sufficiently to keep him in line. Blair had no remorse in killing Maury. It was like stepping on a bug.

CHAPTER 12

BOBBI ANN'S REVENGE

Abe contacted Norris and Dunn. Larry Dunn was extremely helpful. The company had reviewed the emails of the previous auditor, a Greg Tenant, and found the peculiar notation SADIL-110601. The information passed on to Martin Parrish before he went to Wheaton. When Abe asked the nature of Mr. Tenant's death, he was astonished by the answer. Mr. Tenant died in fatal single car accident. The report on his audit was never found, but he had emailed a copy of the preliminary report as an attachment in an email to his company email account.

Abe was beginning to understand the real significance of that notation. Apparently a number of folks had died because they knew about it. It was time to search the Internet.

Although Abe would never be found among the ranks of the Twitter or Facebook crowd, he did find the Internet a useful tool for accessing information that would have normally taken him days to acquire. He grudgingly admitted that it was a time saver. After conducting several searches using different combinations of the number 110601, he could find no significance events or correlation within the Wheaton area. Nothing of major importance happened in Wheaton on November 6, 2001 or on June 11, 2001. What did cause alarm bells to clang in his head was when he dropped Wheaton as a factor. The result was a cause for alarm…. serious alarm.

As Abe starred at the information it became very clear that something with devastating consequences could be on the horizon and probably about to explode in their faces.
He and Jacob had to get to Wheaton quickly. Jacob had pulled out of the drive way just minutes ago. There was still time to catch him before he hit the Interstate. He jumped into his truck and peeled out of the driveway heading down the access road to S1000. He could have used his cell phone but for the fact that Jacob didn't own one.

Jacob had just pulled off the access road and was headed down County Road S1000. About two miles up the road he spotted the car off to the side of the road.

A young woman was squatted at the rear apparently attempting to change a tire on the vehicle without much success. Jacob pulled in behind her and got out of his SUV.

"Got a problem? Need some help?" said Jacob.

"Oh, God, Yes!" exclaimed the woman. "I've been tryin' to loosen these lug nuts for the last fifteen minutes. I'm already late for work, and if I don't get there soon I'll probably get fired."

She was probably in her late twenties, fairly tall, slim and an attractive looking redhead. She was neatly dressed in dark slacks and a cream colored blouse.

Jacob's powers of observation that had been honed through years of police work told him that she didn't look like a person who had been battling lug nuts for fifteen minutes. She had hardly broken a sweat and showed no signs of dirt or grease on her hands which was unusual for someone trying to change a tire.

"Well, maybe I can help. By the way where do you work?"

"I just started work at the Pioneer Café in Maple Grove as a hostess. Do you know it?"

"Yea I've eaten there a time or two. What are you doing way out here?"

"Well, I was coming back to Maple Grove from visiting a friend in Salina. A coworker told me about this shortcut, so I thought I'd try it. Unfortunately my tires have a lot of wear and I blew a tire. Guess I should have stuck to the main road, huh?"

"Yeah, these back roads can be kinda hard on tires. Well, give me the lug wrench, and I'll try to get these lug nuts loose, okay?"

"Great. I'm going to get my cell phone so I can call the café and let them know what happened."

Jacob thought that it was unusual that she hadn't done that already. Something strange is going on here.

Bobbi Ann Henry handed Jacob the lug wrench with the slightest of smiles on her face and walked toward the front of the car.

Bobbi Ann had cursed the flat tire, but she quickly recognized her golden opportunity. When she spotted his vehicle coming down the road, she couldn't believe that it was going to be this easy. Bobbi Ann's father had taught her to change a tire when she was eight. She would pretend to be just another helpless woman. Bobbi was just minutes from doing what she planned for so long. She had him off guard. All she had to do was open the driver side door; reach into the glove compartment for her .38 special; turn and fire at his head from point blank range. He'd never know what hit him.

Her daddy was about to be revenged. Bobbi would drag Jacob's body into the ditch by the road and cover it with grass and leaves in case another car would happen by. She would change her tire and be on her way to Colorado. No clues would be left behind.

As she reached for her weapon, she heard another vehicle pull up. Damn. She dropped the weapon onto the floor mat and quickly stood up and closed the car door. Bobbi Ann was astounded when she saw that it was none other than Abe Lincoln. Shit.

"Hey, what're you doin down there Jacob? Praying."

"Very funny. Come here and give me a hand."

When Abe was close enough Jacob whispered, *"Something weird going on here. My cop sense tells me something isn't right. I don't think that it was a cell phone that she was after before you pulled up, if you get what I mean."*

Abe nodded and moved toward the front of the car.

"Hi there, I'm Abe Lincoln. What's your name young lady?"

Bobbi Ann looked at him rather angrily.

Damn her luck. She had Jacob right where she wanted him and then he shows up. She would have to play it cool, get her tire changed and wait for another opportunity.

"Hi, I'm Melissa Myers. I live in Maple Grove and work at the Pioneer Café. I think that I've seen you in there a time or two."

"Yea, you probably have. Been in there a time or two. How long you worked there?"

Abe maneuvered toward the front door of the car.

"Been there just two weeks."

Bobbi Ann moved into position to block access to the front door.

"What are you doin way out here in the boonies?"

Abe moved to about a foot away from Bobbi Ann.

"Well, like I told your friend I was coming back from visiting a friend in Salina and decided that I'd take this short cut that people at work told me about. Unfortunately, I had a flat tire."

"About got your tire changed." yelled Jacob. "You call the cafe yet?"

"No, I was about to when Mr. Lincoln pulled up. It can wait. I should be there in no time."

"That's okay. Go ahead and make the call. I'm sure your boss would appreciate it," said Abe.

Bobbie Ann was trapped and she knew it. They were on to her. If she opened the car door Abe was sure to see her .38. Maybe she would get lucky. If she kept the car door between her and Abe she could grab hold of her weapon turn and fire it and maybe get him with a lucky shot, then she could take out Jacob. It was awful risky, but what other choice did she have.

"You're right I should call," replied Bobbi Ann

Bobbi Ann opened the front door slightly and lurched for the gun, but she was swiftly pulled backward before her hand touched it. Jacob had stealthily moved up from behind the car and grabbed her around the waist. Abe moved forward at the same time flung open the car door and retrieved the .38 special.

"Well…well what have we here? Plan on doing some target practice on the way to work?" said Abe.

"I carry a weapon for self-protection. It's registered. I take it with me when I'm traveling alone. Now if you don't mind can I have my gun back, and I'll be on my way?"

"Why don't you give up the charade Bobbi Ann Henry? I know who you are and why you're here," said Jacob.

Abe got a puzzled look on his face.

"What the hell is going on here? You knew who she was and still let her go for her gun? You got a death wish or are you just crazy?"

"Relax, Abe. I had the whole thing under control. I had to have confirmation of her intent, so I let her go for the gun. When she turned her back on me to go to the front of the car I had my weapon pulled. I would have winged her before she got off a shot."

"You hope!"

"*How...how did you know?*" stuttered Bobbi Ann angrily.

Jacob let Bobbi Ann loose from his grip.

"Larry Sutton of the Topeka Police Department called me before I left The Lodge and filled me in on your activities Ms. Henry. I had requested a trace on you. Larry did a background and found something very interesting.

It seems that you were living with a small time hood by the name of a Lenny Brunner. It's the same Lenny Brunner that tried to take me out a few weeks ago. Small world isn't it.

While the police were checking out Mr. Brunner they found that he had deposited $2,000 to his bank account the week prior to the attempt on me.

A check of Ms. Henry's bank account showed a withdrawal of $2,000 about the same time. What a coincidence. We've got enough circumstantial evidence for a charge of accessory to attempted murder."

"You son of a bitch!" screamed Bobbi Ann. "You were responsible for my daddy's death. You arrested him and testified against him in court. I was there. I saw it. He was an innocent man. He was framed and you knew it. You and the courts killed him just as sure as if you'd put a gun to his head.

When my father died in prison my mother lost all hope and hung herself. One of your precious policemen that she brought home from a bar raped me right in front of her eyes and then laughed about it. He dared her to do something about it. No one would have believed her because she was a drunk. You killed my family.

Later it was found that my father was innocent after all. You all screwed up. You and your upholding the law bullshit.

You can all go rot in hell! Sure I wanted you dead. Lenny screwed it all up, so I decided to do it myself. So arrest me. Send me to prison. Maybe I'll die there like my Dad. Then you'll have successfully killed a whole family. Better yet maybe I'll just start walking down the road and you can shoot me now. I don't really give a damn anymore."

Bobbi Ann started to move away but Abe caught her and held her in a tight grip.

"You're in very bad trouble here and anger isn't going to solve your problems Bobbi Ann. You've been angry for a very long time and look where it's gotten you. Sure you've had it tough and you've gone through a lot of hell. Yes, there was a miscarriage of justice against your father, and you and your mother suffered at the hands of a rotten cop. If it had been me I'm sure that I would feel the same anger, but seeking revenge by shooting someone who was just doing his job isn't going to fix anything.

You think Jacob doesn't feel bad about that arrest and that the system of justice failed. He knows there were mistakes made in the case against your father, because the investigation wasn't thorough enough.

It pains him deeply that your mother lost her life because of a bastard cop who raped you. But killing Jacob isn't going to undo anything."

Jacob spoke up.

"Look here Bobbi Ann, I know this won't mean much to you right now, but I am truly sorry about what happen to you and your family. After we found out the truth about your father and how he was framed, I vowed that I would never let it happen again. I learned to be painstakingly thorough in all my investigations after that and to make sure of my facts, at least as sure as is humanly possible.

What happened in your father's case was always at the forefront of my mind from that time forward. It was a painful and tragic lesson to learn and at great expense to you. I realize that. If there was a way to make up for the past I would. There isn't.

We did manage to find out the truth about the cop that raped you and sent him to prison. He was killed by other prisoners within a week. As Abe said there is no way to undo what has been done. Killing me may give you a moment of satisfaction, but it will give you a lifetime of grief. I know that to be true, because I suffered grief every time I had to kill someone in the line of duty. Most good cops do feel that grief.

Do you want to be looking over your shoulder for the rest of your life and be constantly on the run? Eventually you would have been caught, because cops never give up when one of their own get murdered. That may not sound fair to you, but it's the truth.

As for shooting you that's not an option. I think that you need to ask yourself one question. Would your father want you to seek revenge in his name? I'm betting that he wouldn't.

The pain and the suffering have to stop now. My only option at the moment is to have the Sheriff take you into custody and hold you on an attempted aggravation charge pending further investigation. Given the extenuating circumstances surrounding your actions, I'm not inclined to press charges against you providing you behave yourself while in custody and take some time to seriously think about those past actions and your future.

Life has given you a raw deal, but hooking up with the likes of Lenny Brunner isn't going to improve your chances for something better. You can either spend the rest of your life living in the past and being an angry and bitter person Bobbi Ann or you can change directions. It's up to you.

You've proven that you've got some brains up there. You just need to channel your energy into something more constructive and away from all the past hate and anger. It's your decision. No one can decide for you. Frankly, I think you've got a lot more potential than you realize. Think about it. Abe, I need your cell phone. I'm going to call the Sheriff."

"It's in my truck."

Bobbi Ann was stunned. Jacob was not at all what she expected. He was far too gentle and soft spoken. There was something about this man Jacob that reminded Bobbi Ann of her father. It was the soft gentle sound of his voice and the way he had of talking to her and not down to her.

He really didn't lecture her. It was more like he reasoned with her and tried to explain things. Just like her father use to do when she was little. Bobbi suddenly realized that the things that Jacob had told her would have been exactly what her father would have said to her. Despite her anger and frustration at the moment she had to admit to herself that her Daddy wouldn't want her to seek revenge in his name.

Suddenly the tears welled up in her eyes and then she let out a wail and fell to the ground sobbing and shaking letting the tears flow out of her. It was like someone had just taken all the pain and hate and anger inside her and ripped it from her soul. She felt weak and empty inside. She was tired. Oh so very tired of it all.

Abe leaned down and tried to comfort her as best he could. He knew then that Jacob was right. This woman was no criminal but merely a victim of all the cruelty that had been visited upon her. Her malice was a reaction to the ugly events that had transpired in her life to lead her to this point on this country road. She suddenly realized that her worst enemy was her own anger.

Jacob ambled back from Abe's truck with the cell phone in hand. He helped Bobbi Ann up from the ground and guided her into the back seat of his SUV.

"Just sit here and relax for a few minutes Bobbi Ann. There are some matters I need to discuss with Abe. Okay?"

"Okay," Bobbi Ann replied in a small weak voice.

She felt like a small girl again and just wanted to close her eyes and rest. She didn't have the strength to argue or discuss anything right now.

Jacob walked over to where Abe was standing.

"I've decided not to call the sheriff for the time being. I'm betting that Bobbi Ann doesn't have the strength or will to follow through on any more attempts. She needs some time to sort everything out in her mind, and sending her to jail even temporarily isn't going to help her do that. I think that she really needs someone to help her sort out her problems, mainly her anger. She needs someone to gain her trust. I think that person would be Miriam."

"What do you have in mind in the short term? When I tell you about what I've found you're going to realize that we need to get our butts down to Wheaton as fast as possible. Something big may be coming down, and we need to get on top of it."

"Bobbi Ann needs to spend some time with Miriam. She appears to be quite capable of quickly gaining Bobbi Ann's confidence and can keep an eye on her for the time being. Miriam could probably use the company as well. What do you think?"

"Well, if anyone can handle Bobbi Ann right now, it would be Miriam. I understand your motives, but aren't you forgetting one small item. Bobbi Ann has committed crimes. Contracting for a murder is nothing to overlook. She solicited the participation of another person in a contract to kill you. That person was killed trying to carry out the contract. I agree that she and her family were victims of a real travesty of justice. But everyone has to take some responsibility for their actions no matter the circumstances.

I fully understand her anger and motivation, but vengeance has no place in the order of things. If we allow that, we invite chaos. The truth is that Bobbi Ann made some serious mistakes in judgment."

"Normally, I'd agree with everything that you've said. I am not making excuses for her behavior and bad judgment. I'm well aware that what I'm suggesting is a circumvention of the system.

But I had to ask myself what would be gained by throwing her in jail even if it were only temporarily. She could easily become more despondent and bitter, maybe even suicidal, given the fact that she realizes that the course of action that she took was dead wrong.

Maybe I'm making judgments here that should be left to the courts, but my years of experience tell me this is the right thing to do. I really don't believe that she is a cold, calculating killer with no feelings of remorse. Lenny voluntarily took out that contract for the money. He wasn't coerced by any means, and was fully aware of the risks. He could have just as easily walked away or reported her to the authorities. He didn't.

I think she has earned some time to sort things out without the threat of jail time. If I'm wrong and she tries to escape or act out again on her need for revenge, Miriam can march her to jail and I'll press charges. My gut feeling is that she won't try to escape or act out.

If you want to go ahead and report her to the authorities, I can't stop you; but I'll refuse to press charges."

"Okay, Jacob. We'll play it your way, but we need to fully explain to Bobbie Ann and Miriam the rules here. On false move and she goes directly to jail."

"Agreed!"

On the way to his truck Abe wondered what had caused Jacob to change his mind about Bobbi Ann. He knew that Jacob and Beth had never had children of their own, because Beth had a medical condition that wouldn't allow her to conceive. They had talked about adopting but never did. Maybe Jacob was thinking of Bobbi Ann in terms of the child that he never had.

Abe knew that Jacob felt responsible for Mr. Henry's conviction and ultimate death. Maybe this was his effort to do the responsible thing for Bobbi Ann and give her another chance at life. God knows she needed one. When Jacob climbed into the SUV he told Bobbi Ann that they were taking her to The Lodge for the time being. He would explain more when they got there.

Bobbi Ann was stunned because she figured that she would be behind bars before nightfall. She just couldn't figure this man out. Most men that she had known would try to take advantage of her or manipulate her in some fashion given the present circumstances. That had been her experience anyway. Actually she was simply too tired to try and figure anything out. She closed her eyes and fell asleep.

Once they arrived at The Lodge Bobbi Ann stumbled up the steps and into the living room half asleep. She lay down on the couch and closed her eyes once again. Abe and Jacob went to find Miriam to explain the situation. Jacob filled her in on Bobbi Ann's background and misfortune, and Abe recounted what had happened in the last hour. Abe explained Jacob's plan for the short term.

Miriam agreed that she could handle the situation. She understood the seriousness of the situation and the need to keep a close eye on Bobbi Ann especially during the next few days. Miriam agreed with Jacob that the girl really needed another chance given what had happened to her over the last several years, but that she would have to earn it by changing her behavior. It would take some time and a lot of patience, because Bobbi Ann had let so much anger and hatred build up over the years. She was carrying a great deal of guilt about her mother's death and her own rape.

She told Jacob not to expect any overnight miracles. Miriam liked this Jacob person. She particularly liked the way that he had handled the situation with this young lady. It showed that he had character and a good heart.

Jacob and Miriam woke Bobbi Ann and took her to what would be her room in the Lodge. Jacob told Bobbi Ann of his decision not to call the sheriff and to allow her some time to think through all that had happened and how she wanted to live the rest of her life. Bobbi Ann would be under a kind of house arrest and her activities would be under the supervision of Miriam.

If Bobbi Ann attempted to leave the premises, create any kind of disturbance, or exhibit any type of violent or threatening behavior, Miriam would call the Sheriff and have her transported to the County Jail. Jacob explained Miriam's background and her capability to handle any type of situation. If Bobbi Ann wanted to talk through some of her feelings or seek advice Miriam was there to help her.

Miriam would outline some daily chores and routines for Bobbi Ann to undertake in a few days. He asked Bobbi Ann if she had any questions about her living arrangements.

Bobbi Ann was stunned for the second time today. She really had some mixed emotions about the whole situation. It had been less than four hours ago that she tried to kill this man.

Now he was offering her sanctuary in his friend's house and a chance to start a new life. She found that hard to believe.

Bobbi Ann had learned the hard way to be suspicious of other people's motives a long time ago and now was no exception. She trusted no one least of all a former cop. There had to be a catch somewhere. She decided that she would bide her time for a few days and see what happened. She needed the rest anyway. If she didn't like what was happening she would figure a way to leave and head for Colorado.

Jacob was so much like her father in many ways that she almost bordered on feelings of admiration for him. These feelings really perplexed her. She didn't feel the desire to harm him like before. All of his recent actions would indicate that he did have true remorse for what had happen to her family.

Deep down inside she really wanted to believe that what he was offering her was genuine, but all that had happened to her in the past still made her wary. She was too tired to sort through it all now. Maybe she could think better tomorrow after she got some rest.

"Although I don't totally understand it, I appreciate the fact that you didn't call the Sheriff," said Bobbi Ann. "Right now all I want is to sleep. I will promise not to give Miriam any trouble.

Maybe in a couple of days I can think more clearly. I really don't have any questions right now, but I'm sure that I will have. What you said about my father is true. He would not have liked what I have done with my life up to now."

"I'll check in later to see how things are going. Meantime get some rest."

"Yes, I need to."

Jacob left the room and went to find Abe.

"You have a private bathroom and that's the door to your left. I'll show you where the towels and wash clothes are. The bed has been remade with clean sheets. I'll show you how to work the intercom if you need to call me for anything. We are going to lock your door for a while, so you'll have to call me if you want out of your room. I'll show you where things are tomorrow. Okay?" said Miriam.

"Sure, fine," replied Bobbi Ann.

Jacob found Abe in his room packing a bag for the trip to Wheaton.

"What's up?" said Jacob.

"Well, the information that I retrieved from Martin's former boss and the Internet tells me something very nasty is about to come down on our heads.

That notation that Parrish left is the key. It represents the month, day and year that Timothy McVeigh was executed for the Oklahoma City bombing. June 11, 2001. The letters preceding the numbers represent the name of a far right political group called the Sons and Daughters in Liberty. I took a look at their website.
Basically they advocate a drastic downsizing of the role of Federal, State and Local Government."

"Interesting," said Jacob. "I've got a contact in the Counterterrorism Unit of the FBI. Let's get on the road and I'll contact him. They may have something on this group."

Abe handed his cell phone to Jacob.

"Alright, but we're getting you a cell phone. You're going to need it."

"Okay, but I'll pay for it."

Jacob was able to get through to his contact and spent the next twenty minutes getting a run down on the Sons and Daughters organization.

Jacob explained, "According to my contact they've had the Sons and Daughters in Liberty under low level surveillance for over a year; but the organization has no record of domestic violence or even advocating violence as part of their agenda. Apparently the organization has a budget around $10 to $20 million. What concerns me is that according an FBI informant the organization has 350 members, and Harvey Bacon is on the list. Maury Williams is listed as a member and has had extensive ties to radical organizations in his past including such groups as the Weathermen. Maury has been seen in the company of Harvey Bacon and a wealthy lady by the name of Blair Logan.

Blair Logan as it turns out is the Director of the Sons and Daughters organization. All three have had several meetings in Ms. Blair's Wichita luxury apartment. The informant believes that Harvey, Maury and Ms. Blair are the decision makers behind the organization.

Ms. Blair is a strong Bircher and has contributed generously to the cause of several radical right wing groups. According to FBI sources she has remarked on several occasions that Ronald Reagan and Barry Goldwater were too moderate and Rush Limbaugh is a loud mouth idiot.

The FBI also picked up rumors that some of those folks who joined the Sons and Daughters and who had a falling out with the organization have mysteriously disappeared over the last few years or been killed in rather freakish accidents.

The informant told the FBI about a month ago that he learned of a big event that was in the planning stages that would literally shake the foundations of the Federal Government.

Unfortunately the informant has gone missing and hasn't been heard from in weeks."

"Well Larry Dunn at Norris and Finch told me that the previous person to audit the Citizens Group, a Greg Tenant, was killed in a one car accident on his way home from the audit. The hard copy of his audit report was never found, but he had emailed a copy of the report to his company email address. The report had a special notation labeled SADIL-110601. Martin Parrish had a copy of that report. Knowledge of that notation seems to be very fatal. My gut feeling is that Mr. Parrish and anyone who he associated with in his last few days were targeted because of his knowledge of the notation."

"That's not good news," exclaimed Jacob. "The only problem is that all this information is circumstantial. We may have a hard time selling the theory to the Wheaton Police or any law enforcement agency without more solid proof. Based on what you've discovered I wouldn't have a hard time believing that we're looking at another Oklahoma City style bombing. The question is where and when?"

"Those were my thoughts exactly. I'm thinking maybe I'll give Lisa a call and bounce some of this information off her. See what her instincts tell her."

"Not a bad idea, but you sure that's the only reason for calling?" Jacob said with a big grin.

"Why, Jacob what other reason would there be?" replied Abe with a shrug of the shoulders.

"Come on Abe. You're talking to a seasoned detective here. You think I don't notice things. Give me a break. Your behavior and motives are as obvious as that big nose on your face, buddy."

"Well, not much gets past you, but any ulterior motives are on hold until we actually find out what's going on here."

"I understand that. Just couldn't pass up the chance to needle you a little."

"Well, now that we're on the subject and to even things up I've detected some behavior changes in you and a great deal of interest developing in one certain Israeli ex-patriot. Care to comment?"

"Now hold on a minute ol' buddy. I just admire her intellect and the fact that she seems to be able to keep you in line most of the time without much effort. Any interest is purely platonic."

"Sure….sure…..platonic my ass. Just curious."

"You know about curiosity and the cat right."

I called Lisa's cell phone number. She picked up on the third ring.

"Abe?"

"That'd be me. You where you can talk?"

"Is this business or personal?"

"Strictly business."
"Call me back in ten minutes. Better yet I'll call you."

"She'll call me back," said Abe.

"Strictly business …..very interesting," replied Jacob.

"Okay, Jacob. You've had your fun."

"What are you going to tell her?"

"Everything. No need to hold anything back. We need to convince her and her superiors that this is extremely serious and probably goes well beyond a local case of murder."

"Amen to that. After Oklahoma City and McVeigh's execution I often wondered when one of these radical groups would go off the deep end to raise some real havoc and try to top him. Surprised it hasn't happened before now."

"Whoever these people are, they've kept a damn tight lid on things until now. I'll give them credit for that. Frankly I was about at a dead end until those jokers tried to tenderize me with baseball bats and then killed two more of Mari's friends. Kinda of a dumb move on their part. Up to that point they really hadn't made any mistakes."

"It's the nature of those kinds of groups. They always go to the extreme to cover themselves and end up making the big mistake. Go figure. Guess that's why they call them extremists."

"Well whoever's leading this charge just plain outsmarted themselves. We still don't have a clue who the brains behind this group really is. It could be Harvey Bacon, Maury Williams, or Blair Logan for all we know; or Mr. David Peterson, the banker, or someone we've never heard of. We're going to need a major break and soon."

My phone rang. It was Lisa calling back.

"Okay, Abe. What've you got for me?"

"Well for starters I think we figured out the strange notation in Parrish's notes, the SADIL-110601. Jacob and I think that the letters stand for a domestic radical political group called the Sons and Daughters in Liberty.

We believe numbers represent the execution date for none other than Timothy McVeigh, the Oklahoma City bomber that being June 11, 2001. You understand that right now this is all speculation on our part, but we believe that the motive for killing Martin Parrish and all who associated with him in his final hours was the notation found in his notes.

The party or parties involved probably thought the notation was destroyed in the blast until I came snooping around asking questions about it. Why they didn't just kill me is anyone's guess. Maybe they thought another death in such a short period of time would raise an alarm and intensify the investigation. There simply is no other plausible explanation for the killings."

"What if the killings weren't related or maybe they are the work of a serial killer?"

"I wouldn't totally rule those ideas out, but I have two questions for you.

When is the last time you had three suspicious deaths occur in three consecutive days involving Wheaton citizens, not to mention the additional deaths of Red Francis and Randy Miller?

Second if it is a serial killer where is his or her signature? Show me some similarities among the victims. Typically serial killers have those markers. There is none here."

"You have a point for now. Go on."

"It appears that some local folks in the Wheaton area have strong connections to the Sons and Daughters organization. Through one of Jacob's sources in the FBI who have kept a low level surveillance on the group we've found out that Harvey Bacon is a bona fide member and maybe a leader.

Apparently a prominent business woman in the area by the name of Blair Logan is the Director of the organization. It, also, appears that our disappearing bartender friend Maury Williams is a bona fide member of the group.

Now granted I'm not one for guilt by association nor does the FBI have any indication that this group is militant or promotes violence but there seems to be a hell of a lot of coincidental information floating to the surface.

Right now all of this information is like a giant jigsaw puzzle, and I'm anxious to see how the pieces fit together if they fit at all. Jacob and I have a very strong gut feeling that this group of folks have a timetable in place for something very bad to happen and are protecting that timetable at all cost. That feeling has been given some creditability through an FBI informant that has been planted in the organization. Unfortunately he has disappeared.

The relationship of the date in the notation or code and Timothy McVeigh is frightening in and of itself. Our worst fear is that the group is planning an Oklahoma City style bombing to make some kind of political statement or to create some real panic. I know that the information is thin, and it requires a real leap in imagination to support our gut feelings but then the FBI didn't know about these local killings and the notation. Now they have an informant that is missing. They may well be reevaluating their scrutiny regarding the Sons and Daughters."

"I see. I can understand the need for concern, but isn't your information rather weak as a basis for assuming that some kind of terrorist attack is imminent?

If the FBI had the Sons and Daughters organization under low level surveillance that would indicate to me that they are not any kind of immediate threat, and according to what you said the FBI doesn't have any evidence that the group actually promotes violence or is militant."

"Normally I'd say everything you said is true, but for a couple of disturbing factors. Most domestic radical groups are underfunded and don't have the resources or expertise to undertake a well-planned coordinated and sophisticated terrorist attack. McVeigh got lucky in that security was lax, and he had some expertise in explosives and worked alone except for one accomplice. After Oklahoma City the chances of getting any kind of unattended rental truck even close to a federal building would draw all kinds of scrutiny.

The fact is that the Sons and Daughters organization has a very robust treasury that is estimated to be in the $10 to $20 million dollar range according to FBI sources. The second factor is that one of their members has a rather large dossier at the FBI of association with and participation in radical left wing groups of the 60s and 70s namely groups lead by Tom Hayden, Jerry Rubin, and believe it or not the Weathermen. That person is none other than Maury Williams.

It seems that our Mr. Williams was rather busy in his youth dropping out of college and traveling the country heavily involved in and learning militant tactics and techniques.

It is a matter of record that he participated in the debacle at the Democratic Convention in Chicago in 1968 and was arrested for attempting to incite a riot as well as aggravated assault. His well-connected parents managed to get him out of that mess.

Eventually he drifted back to college where he became a close friend and roommate of our Mr. Harvey Bacon. It was during this time that he switched sides and joined the ranks of the right wing conservative movement.

After that Maury sort of blended into the woodwork until he emerged a few weeks ago. What we could have is an organization within an organization here. By the way what do you know about Blair Logan?"

"Professionally or personally?"

"Both!"

"Professionally she has been quite successful. She owns a string of beauty salons and spas throughout the Midwest and built her business from the ground up.

I've been in numerous meetings with her, and she appears to be a very bright and articulate woman. Politically speaking I would say her views are extremely conservative. I have had several conversations with her, and she seems to be very opinionated and inflexible. Although I've never observed it, others tell me that she has a very sharp tongue and is quick to cut others down.

It is a widely held rumor that she and David Peterson have had an ongoing affair for years. He was the banker who gave her the first loan to get her business started. The have been other rumors that she has taken on several of her female employees as lovers from time to time and prefers women to men.

Obviously there are people in the community who resent her and are jealous of her financial success. She has no criminal record not even a parking ticket. That's about it."

"You think that she would be capable of getting involved in political violence?"

"Hard to say. I really don't know enough about her to make that kind of judgment. As we both know from experience given the right circumstances anyone is capable of violent activity.

In her case I would say that there would have to be some definite monetary gain involved. Others have told me that once she commits to something she will not tolerate failure."

"Good to know that. What are the chances of us getting an audience with David Peterson?"

"I'm sure that can be arranged. Does that mean you're on your way back down here? And who is us?"

"As we speak! Jacob is with me."

"I'm honored. What kind of pretext did you have in mind for this meeting?"

"I'll leave that to your imaginative mind, probably something along the lines of the continuing investigation into the recent deaths of Martin Parrish and Mari Denton. We need to really turn up the heat and see what develops. You and Jacob will have to participate, since I'm supposed to be out of the picture. You can introduce Jacob as a consulting investigator."

"Oh, now I have an imaginative mind. Well, at least Jacob and I are savvy enough to avoid the bat treatment."

"I swear one little miscue and you never stop hearing about it. At any rate somewhere in the conversation you need to bring up Blair Logan and Harvey Bacon and their connection to the Sons and Daughters to get some kind of reaction. Either Peterson is party to what's happening or he's totally ignorant.

I'm inclined to believe that he really doesn't know what's going on.

He was totally puzzled when I brought up the notation 'SADIL -110601' found in Parrish's notes about his Citizens Group Foundation funding ledger.

I'm betting that funds were being transferred from his organization to the Sons and Daughters for a specific purpose without his knowledge. Ask him what his Chief Accountant told him about the notation.

We really need something out of Peterson to give us an excuse to interview Blair and Harvey and shake them up. Any ideas on the whereabouts of Maury Williams?"

"Not a clue. We have searched everywhere and talked to all our usual sources and come up empty. He seems to have completely disappeared."

"That really concerns me. It could mean that whatever is going down will happen very soon. We should be there in about another hour and a half. Jacob already has a room at the Holiday Inn Express, so we'll operate out of there.
Find out where Harvey is, and I'll follow him around while you two are busy with Mr. Peterson. Maybe he'll lead me to Maury. Any thoughts?"

"You believe something very sinister is going on around here don't you?"

"Absolutely! According to the FBI there have been numerous reports of members of the Sons and Daughters suddenly disappearing never to be found, or meeting with unusual fatal accidents over the past couple of years which could mean this group has a method of permanently terminating recalcitrant members; or maybe it's all coincidental but I doubt it.

From my experience there are just too many signs that someone is trying to hide something critically important to this organization. Jacob's instincts tell him the same thing. I think that the missing FBI informant confirms that."

"That's good enough for me. I'm going to have my intelligence unit see what they can uncover about the Sons and Daughters in this area. I know that they've had a couple of rallies in the area protesting taxes and government regulation, but it was all very peaceful and certainly non-violent. If I remember, I think that they drew crowds of between 150 to 200 folks which is normal for those kinds of things.

"Sounds like a good idea. See you soon."

"Okay, you want me to meet you at the motel?"

"I'll call you when we get in. We need to sit down and figure out the best way to move on this."

"Sounds like a plan. Bye for now."

"Bye."

Abe stopped at a well-known cell phone distributor in Wichita and bought Jacob his own cell phone. Jacob had used them while on the job, but never bought one for his personal use. He didn't feel the need after his wife died.

CHAPTER 13

TEDDY SEXTON'S NIGHTMARE

Dusk had begun to descend upon the small village just north of Kabul when Dan Sexton and Eric Stiles crept up the side of a hill overlooking their mission target. Dan and Eric were military assassins assigned to take out Taliban leaders who were mounting offensives against American troops in Afghanistan

Their mission tonight was to take out a very troublesome leader who had done a great deal of damage in this sector. Neither Eric nor Dan had any qualms about assassination. They figured that it was just part of the job. Neither person had the slightest hesitation even though innocent civilians were sometimes collateral damage victims as a result of their tactics.

As darkness began to envelope them they slithered down the side of the hill and worked their way toward the location where their victim was allegedly spending the night. Tonight there weapon of choice was a M202A Flash Assault Shoulder weapon that had a bazooka type design and held four launch tubes. The rockets themselves contained an incendiary mixture that would torch its intended victims and anyone near them. When they reached their attack position Dan shouldered the weapon and prepared to fire. Eric acted as a spotter and look out.

"I hope the Intel on this is spot on this time"
declared Dan.

"According to the boss, the source is 100%," replied
Eric.

At the very moment Dan was squeezing the trigger
automatic fire erupted behind and above them from
the hill. Eric and Dan immediately knew they had
been set up. In the Nano second that Dan swerved a
rocket was launched and hit the hut next to the
intended target. Women and children came
screaming from the hut ablaze in a phosphorous
fire. Automatic fire erupted from the target hut. Eric
was hit twice in the calf.

Luckily they weren't disabling wounds, but they
hurt like hell. It was the first time either person had
ever been hit by enemy fire. Dan swerved and fired a
rocket at the attackers and obliterated the whole
group in a fiery ball. He then turned and fired a
rocket at the intended target and set the hut ablaze
in phosphorous flames. The screams from the
victims were indescribable.

As Dan aided Eric in moving away from the area he
noticed that he had been hit in his left forearm. Both
men knew that it was Dan's quick reflects that had
saved them from certain death. Eric would be
indebted to Dan. It would never be mentioned, but it
was the unspoken code that was honored by
everyone in their line of work.

"Damn I hope that we got the son of a bitch,"
murmured Eric. "Too bad about those women and
children."

"Shit happens," casually remarked Dan. "Shit Happens. Casualties of War or I guess the term now is collateral damage."

As it turned out their intended target had escaped the attack.

After completing two tours of duty as an Army Ranger assigned to Delta Force, Dan Sexton came home and married his high school sweetheart. He went to work as sheriff's deputy for Madison County. Dan never mentioned his activity while overseas, but then most who had been there in his line of work didn't and couldn't according to military law. Eric Stiles followed Dan to Madison County and became a Deputy Sheriff as well.

When Dan joined the Sons and Daughters organization, Eric didn't. Eric wasn't a joiner.

Dan's pride and joy was his son Teddy. Teddy Sexton always admired his Dad. Dan Sexton stood 6'3", 240 pounds with an athletic build and curly blond hair. He was what women would call 'hot'. Teddy wanted to grow up to be just like him.

Dan Sexton had been an exceptional father. He spent a great deal of his off duty time with Teddy teaching him how to fix things, fish, hunt, throw a football and baseball, shoot a basketball all those things that kids need to learn from a Dad.

At age 15 Teddy could fix anything that ran on a small engine, change the oil, fix a flat tire and do minor repairs around the house. He could clean and reassemble most of the guns in the house. Teddy was an above average student at school and excelled in most sports.

Right after school started in the fall Teddy began having some rather disturbing nightmares about his father. At first they terrified him, and he was afraid to even admit to having them. It wasn't long before Teddy's grades began to slip at school, and he would miss days at a time with terrible headaches. His mother kept asking him what was wrong, but Teddy would say that he didn't know what was wrong.

Finally his mother took him to the doctor who ran a series of tests but could find nothing physically wrong with Teddy. The doctor suggested that the mother consult a family therapist. Dan Sexton exploded. He exclaimed that his son was not crazy and absolutely didn't need to see a shrink.

He told his wife that it was probably an adolescent phase and Teddy would get over it.

But things got worse. Teddy would spend hours at a time in his room and barely spoke to his parents. He could barely sleep at night for fear of having the same nightmares. He was benched by the football coach for making too many mistakes and lack luster play. He grades continued to suffer.

Dan had noticed that Teddy appeared to be avoiding him and seem to be uncomfortable around him. Dan could not bear being ignored by his son. He had confronted Teddy on several occasions but Teddy would deny his behavior.

Each nightmare was the same. It never changed. His parents would come into his room and tell him good night. In the dream his Dad would leave fairly late in the evening on some days and not return until early the next morning. Teddy asked his Dad about it, and his Dad would only say that it was a special mission. Teddy was naturally curious and decided to hide in his Dad's truck one night to see what kind of a special mission his Dad was undertaking.

After they left his room he would get dressed and sneak down the stairs and out the back door and climb into the bed of his Dad's pick-up. Teddy would hide under a tarp in the back of the truck bed. His Dad would get in his pick up and drive for about a half hour to a specific location in the country. Once at the destination his Dad would park the pickup in a semi-circle with other trucks and leave his head lights on.

Teddy would slip out from under the tarp and hide by the rear end of the truck. The location was a clearing surrounded by trees with a dirt road the only access. His Dad would talk with about five other men for a few minutes when a large truck would pull in. Two men would get out of the cab and walk to the back of the truck. All the men would surround the truck and pull their weapons.

A whole group of people would be unloaded from the back of the truck. It appeared that they all had their hands and arms bound behind them. Teddy remembered that they all looked scared. Some would be weeping and sobbing others were silent.

They were lead in front of the semi-circle of trucks and then several yards where they were forced to kneel in front of a large hole that had been dug in the ground. His father would read something from a piece of paper, but Teddy could never hear the exact words. Teddy thought one of the words was 'traitor'.

His Dad and each of the other men would stand to the side of each person place their weapons against the person's temple and fire. The people who were shot would just pitch forward into the hole in the ground. His Dad and the other men would then cover the hole with dirt and limestone using a bulldozer.

Teddy was too stunned to react. He didn't even remember crawling into the back of my Dad's pick up and pulling the tarp over himself.
Teddy would sit there for a moment and then silently begin to weep for those people. That's when the nightmare would end.

Teddy knew that his Dad would never do anything like that, but it was all so vivid and real. Eventually the nightmares decreased and visited Teddy no more. His grades improved, and he began to spend more time with his parents, especially his Dad. He got his starting job back with the football team. Perhaps it was just a bad adolescent dream.

Lisa discovered that Harvey Bacon was vacationing at his condo in Idaho and would be gone for a week. Harvey had been under surveillance ever since the beating received by Abe. It was determined that Harvey had visited Blair Logan in her Wichita apartment on several occasions the last time being just three days ago. He had come from that meeting looking rather shaken and disoriented. Wonder what that was all about? Given Blair's preference for women, Lisa doubted that it was a lovers tryst.

Common knowledge was that Blair didn't have sex with men unless she wanted something from them. Harvey wouldn't have anything that she wanted. She already had his boss by the nuts. Lisa's Intelligence Unit could find nothing disturbing about the Sons and Daughters organization in the Wheaton vicinity.

It appeared that they did have several meetings over the past six months at their facility fifteen miles south and west of town called simply 'The Barn'.

The organization contracted for its own security force with a local business called Sexton Security. Lisa had met Dan Sexton on several occasions and considered him to be very knowledgeable about security methods. She knew that he had previously been a sheriff's deputy and accused several times for using excessive force in his arrests, however he was never cited or disciplined to her knowledge.

Her unit had not observed any of the local meetings, because the organization and its security force did not allow non-members to attend the meetings. There had been no reason up to now to try and penetrate the organization.

There was one piece of intelligence information that did bother her. It was reported that an unusual high number of missing person cases had gone unresolved within the last two years in the Wheaton area. There were about fifteen missing person cases pending which was highly unusual.

This information coincided with what Jacob learned from the FBI. Whatever was going on disturbed her. Were these folks local members of the Sons and Daughters? She decided that she would personally review those cases this evening to cull any similarities.

A few minutes later Abe called to say that they had arrived at the motel and to meet them in Room 102 in fifteen minutes. Lisa felt a bit of a twinge in her stomach. Really, she thought, I'm a little old to be acting like a school girl.

She did have feelings for this man. He certainly wasn't the most handsome or accomplished lover that she had known, but there was something about him that connected with her. He was fun to talk to, and she felt totally comfortable around him. Those feelings would have to be put on hold for now. There was some serious business to conduct perhaps with a great many lives at stake.

When Lisa walked into the room Jacob was stretched out on one of the beds with his St. Louis Cardinal baseball cap pulled over his eyes and was sipping a cold Tecate. Abe was slouched down in a chair hovering over his laptop staring intently at some information on the Sons and Daughters website with a Tecate sitting next to him.

"There's beer in the bathroom sink if you want one. If you don't like Tecate there's Bud draft."

"Thanks, I like Tecate. By the way Harvey is at his condo in Idaho until Saturday. Looks like you'll have to find another target to tail."

"That's okay. I think that Blair Logan might be a more interesting target. According to this information she's a charter member. Apparently Harvey has a membership but holds no office. Didn't see Maury mentioned at all."

"I can tell you that we've had no luck trying to track down the illusive Maury. He's just disappeared. My Intel unit has been unable to find anything of a really sinister nature regarding the Sons and Daughters organization. They did report that our Mr. Bacon has made several recent visits to Ms. Logan's apartment in Wichita in the last two months. Intel reports that he came out of her apartment just three days ago looking shaken and disoriented. Something of a disturbing nature must have happened. The question is "What?"

The Sons and Daughters have a meeting place in this area just fifteen miles south and east of town in a place called 'The Barn'. Apparently they've had several meetings in the past two months. Members only are allowed in the meetings, so we haven't been able to monitor them.

A local private firm handles their security. The head of the firm is a Dan Sexton who used to be a deputy sheriff with a reputation as being overly aggressive in dealing with arrests. He had several complaints filed against him while on the job but was never charged with anything. He has no citations or suspensions. The complaints were dropped.

Dan started his own firm a few years ago with a sizable loan from the bank where Harvey Bacon works.

He has security contracts in five states. He and Harvey are apparently close friends. Their families spend a great deal of time together, and they hunt and fish together.

What disturbs me most from the Intel report is the increasing number of unsolved missing person cases in the Wheaton area over the past two years.

Normally in a town like Wheaton missing person cases are rare and almost always resolved in a couple of months. It fits with what the FBI told you."

"Figures. I'd bet that we'd be hard pressed to find any former Sons and Daughters members still alive. It's how they keep them in line. They know the consequences if they leave or interfere with the organization's plans. On the surface they look like any other harmless right wing organization, but beneath the surface this group is beginning to look like something very lethal."

From beneath his cap Jacob said, "I'd bet a month's retirement pay that the Sons and Daughters are about to spring something major. Based on what you've told me I'd bet Mr. Sexton and his firm have been rather busy in the area of enforcement. I've known a number of former cops with his kind of mentality who got into the security business because they can make their own rules about enforcement.

We've got to find ourselves a member who is disenchanted with all this business and offer them protection in exchange for Intel and fast. I wouldn't be surprised if we're not in the countdown phase of whatever is going to come down on us."

"I don't doubt what you say is true, but getting a member at this stage that'd trust us is doubtful," replied Lisa. "It takes a little time to build that trust, and my Intel unit hasn't had cause until now to infiltrate that group. Got any other ideas?"

"We've got to shake them up," said Abe. "You and Jacob need to meet with Peterson immediately and try to determine his level of involvement. According to the informant's list he isn't a member and doesn't appear to have any connection except through Harvey and Ms. Logan. I'm betting that he doesn't know much. We need to shake Mr. Peterson up in order to get him to contact Bacon or Logan.

My suggestion is that you strongly hint that you've come across information that may implicate the Sons and Daughters organization in the recent deaths of Mari Denton and Martin Parrish. You know the drill. If he asks you the source of your information, you can't divulge it due to an ongoing investigation. Let him know that you know that Harvey and Blair are connected to that organization.

We'll see what develops. Hopefully they'll panic and make a mistake. I'll stake out Ms. Blair and see what she does, however I'm betting that Harvey is the weak link here."

"Which is probably why he's unavailable," said Lisa.

"Knowing Blair I doubt that she'll panic, but when Harvey gets the word he might do something stupid."

"We can always hope," said Jacob. "If not, Abe and I may have to break into 'The Barn' and do some snooping for information. It may be the only way to catch a break here."

"Just remember anything you find will be tainted," replied Lisa.

"I know, I know, but desperate times call for desperate measures. We must find something that will blow the lid off whatever is going on or at least delay their plans until we get some hard evidence."

CHAPTER 14

CONFRONTATION

David Peterson had one terrible headache. His third wife was off in Europe somewhere spending his money buying hideous art works and antiques. His children were all grown, moved out of the house and making their own way in life thank God.

Part of his headache was the report that he'd verbally received from his Chief Accountant on the financial status of his nonprofit corporation called the Citizens Group Foundation. David had wanted to know about the ledger entry that had been reported to him by Martin Parrish and Abe Lincoln. He still couldn't get use to that name or the fact that the man had misled him by posing as an insurance investigator.

What the hell was the world coming to when you couldn't even trust a man with a name like Abe Lincoln?

That was the least of his worries. Apparently the 'SADIL-110601' was a ledger item that allowed the transfer of monies from the Citizens Group account to a separate account set up for an organization called the Sons and Daughters in Liberty. The sum was seven million dollars for Christ sake.

Although David had heard of the organization, he had no idea that his Citizens Group was providing them with funds. He was dumbfounded because this had all happened over a period of several years without his knowledge or consent. Further digging revealed that the person responsible for setting up the account was none other than Harvey Bacon. Damn that Bacon. He had treated him like a son, and this is the payment he got.

Peterson had tried to contact Harvey twice without luck. He'd have Harvey's head on a platter for this. He was about to call Blair to see if she could contact Harvey when Ms. Neufeld paged him on the office intercom.

"Mr. Peterson, Chief of Detectives Lisa Hamel is here and wants a few minutes of your time. She has a Jacob Grant with her."

"She say what the nature of her business was?" replied David.

"Just that it relates to an ongoing investigation into the deaths of Mari Denton and Martin Parrish, sir."

"Give me a few minutes and I'll buzz you to let them in. But tell them it'll have to be brief."

"Yes sir."

What the hell is going on? Why on earth would they want to talk to me thought David? I hardly knew the woman, and I had a total of one conversation with Mr. Parrish. Coming on the heels of the report from his Chief Accountant this was not a good sign. He had to get his thoughts together. Lisa Hamel was a damn sharp woman and wouldn't ask for a meeting unless she had uncovered something very relevant that involved him. But What?

He would have to be very careful in how he worded his responses. He could most certainly not divulge any of what his accountant had told him. Thank God his Chief Accountant was on his way to France on a belated honeymoon. If Lisa had established some kind of a link between the organizations he would have to act dumb.

"Okay, Ms. Neufeld let them in."

"Detective Hamel, it's good to see you. You'll have to forgive me, but I have a busy day so this will have to be brief. How can I be of help?"

"Mr. Peterson, I appreciate your agreeing to see us on short notice. This is Jacob Grant, retired Police Detective from Topeka. We have retained Mr. Grant's services as a consultant to assist us in the ongoing investigation into the murders of Mari Denton and Martin Parrish. Mr. Grant has had a high degree of success in the past in solving cases of this nature, so we decided to draw on his expertise."

"Please to meet you Mr. Grant."

Peterson walked over to Grant and shook his hand. Grant noted that Peterson had an overly aggressive hand shake. Peterson noted that Grant had a very stern look about him. He was probably the type of person who would cut right through any bull shit thrown at him.

"Please be seated. Can we get you anything? Coffee? Juice?"

"No, thanks," said Lisa.

"I'm not sure how much help I can be in the matter under investigation. I had a total of one meeting with Mr. Parrish, and although I knew Ms. Denton I'm afraid that I didn't know her very well."

"I'll get right to the point Mr. Peterson," replied Lisa. "It's the meeting with Mr. Parrish that we're most interested in. I believe Mr. Parrish was auditing the nonprofit organization Citizens Group which is under your direction. I assume the meeting was about that audit. Am I correct?"

"Yes....that is true. He was giving me a preliminary update."

Grant noticed that Peterson had suddenly begun to fidget a bit and beads of sweat had begun to appear on his forehead. His early self-confident manner had faded, and he'd suddenly become very uncomfortable.

"Although most of Mr. Parrish's papers and documents related to the audit were destroyed in the bomb blast, we were able to retain his personal notes that were left in the motel. Apparently Mr. Parrish was quite puzzled by a ledger entry. Did you and he discuss any particular ledger entry that you remember?"

"*I....I'm* not sure what entry you're referring to?" stammered Peterson.

Grant noted that Peterson was getting very nervous. Apparently they had hit a nerve. Wonder what he's hiding?

"I'm not here to play games Mr. Peterson. Are you being evasive?"

Grant suddenly gained a great deal of admiration for Lisa. She certainly knew how to put someone on the defensive rather quickly. You didn't bull shit this gal. Go girl!

Peterson suddenly found himself in a real dilemma. If he admitted that he knew about the notation and what it meant then eventually he'd have to reveal what the Chief Accountant had told him.

Lisa Hamel was no one to fool with. He'd seen her work before. Eventually, she'd find out the truth. Do I tell her now and save myself some grief, or do I stall until I get some answers on my own? Peterson decided to stall for time.

"No, I'm not being evasive Detective Hamel. We discussed several ledger entries. That meeting was several weeks ago, and I've had a number of meetings since then, so I've forgotten most of what was said. It was a very brief meeting, so if you'd be so kind as to refresh my memory I'd be appreciative."

"The entry that I'm referring to Mr. Peterson is 'SADIL-110601' which we believe was a ledger item. I must warn you Mr. Peterson that this investigation is a very serious matter, and if I suspect for one minute that you are in any way impeding the process I will personally arrest you for interfering in an investigation. Is that understood?"

"It's understood," was Peterson's very tight lipped response.

Grant had to smile to himself. He thought that he might have to be the heavy in this interview, but Lisa was doing one hell of a job. She knew when and how to hard nose.

"Well, what do you know of the entry?" responded Lisa.

"I turned all the information over to my Chief Accountant to further investigate and am awaiting a report. What does this have to do with the murders might I ask?"

"You turned it over to him when?"

"After my meeting with Parrish Detective Hamel."

"Don't you think that sufficient time has passed to get a response to a simple fund ledger item, Mr. Peterson?"

"Not if it isn't a high priority issue, Detective, and at the time I had no reason to believe that it was a high priority issue. My Chief Accountant is a very busy man and has other priorities as well. Maybe if you would tell me what this is all about, then I could expedite the matter if need be."

"I swear Mr. Peterson if you know something and are stonewalling me I will haul your ass to jail. Do you understand me?"

"Okay. Okay. I understand. You don't need to make threats. Just tell me what it's about and I'll get the Accounting Department right on it."

"May we talk with your Chief Accountant to check on the status of his progress?"

"He is on vacation in France and asked not to be disturbed. Actually he's on a belated honeymoon."

"How convenient for him. When will he be back?"

"The first of next week, but I can get the inquiry underway if you'll just tell me what the urgency is about?"

Grant decided that this was the perfect time to plant the seed and see what happened. Lisa had set the situation up perfectly. He was actually going to get the chance to play good cop for a change.

"You right Mr. Peterson you have every right to know why this bit of information may be vital to our case. Detective Hamel, if you don't mind I'd like to explain the situation to Mr. Peterson? I'm sure that after he knows the full story, he'll be more than happy to cooperate."

"That would be helpful," said Peterson.

"Very well Mr. Grant but we'd better see some results and quickly. I don't care if we have to bring the Chief Accountant back under a court order; we need to get some answers."

Lisa was keeping the pressure on and that was good.

"Thank you Detective Hamel. Mr. Peterson, are you aware of an organization called the Sons and Daughters in Liberty?"

"Yes, I've heard of them," replied Peterson warily.

"Unless your investigation into the ledger entry proves different, we have information which would indicate that the letters in that entry stand for the Sons and Daughters in Liberty or SADIL. What we suspect is that there may be a connection between that entry and the deaths of Mr. Parrish, Ms. Denton and Elaine Myers.

"How so?" replied Peterson.

"There are some details that I cannot divulge since this is still an ongoing investigation Mr. Peterson.

What is even more curious is that your Assistant Bank Manager Harvey Bacon is and has been heavily involved with this group, and your good friend Blair Logan sits on their Board of Directors.

So you see Mr. Peterson this is high priority.

The fact that this ledger entry appears on the books of an organization for which you are the Director begs the question as to whether or not there was some financial manipulations taking place to fund the Sons and Daughters, and if Harvey and Ms. Logan and maybe even you were somehow involved. That is why Detective Hamel feels that this is an urgent matter that requires some truthful answers, if for no other reason than to clear your name.

So if I were you I'd get on the phone today to my Chief Accountant and get him back here to look into this high priority item. Otherwise we will be required to take you, Ms. Logan and Harvey Bacon in for further questioning as persons of interest."

David Peterson was in turmoil. Had he heard them correctly? He was a suspect in a capital murder case. What the hell is going on here? First I learn that someone is embezzling money from the Citizens Group and now I'm involved in a murder investigation. Was it time to call my lawyer? Peterson took a few moments to collect his thoughts. He decided that it was time to take the offensive.

"Let me understand you correctly. Based on conjecture you have deduced that Mari, Elaine, and Mr. Parrish were killed because they knew or might have known about this ledger entry? You think that the letters in the ledger entry stand for the Sons and Daughters in Liberty and the murders may be related to some financial manipulations at my Bank? On that basis and that basis alone you think that this group, the Sons and Daughters, carried out acts of violence that involves one of my most trusted employees and a very well respected business woman in this community.

You suspect Harvey, Blair and I of murder? Good Lord those letters could mean anything but that and probably do!

I'm sorry Detective Hamel but I think that your case has more holes in it than Swiss cheese. I realize that you must be under a great deal of pressure to solve these unfortunate murders but this is really reaching into left field.

You want me to call my Chief Accountant and have him interrupt his honeymoon to come back here and help verify your shaky theory about what happened to those unfortunate people.

I have no idea why Mari, Elaine, and Mr. Parrish were killed, but I cannot believe that it's over this ledger entry. Have you even checked out the other possibilities, maybe a jealous lover or maybe even a drug deal gone bad? I think that you're totally shooting in the dark.

I really don't have time for this. If you're going to cuff me then do it. My lawyer will have me out in thirty minutes. If you charge me based on this flimsy circumstantial evidence I will sue you both and the Police Department and probably win."

"Mr. Peterson let's talk about this circumstantial evidence," said Jacob. "The FBI has had the Sons and Daughters in Liberty under surveillance for over three years. The FBI has a list of the membership. Mr. Bacon, Ms. Logan of course, and a Maury Williams are listed as members

We have investigated all other possibilities into the cause of the deaths of these three folks and can find not one iota of evidence that jealousy, revenge, greed, drugs, or any other cause was involved. That only leaves the one thing that they all had in common and that is possible knowledge of this ledger entry."

"I can't believe we're having this conversation," said Peterson.

"Let's talk for a minute about this business of cuffing you and hauling your ass to jail for questioning. We can certainly do that without the fear of being sued, and your lawyer may well have you out in thirty minutes.

The one thing that I can guarantee is that the impact of hauling your ass downtown will have non-legal repercussions for you.

You are a banker, sir. People put money in your bank because they trust you. Your whole livelihood depends on that bond of trust. If word gets around this community, and believe me it will, that you're a suspect in a capital murder case that may not set too well with some of those fine folks who bank with you.

In short the big risk is that you'll lose business and most certainly won't gain any new business. People are gonna, rightly or wrongly; ask themselves the question do I want to bank with someone who might prove to be a criminal? In your business sometimes the facts don't matter much but your image in the eye of the public sure as hell does.

Now we really don't have to go that route do we? All you need to do is make a couple of calls. Who knows you may prove us wrong? Somebody created that ledger account 'SADIL-110601', and I'm willing to bet that either Mr. Bacon or your Chief Accountant knows something about it. You can call Harvey or your Chief Accountant and put this whole business to rest right now without anyone having to travel anywhere. If you want us to step out of the office while you call we will. No problem. If we're wrong then we'll just leave and you won't be bothered again by us. The decision is yours."

"Just a reminder Mr. Peterson," said Lisa. "I'm perfectly within my rights as a law enforcement officer to cuff you and take you downtown for interrogation on the basis of your refusal to assist in the investigation of a capital murder case. Call your lawyer if you don't believe me. I may not be able to hold you for long but I do have the right to question you, and you have no legal recourse."

Peterson knew that his ass was against the wall on this. They were going to find out about the link between his organization and the Sons and Daughters. Why in the hell had he allowed Harvey to manage the Citizens Group account in the first place? He should have known early on that Lisa would force his hand. Grant was certainly right about the repercussions. He'd seen it happen before to others in his profession for lesser reasons.

"Okay. If you agree to step outside I'll see if I can get some answers. It may take a while especially if I have to call overseas, so if you have other business; I can contact you when I learn something. I may not be able to get a hold of Les Miles, my Chief accountant, right away. I promise you that I'll have some answers within 24 hours."

"That sounds reasonable to me. Do you agree Detective Hamel?"

"That's acceptable, but if we don't hear from you within 24 hours; I will make good on my promise to haul you in for questioning."

"I understand. I know the consequences, and I assure you that I will cooperate."

"Very well Mr. Peterson. We look forward to hearing from you," replied Jacob.

Lisa and Jacob left the room and walked to the elevator.

"I think that went rather well," said Lisa.

"You did good. Nothing like a good dose of 'good cop, bad cop' to light a fire," replied Jacob.

"You weren't bad yourself," responded Lisa.

Abe was bored. Stake outs were one of his least favorite activities. Apparently, Blair had no need to venture out of her apartment. She'd been in there all morning. Lisa had called about fifteen minutes ago to bring him up-to-date on the meeting with Peterson. If Blair was going to panic, it could come at any time assuming that Peterson called her. The question was would she? Abe doubted it. From what Lisa had told him, Blair probably has a deep seated contempt for all men and Peterson was certainly no exception.

Blair was about to leave the apartment to do some shopping and stop by her office when her cell phone rang. What now Blair thought?

"Blair, this is David. I hate to bother you at home but I have some rather disturbing information that I need to discuss with you preferably not over the phone. Can you come to my office?"

"You want me to drive all the way over to Wheaton. Its mid-afternoon and I have to get ready for a dinner this evening. Why can't we discuss it over the phone? You think that your phone is tapped or something?"

"I don't know, but it could be. I just had a visit from the Lisa Hamel, Chief of Detectives and some consultant by the name of Jacob Grant that they've hired to investigate the Denton and Parrish murders. I really need to talk to you and Harvey Bacon. Harvey isn't returning any of my phone calls. Would you know why?"

"I wouldn't have a clue. I know that he was going to his cabin in Idaho to play macho woodsman for a few days, but he should be back by the weekend. Can't this wait? I mean what the hell do those murders have to do with Harvey and me? It wasn't like Mari and I was best friends, and I never met the Parrish fellow. Did Harvey have something going with Mari?

"Not that I'm aware of. Okay, look I'll drive over there. I should be there in thirty minutes. The point is that it can't wait. I've got twenty four hours to come up with some information or I'm going to be hauled in for questioning."

"Are you serious? David, what the hell is going on? If you want my help I need to know exactly what the fuck this is all about."

"You, Harvey and I are suspects in the capital murder case involving Mari Denton, Elaine Myers, and Martin Parrish."

"WHAT! You've got to be kidding me. Get your ass over here right now. This is ridiculous. Has Lisa gone mad?"

"I don't know, but I'm on my way."

Blair was furious with Peterson. In the beginning when she first seduced him to get her loan, she thought that he was strong and decisive. After a time she began to realize that he was just like all other men weak and self-indulgent. When Blair reached the point of having little need of him she withdrew her sexual favors and passed him on to her girls. It appeared that he may become a liability. After she got the information out of him that she needed Blair would make arrangements for him to become another victim. If his wife knew of his escapades, she'd probably give Blair a medal. Blair placed a call to Dan Sexton.

Abe was about to nod off for the umpteenth time when he spotted David Peterson pull into a parking space three cars to the West of him. Peterson got out of the car and proceeded to look around to see if anyone was following him. He ran across the parking lot and into the lobby rather quickly. Very interesting thought Abe. Maybe he'd been summoned after making a phone call to Blair. Our Mr. Peterson may not be so innocent and in the dark as we thought. Looks like that meeting might have generated some activity.

After Peterson went into the building Abe spotted three men in coveralls get out of an unmarked white van parked in the next row behind Peterson's car.

One person used a locksmith key to pop the lock on the driver's side and open the hood. Another short stocky man shimmed underneath the car. Apparently the word had gone out to have Mr. Peterson become road kill.

Once they were finished the men got into the van and drove away. Abe would confront Peterson when he came back out. After he showed Peterson what was in store for him, he would sing like a bird. Abe was going to need Jacob and called him on his cell phone.

"Jacob Grant speaking."

"Listen, David Peterson just went into Blair Logan's apartment. Looks like the meeting paid off. After he went inside three thugs showed up and tinkered with his car. I'd bet they're employees of Sexton's. I'd say our Mr. Peterson is a marked man. I need for you borrow Lisa's car and swing by here. When Peterson comes out I want to show him what was in store for him. I need you to take him to the motel. I'm betting whatever he knows we'll know fairly quickly.

I need to stay here to see if Blair leaves to make contact with someone. I think we've succeeded in shaking them up."

"Sounds like it. Lisa's with me now. She says that she'll get a ride to Police Headquarters. I should be there in a few minutes."

"Okay, make it as quick as you can. No telling when Peterson will come back down."

"Right. I'm on my way."

David could tell that Blair was agitated when he walked into the apartment. She was pacing back and forth with a very stern look on her face and biting her fingernails. Never a good sign.

"Okay David, as calmly as you can, will you please tell me what the hell is going on. I need every detail, so you better not hold anything back. If I find out you lied to me or held something back your wife and your Board of Directors are going to get some very interesting mail. Do you understand me?"

David knew that Blair never made idol threats. She had him by the balls and he knew it.

"Several weeks ago I had a meeting with an auditor by the name of Martin Parrish who was performing a routine audit on the Citizens Group nonprofit organization. As you know I'm the Director. He asked me about a ledger entry labeled 'SADIL-110601'. I told him that I had no knowledge of the entry and would consult with my Chief Accountant and get back to him. Frankly, Harvey Bacon was assigned the Citizens Group account and had complete control of the activity. I asked Harvey about it, and he told me that he would have to check into it. As you know Martin Parrish was killed in a car bombing the day after I met with him. We all figured that he was a victim of a drug deal gone badly or something.

A few weeks later I get a visit from an insurance investigator by the name of T.J. Bonham, asking me questions about the same notation. Turns out that T.J. Bonham is a man named Abe Lincoln. Can you believe that? Someone named their kid Abe Lincoln for Christ sake. Apparently Abe Lincoln is some kind of private investigator.

Again I ask Harvey about it, and he tells me that it's complicated and he's checking into it. Later I learned that Abe Lincoln aka T.J. Bonham was mugged in an alley and was in the hospital. I told the Chief Accountant to follow up with Harvey.

Just yesterday the Chief Accountant told me that Harvey had told him that the entry represented purchases by the Citizens Group for an organization called the Sons and Daughters in Liberty that ran to seven million dollars. He had no idea what the numbers stood for. He assumed that it was a random number assigned by Harvey. Harvey told him that the purchase was for transportation and communications equipment.

I've tried to get a hold of Harvey, but he's not responding to my calls. I'm going to fire his ass and have him arrested for embezzlement.
Today, I get a visit from the Chief of Detectives, Lisa Hamel, whom you know and some contract investigator by the name of Jacob Grant. They're investigating the homicide deaths of Mari Denton, Martin Parrish and Elaine Myers.

According to Lisa and Mr. Grant the deaths are related. The common denominator is the notation 'SADIL-110601'. It is their belief that Mr. Parrish was killed because he asked about the entry, and the others were killed because they might have gained knowledge from Parrish. Can you believe that?"

"Go on David. I know there's more. Where do I fit into the picture? You said that you, Harvey and I are suspects."

"Well, this is where it really gets speculative. It is their theory that the letters stand for the Sons and Daughters in Liberty organization which they do. According to Hamel and Grant, the FBI has had the Sons and Daughters under surveillance for some time and has information on the membership.

According their information you and Harvey are members of that organization, and you sit on the Board of Directors.

Hamel and Grant believe, based on the information that they have, Harvey and maybe you have been making purchases through the Citizens Group for the Sons and Daughters.

It appears that our association with the Citizens Group and the Sons and Daughters tied to their theory about the murders and the ledger entry make us suspects in the ongoing homicide investigation. That is the sum of what I know. Now it's your turn to tell me what you know, Blair. Just remember if you take me down, you're going with me. I can provide some interesting mail as well that could ruin your reputation for good."

Blair was stunned. She couldn't believe that the information that had been acquired by Lisa, Abe Lincoln, and this Grant fellow was so on target. She knew Abe Lincoln might be a problem, but this was beyond belief. Maury should have killed him.

Blair had no idea that they had been under FBI surveillance or that the FBI had their membership listing. Maury had told her that they believed that there was an informant, but how did he get the membership list? It was kept in a vault and only she, Maury, Maury's Assistant, and Harvey had access to the combination.

Maury's assistant, Shelia MacMurphy, compiled and updated the list. Shelia was one of her girls and totally loyal to the organization, but somehow she must have been compromised. Shelia would have to disappear. They had caught the informant after the last meeting and disposed of him. Abe, Lisa and Mr. Grant didn't have the details of what was planned, but they were getting too close for comfort.

"Yes I am a member of the Board of Directors for the Sons and Daughters organization," replied Blair. "Harvey is a member of the organization as well. Apart from that the rest is total bull shit. The Sons and Daughters are a nonviolent society dedicated to the downsizing of government by peaceful means. We sponsor rallies and support candidates at election time who are in tune with our beliefs. We sure as hell don't plan the killing of innocent citizens.

As for the money transaction, you'll have to ask Harvey about that. I don't get involved in the day to day financial transactions of the organization. He's your employee for Christ sake!

It sounds to me like Lisa and her friends are shooting in the dark. Apparently the pressure is on her to solve those killings, and they're grasping at straws. The only fact that they have straight is that we're members of the organization.

Now, if you don't mind I have other business to conduct. If they want to come arrest me, let them. I'll sue them into obscurity. Keep me posted if you get any more solid information. I'll see if I can get a hold of Harvey."

"Very well, Blair. Just remember you aren't the only one with damaging information."

"Yes, David I am well aware of that fact."

David let himself out of the apartment. He had known Blair for a very long time and could usually tell when she was lying. He had no doubt that she was lying in this case. He knew that he would probably not hear from Harvey any time soon. David was ready to tell the cops everything that he knew about the ledger entry.

Blair needed to make a trip to The Barn to call Harvey on a secure line to let him know what had happened. It would take a maximum effort to keep him from panic. Maybe Maury, despite his traitorous nature, had been right. Maybe it was time to think about letting things cool off for a while. She also needed to talk to Dan Sexton about Shelia.

Jacob Grant made it to the Hilton with two minutes to spare. As he climbed into Abe's car, they both saw David Peterson emerge from the lobby.

"Better go grab him Jacob, before he becomes another accident fatality."

Jacob scrambled from the car and intercepted David before he opened his car door.

"You may want to come have a little chat with a friend of mine," said Jacob. "It would seem as though he saw some folks messin' with your car while you were inside talking to Blair."

"Are you serious? Why would anyone do that? Have you been tailing me? I think I need to call my lawyer."

"Okay. Get in your car and drive away. But don't say that I didn't warn you. You want to be another freak fatality, go ahead be my guest."

"Who's your friend?"

"Abe Lincoln and we know that he doesn't lie."

David felt sick to his stomach. He couldn't believe it. His life had become total chaos. Blair was lying through her teeth. She wanted him dead. Damn that bitch.

"Show me," replied David.

"Pop the hood on your car."
David got in his car and pulled the lever for the hood latch. Jacob pulled the hood up and secured it. He pulled back the cap on the brake fluid reservoir.

"Well, well look here. Those boys were busy. They drained most of your brake fluid. Maybe you had enough to at least make it out of town. From the marks on the steering column, looks like they may have tinkered with it as well which would buy you an additional disaster. Let's pop your wheel covers. Jacob pried loose the wheel covers on the front wheels. My, my they didn't leave anything to chance. Looks like your lug nuts have been loosened. These guys were very serious. You're dealing with some very dangerous people here, David."

"Damn that bitch, I knew she was lying to me. Okay. Let's go talk to Mr. Lincoln. I think I can confirm some of what you've told me. She's total nuts. Obviously, Harvey and Blair have been using my bank and my nonprofit organization as a front for their organization. They both belong behind bars."

Jacob took David over to talk to Abe, and then Jacob took him back to the motel in Lisa's car to write down everything that he knew about Harvey and Blair's activities.

Abe recognized Blair Logan as she pulled out of the parking garage. Lisa had given him a picture of her, and David gave him a description of her vehicle.

He pulled into the street and made sure to stay two cars behind her if possible. Blair headed West on Kellogg to the 135 bypass, then South to the 96 exit, then headed northwest toward Wheaton. Blair got off at Haven and onto the East Arlington Road to Arlington then South on South Hodge Road for five miles. She made a turn onto a gravel road heading East to what looked like a deserted Red Barn off on the right. There was a rather large paved parking lot next to the barn. Blair hadn't noticed the grey Honda sedan that was tailing her.

She was too busy trying to determine what she would tell Harvey. Blair knew how agitated he got, and she didn't need for him to be freaking out. Harvey didn't need to know about the potential arrest as a suspect in a murder case. Blair would frame her report in the context of how flimsy their suspicions were, but she would tell him that for the time being operationally they needed to stand down. They could reschedule the attacks in three months after things had cooled down. With David Peterson out of the way more than likely Harvey would become the Bank President which would make things infinitely easier for them.

Abe decided to park his Honda rental in a little alcove used by fishermen and hidden by the surrounding trees and vegetation about a mile back up the road. He followed the tree line on foot along the road until he could see the Red Barn. He took note that there was about a 150 yard clearance created all the way around the barn with no vegetation available for cover.

He suspected that there would be heat sensors implanted at strategic points around the barn as well as video cameras set up for early detection of any intruders. So much for the element of surprise.

Abe's options were simple. He could wait here on the chance that Harvey or Maury would show. If they didn't show, he could always follow Blair to her next destination which might be back to the Hilton; or he could try to gain entrance to the Red Barn after she left and see what he could find. His second option would be to hook up with Jacob and Lisa and see what David Peterson had to offer them.

He saw no real point in sticking around. It was too light outside, and he wasn't equipped to penetrate the perimeter in broad daylight. Now that he knew the location and layout maybe he and Jacob would visit the Red Barn at night. He was almost certain that Blair would head back to the Hilton.

He doubted that Harvey or Maury would show, because Blair obviously came out here to contact Maury or Harvey or both using a secure phone line. He trotted back to his Honda and headed toward the motel.

Blair let herself into the Barn through a side door that was rigged with a silent alarm. She used the code to disarm the alarm once inside. She took a small whistle out of her purse and blew into it twice which emitted a sound frequency that only dogs could hear. That would bring the two Dobermans, Mutt and Jeff, to heel. They were added insurance in case of a successful break in and were allowed to roam free at night. The dogs would not bother Blair, since they knew her scent.

Blair made her way to the office that she had shared with Harvey and Maury, punched in the correct cipher key code and entered the room with the secure satellite telephone link that was the property of Sexton Security and purchased with funds funneled to them by Harvey. It was this link that was to be used to communicate with the strike teams in the various cities that were targeted. Blair dialed Harvey's number.

Harvey answered on the second ring.

"Blair?"

"Who else did you think that it would be? You need to get your ass back here as quickly as you can. We've got some serious problems and some decisions to make."

"What the hell happened?"

"Abe Lincoln and the FBI happened. Apparently, the FBI has had us under surveillance for over a year. Something Maury never mentioned. The FBI had somehow placed an informant among us. Dan Sexton had suspicions but didn't nail down who it was until the last meeting. The informant got access to our membership list and transmitted it to the FBI before he was caught and eliminated. I think that Shelia must have cooperated with him. I've instructed Dan to take care of her.

Abe Lincoln has the membership list from a source in the FBI, and of course our names. Based on the notation that he found among Martin Parrish's effects, he, Lisa, and a consultant that they hired, a Jacob Grant, believe that the Sons and Daughters in Liberty have some violence planned in the near future. They believe that you and I are involved and that you have been funneling funds from the Citizens Group account to the Sons and Daughters to implement operations."

"Who the hell told you all this? What kind of proof do they actually have?"

"David Peterson contacted me. Lisa and this Jacob Grant paid him a visit a few hours ago probably to determine to what degree he might be involved. As far as I can tell it's all speculation without hard facts. David appeared to be very shaky when he came to my place. He knows that you've been funneling funds to the Sons and Daughters, but I've taken care of that little problem."

"Blair, are you nuts! I mean is that smart? Surely Abe and Lisa will connect the dots and throw more suspicion on us."

"Quit worrying and get some balls. It'll totally look like a bona fide accident. You just get yourself composed, because you'll probably ascend to the Bank President's chair.

Get back here as soon as you can. Go directly to the Red Barn not to my place. I'm sure that I'm being watched. I'm going to stay here tonight, then go back to my place tomorrow to take care of some business. We may have to delay the operation for a few months."

"Is that wise? Won't that give the FBI and this Abe Lincoln more time to put the pieces together?"

"Harvey I told you to quit your damn worrying. Get back here and we'll discuss it."

"Very well. I'm on my way. I should be there by tomorrow night. See you then."

Harvey hung up before Blair could hurtle any more insults at him. The bitch. Maybe he and Dan needed to have a little discussion about Blair.

CHAPTER 15

PEOPLE TALK AND BOBBI ANN IS REBORN

"Where is Peterson?" asked Abe.

"Lisa has him tucked away in a safe house for the time being," replied Jacob.

"What'd he tell us?"

"Peterson didn't tell us much more than we already know. His Chief Accountant confirmed that the ledger entry was a transfer of funds made by Harvey Bacon from the Citizens Group account to the Sons and Daughters organization allegedly to purchase communication and security equipment," responded Jacob.

"Must have been expensive equipment," Abe replied.

"Tell me. In the beginning Blair was insistent that Harvey handle the Citizens Group account. She hinted that she had video of some of his sexual exploits and documents of him approving questionable loans and padding his expense account. After Elaine died it was Blair who insisted that Harvey be put in charge of the property. Apparently, she had Peterson by the balls."

"I'd say that's a valid observation. I think that it's about time that we pay a visit to the Red Barn tomorrow night. I followed Blair to the location. I'm fairly sure they've placed heat sensors and video cameras around the place. There's a 150 yard clearance all around the barn offering absolutely no cover, and I wouldn't be surprised if they have a couple of Dobermans running around at night."

"Oh! Great! I hate those damn dogs. Got any ideas on how we might penetrate this mini fortress?"

"Very Carefully, very carefully!"

***

Teddy Sexton's nightmares had dissipated. Teddy was relieved and no longer felt uneasy around his father. It had been over a month since his last nightmare episode. It was early afternoon and school let out early for teacher's conferences. Teddy decided to pay a visit to his Dad's office and surprise him. When he opened the door to the outer office his secretary wasn't at her desk. He figured that she must have gone for coffee or something. Teddy noticed that the door to his Dad's office was closed. As he tiptoed slowly toward the office to surprise him he could clearly hear him on the phone.

He heard his Dad say, *'I'll take care of it Blair. It'll look like a freak accident just like all the others.'*

Teddy was stunned and wondered what his Dad meant by that. Then his Dad dialed another number. Teddy was frozen in place and afraid of what he might hear, but he wanted to know what his father was doing. He heard his father tell someone on the other end that they needed to get a couple of the guys and head over to Blair Logan's apartment at the Hilton in Wichita. He told them to fix David Peterson's BMW so that he'd lose control and have a freak accident.

Teddy heard enough. He got out of there fast as he could and ran and ran for a long time until he couldn't run anymore. He hid for a couple of hours in an old club house that his friends and he used a long time ago. Teddy buried his face in his hands and cried for a long time.

He didn't know what to do. If he went to the police, they wouldn't believe him. Would they take his word over that of his Dad, a former sheriff's deputy? Teddy didn't think so. He didn't want to believe what he'd just heard. My own father is a killer. Then it all started to come back to him. He had actually hid in his Dad's pick up that night to find out where he was going late at night. It was no nightmare. It was real. He did see all those things that he thought were a nightmare. My father is a cold blooded killer. For a few moments Teddy was paralyzed with fear and confused about what to do. Then it all became very clear to him. He would have to do something for poor Mr. Peterson's sake and fast. He would do what his father had taught him to do.

There was one member of the police force who might believe him. His mother had always spoken highly of her as being honest and fair minded.

Lisa wasn't in her office when Teddy called from a pay phone, but her secretary told Teddy that she would try to locate her and to call back in about 15 minutes.

Teddy decided to wait in the phone booth.

Lisa received a call from her Secretary and wondered what could be so urgent that Teddy Sexton had to talk to her immediately.

When Teddy called her Lisa could tell that he was very upset almost to the point of hysteria. She told him to stay where he was and she would come to pick him up. Apparently it had something to do with his father, but Teddy wasn't very coherent over the phone.

Lisa called Abe and Jacob and told them about the new development. She would brief them when she knew what it was all about.

When she picked Teddy up he was shaking like a leaf and not making much sense. He kept muttering something about his father and nightmares that weren't nightmares at all. When they were all settled in her office with the door closed Teddy began to talk more coherently.

Teddy took a couple of deep breathes, moaned and let out a couple of prolonged sobs and then was quite for several of minutes. Finally he began to speak in a soft but shaky whisper.

"I....I.....can never go home again. I can't....I know that I can't. I .....I could go home if it was just my mother there, but I....I can't go home if my father is there. I....I know that my father is a murderer. It's no nightmare, it's true. Just as true as I am sitting here. I know it. I didn't dream those terrible nightmares. Those things really did happen."

Teddy's body was trembling at first as he spoke, but then he began to calm down. His voice became more firm and determined.

"Teddy, you need to tell me what has happened," responded Lisa.

Lisa could tell by Teddy's body language that this was not something that he was making up and that something very traumatic had happened to cause him a great deal of pain. Teddy was being very brave, because many kids Teddy's age under these circumstances would have gone catatonic or engaged in some kind of bizarre behavior.

"This afternoon, school let out early for teacher's conferences. I decided to pay a visit to my Dad's office and surprise him. When I opened the door to the outer office his secretary wasn't at her desk. I figured that she must have gone for coffee or something. I noticed that the door to my Dad's office was closed.

As I tiptoed slowly toward his office to surprise him I could hear him on the phone. As he finished his phone conversation, I clearly heard him say, *'I'll take care of it Blair. It'll look like a freak accident just like all the others.'*

I was stunned. I wondered what he meant by that. Then I heard him dial another number. I feared what I might hear, but I wanted to know what my father was doing.

I heard my father tell someone on the other end that they needed to get a couple of the guys and head over to Blair Logan's apartment at the Hilton in Wichita. He told them to fix David Peterson's BMW so that he'd lose control and have a freak accident.

I'd heard enough. I got out of there fast as I could and ran and ran for a long time until I couldn't run anymore. I hid for a couple of hours in an old club house that my friends and I use to use. I didn't know what to do. I didn't want to believe what I'd just heard. Then it all started to come back to me. At first I thought it was a nightmare. I'd hid in my Dad's pick up one night to find out where he was going late at night. I did see him and his friends kill all those people and bury them in a mass grave. My father is a cold blooded killer. I must have suppressed it.

That's when I decided you were the only person who might believe me. My mom always said that you were fair minded.

I can't go home Ms. Hamel. I can't. You need to tell someone so they can stop them before the kill poor Mr. Peterson. Please......please you need to do something!"

"Take it easy Teddy. I believe you. Mr. Peterson is safe and in hiding. You need not worry about him, okay?"

"Okay, but how did you know what was happening?"

"We have some very resourceful people working on this, believe me. I agree that until they arrest your father it would not be in your best interests to go home. When that happens you mother will certainly need to have you at home. For now you can stay with me. Eventually, we will need to take a statement from you and take you into protective custody to keep you safe. When are you expected home?"

"We usually don't eat until around 6pm. I guess that I could call my Mom and tell her that some friends and I are playing video games until supper."

"Let's wait on that and see what develops. I'm thinking that it might be better if I call your Mom later and tell her that you've with me and we need to talk to her. I tell her not to worry that you're not injured or in trouble. That should buy us some time until we can take action.

I'm not going to sugarcoat anything for you Teddy. You've been a very brave young man up to now, but the hardest part is yet to come. You'll have to testify against your Dad. You'll have to retell the story under oath of exactly what you saw and heard. Most importantly, you'll have to do that in front of your father. I want you to know that. I will help you all I can, but you will have to face your father on this."

"I know Ms. Hamel. I know that. I know that he's my father and all, but it was he and my Mom who taught me right from wrong and to always be truthful and never lie. He's been good to me and my mother, but he killed those people, and they have families too. I can't help but think about that. They didn't deserve to die not in that way. My father needs to be punished for it. I'm just going to have to be brave and do what's right."

"You're right. You always have to do what you think is right. Sometimes it's the hardest thing to do in this life."

"I know. Is there some place that I can lay down for a while? I'm kinda tired."

"Sure. There is a couch in the other room. I'll come get you if I need you."

Lisa dialed the home number for Betty Sexton dreading this call more than any call that she'd made in recent history.

Shelia MacMurphy was in trouble and she knew it. Randy Lewis had not called her or come to see her in three weeks. He had simply disappeared. She called and left messages and had been by his apartment three times only to find him not there. She had sat outside his apartment two evenings in a row until morning and no Randy. Obviously, he had skipped town or worse had been found out. If it were the latter, she was in big trouble.

Randy had been hired by Harvey Bacon a year ago as an accountant in the financial unit of the Sons and Daughters organization. Like Shelia, he had made it through the screening process and become a member of the organization.

Shelia and Randy had become acquainted at a social gathering three months ago. They became friends, then dated and finally became lovers. Randy would call her every day and stay with her in her apartment at least three nights a week. That had been their routine for over a month

Originally, Shelia had worked for Blair Logan as a cosmetologist in her shop in McPherson. Shelia had been to several of Blair's parties and eventually was enlisted as an escort of sorts. Shelia was very attractive with golden blonde hair, deep blue eyes, and a very nice figure at five foot ten and a hundred twenty pounds. Shelia was never comfortable entertaining men selected by Blair but the money was good. Shelia never spent much on herself, but used the funds to pay for her mother's medical expenses.

Her mother had heart problems and was a diabetic with no health insurance. Her father had abandoned them when Shelia was eight, and her mother had to get a job as a cashier in a local grocery store.

Her mother went through an assortment of boyfriends but never remarried. When her mother turned fifty-five she had a heart attack and nearly died. It was during this time that she learned that she was a Type One Diabetic. Eventually, her mother had to quit work and go on disability.

Shelia met Harvey Bacon at one of Blair's parties and had become a favorite of his. Shelia knew that he was married and would probably never leave his wife, but he was fun to be with and he had always treated her well. Shelia had taught herself computer skills and had become very proficient with word processing.

During one of their liaisons Harvey told Shelia that Maury Williams was looking for an assistant to help him with clerical functions at The Barn. Shelia mentioned that she was very proficient on the computer. Harvey arranged an interview with Maury, and the next day Shelia was hired as Maury's assistant.

It didn't take Shelia long to learn that Maury was an arrogant asshole. He was continually trying to hit on her, but she always managed to fend him off except for the occasional butt pinch. She literally hated working for him, but the money was too good to pass up.

At least she didn't have to earn extra cash as an escort anymore or stand on her feet all day giving perms to blue haired old ladies. Shelia had access to most of the sensitive files related to the Sons and Daughters, except the plan that Blair, Harvey and Maury were working on. She could get into the storage vault where it was kept, but the plan itself was kept in a black metal box in a wall safe with a different lock. For the first time in her life Shelia felt like a real VIP.

In the beginning Shelia had developed a mutual relationship with Blair. They both came from broken homes, and were the primary financial support for their mothers. Things cooled off between them when Shelia refused Blair's advances on several occasions. Shelia had no interest in messing around with other women. Blair never forced the issue for which Shelia was thankful.

As time went by Shelia began to see the real Blair Logan. Blair seemed to be devoid of any real emotion other than rage. Shelia saw her as being very manipulative of men, especially Harvey and Maury, and had never shown any compassion for anyone other than her mother.

Blair seemed to have one single obsession and that was the Sons and Daughters organization. You would have thought that Blair gave the organization birth and was the only one who nurtured it.

Shelia was not really dedicated the Sons and Daughters cause. It was a job to her that paid very well. It gave her financial security, status, and self-esteem. It seemed to her that the goals and objectives of the organization were nothing more than platitudes on paper. So much of what went on within the organization seemed secretive. Security was very thorough. Every time that Shelia created a new membership list, she was required to shred the old one. She could not take the list out of her office area. The list was distributed by Maury to Harvey, Blair, and Dan Sexton and no one else. The odd thing to Shelia was that she was generating a revised list at least once a month. Dan Sexton provided her with the necessary information to generate the revised listing.

Some events transpired that began to alarm Shelia. Two of her friends who had cleared the screening process with her had recently been taken off the membership listing. When Shelia tried to contact them, they had disappeared.

One evening Randy told her that he had learned some disturbing things about the Sons and Daughters. He broke down and admitted to her that prior to coming to work for the Sons and Daughters; he had been a CPA with a large financial institution and had been arrested in a mail fraud scheme. In order to avoid going to prison he had become an informant for the FBI Intelligence Unit.

Randy was directed to join the Sons and Daughters organization and attempt to get a job in their financial unit. The FBI set up a phony employer contact in case the Sons and Daughters checked on his previous employment. He was to see what he could find out about the organization and their true purpose. Randy asked Shelia if she could get him the revised copies of the membership list. She remembered their conversation like it was yesterday.

"Randy, I can't do that. That's classified material and you know it. What would you do with it?"

"Shelia, you don't realize what's going on around here. The FBI wants the listing. The FBI believes that members who choose or are asked to leave the organization are being systematically eliminated. Some have freak fatal accidents; some just disappear never to be heard from again."

"Oh! My God! That must be what happened to Jean and Rachel. They joined the organization when I did. I haven't been able to get a hold of them for weeks, and their names were removed from the membership listing. Christ! What have I gotten myself into?"

"Calm down. I need that listing Shelia," replied Randy. "I don't want the same thing to happen to you. If what the FBI says is true, none of us are safe. I've heard bits and pieces of conversation about a major initiative in the planning that will literally shock the country. I've been trying to get my hands the details of those plans, but right now only Blair, Harvey and Maury have access."

"Alright, Randy I'll get you a copy of the listing. But please be careful. I care about you, and I don't want you to turn up disappearing on me. I don't know what I'd do. Lord knows they probably know we've been sleeping together. If they find out that the FBI has the list, I'd be the first person that they would suspect."

"If something happens to me get out of here. Go someplace where no one knows you and lay low. My gut feeling is that these people play for keeps, because they're dead serious about their plans. I would stay clear of Dan Sexton. I have a feeling that he's behind these disappearances and accidents."

"Don't worry about that. When he looks at me he gives me the creeps. It's like he can see right through you. The less contact that I have with that man the better I like it."

Randy disappeared the following week. Shelia didn't leave right away, because she thought that maybe the FBI had pulled him out. The new membership list came down from Dan two days later and Randy's name was still there. When she asked Vivian Pearce who worked in Randy's unit about him, she was told that he had gone to Chicago on business for the Sons and Daughters.

The very next day Maury didn't show up for work. Harvey called Shelia and told her that Maury had resigned and she would be reporting to him.

Harvey told her that he would be vacationing in Idaho for a week, so if she needed to take some time off go ahead and take it.

Shelia indicated that she needed to take a few days off. None of this resignation business made any sense to Shelia, because for Christ sake Maury had been one of the leaders of the organization. Why would he up and resign, particularly if what Randy told her about a major initiative was true?

Furthermore, Randy would have never gone to Chicago without letting her know. Shelia was frightened. It was time to get her things together and create her own disappearing act. She knew exactly where she would go.

The next morning while Shelia was packing and making arrangements to shut down her apartment, she received a FedEx letter from Randy Lewis. Could he still be alive?

She opened the letter and unfolded a note. The note was in Randy's handwriting and informed her that if she got this letter he was dead. He told her to run. When she was safely away from the Sons and Daughters she was to call the number in the note and ask for Jacob Grant or Abe Lincoln. She was to give them access codes to the Red Barn, the combination to the storage vault, and the wall safe if she had it.

Shelia was in shock. She broke down in tears at the thought that Randy was dead. She really had loved him despite the short time that they had been together.

She couldn't believe what she was reading. Abe Lincoln? Had Randy gone completely mad? Abe Lincoln had been dead for decades. What in hell was he thinking?

After she was able to get her emotions under control and was safely on the road, she used a new cell phone that she had acquired and dialed the number not knowing what to expect on the other end. Abe Lincoln for Christ sake!

***

Bobbi Ann Henry spent a great deal of time the next two days sleeping off her exhaustion, only getting out of bed to eat the meals that Miriam had prepared for her. Bobbi Ann was deeply puzzled by the kindness that Miriam, Abe and Jacob had shown her. She just couldn't figure it out.

After the death of her mother and father most of her life had been a harsh experience. It seemed as though everyone she met and befriended were only interested in using her for their own benefit. Her aunt and uncle were only interested in the foster care payments that they received for her care. Bobbi Ann was expected to clean the house and prepare most of the meals and in return received a minimal amount for clothing and necessities. Her girl friends at school hung around with her only because she was good looking and had a mature figure that attracted the boys. Once they hooked up with a boy they would barely talk to her. The boyfriends that she hooked up with only wanted to get in her panties. Once they tired of her, they were gone.

Bobbi Ann had learned early on that people were only nice to you because they wanted something from you and for no other reason. She had no one that she could talk to seriously about her feelings, her hopes and dreams, and her troubles. After all that she had done to destroy Jacob Grant, to think that he and his friends were willing to have some faith in her and take a risk that she wouldn't cause further trouble was enough to make her want to stick around to find out what their angle was. What did they want from her?

On the third day Miriam enlisted Bobbi Ann's help with the chores around The Lodge. Miriam didn't demand that she help. Instead Miriam asked if Bobbi Ann would be willing to help. Bobbi Ann was ready to do something to get her mind off her troubles and agreed to help clean the rooms and serve meals to the two groups of fishermen staying at The Lodge. Even the fishermen were nice and treated her kindly. Most of them were older businessmen taking a break from the pressures of work who wanted nothing more than to spend a relaxing week just fishing.

What surprised her most was that none of them tried to hit on her. All her experience had taught her that most men were only after one thing. She had heard plenty of stories about fishing and hunting parties and what normally happened when good looking women were available. Bobbi Ann wasn't vain, but she knew that she was young and attractive.

These men were different. They treated her with respect which was a brand new experience for Bobbi Ann. Maybe it was because many of them had daughters at or near her age. Or maybe this lodge had certain rules about such things. Bobbi Ann sensed that Miriam probably wouldn't tolerate such behavior and Miriam looked as though she could handle herself in any situation.

One morning after the groups had departed for a day of fishing on a nearby lake, Miriam sat Bobbi Ann down at the breakfast table.

"Bobbi Ann, you've been a big help around here the last few days. I want you to know that I appreciate your effort. You've given me absolutely no trouble, which I also appreciate. I've talked to Abe, and we both agree that you need to be compensated for the work that you do. I don't know how long you'll be here, but for the time being is $450 a week satisfactory?" said Miriam.

Bobbi Ann was speechless. They actually wanted to pay her after all that had transpired. I don't get it. What's their angle?

"You really don't need to do that," replied Bobbi Ann. "After all I'm getting room and my meals. Besides aren't I under some kind of house arrest?"

"Yes I suppose you are to a certain degree, but that doesn't mean that you can't be paid for the work that you do.

It's money that you can save and use once you're free to go. I don't think that Abe and Jacob plan on holding you here indefinitely.

They're tied up in another urgent matter for the moment, but when that's resolved; I'm sure they plan to sit down and talk to you about your future."

"If you want to pay me that's fine, Miriam. Frankly I'm puzzled about this whole arrangement. I mean for Christ sake I tried to kill Jacob twice. I mean I guess that I don't get the angle. My whole life after my folks died has been filled with people trying to use me for their own benefit. I don't get it. Why are you all being so nice to me? What is it that you people expect to gain from all this?"

"Bobbi Ann, I understand how all this puzzles you. Believe me I do. I was in a similar situation at one time. I didn't actually attempt to kill someone, but I did think long and hard about doing it. I was angry after losing my husband and my son in Israel. They were killed by a street bomber while shopping for tennis shoes for my son. I was a member of the Israel Army at the time and thought of a thousand ways that I could extract my revenge on the Arab population. I was actually praying for another war to start, so I would have a legitimate reason to kill Arabs. Like your father and mother in a way, my family was innocent victims of violence.

After they were gone I insulated myself from everyone. I didn't trust anyone and would not let anyone get close to me.

When my enlistment was up, I packed my bags and came to the United States. I couldn't stand to stay in Israel because of all the memories of my husband and son that still haunted me. I had a cousin living in Wichita who invited me to move in with his family until I got settled and found my own place.

I found a job with a security firm and led a solitary life for some time. There was an Arab family living down the block from us whom I totally ignored. Their mere presence evoked anger in me.

One evening as I was taking my walk I passed the school yard and noticed that five neighborhood kids had surrounded this little Arab boy and were calling him names. I didn't pay much attention because I figured that they were just being boys and would soon tire of the activity. Then I saw one of the boys shove the little boy and another grabbed him. It was apparent that they were going to beat on him. The little boy started crying.

Before I realized what I was doing I ran into the fray and snatched the little boy away from them. I told the other boys that if I ever heard of any of them harming the little boy they would have me to reckon with. One of the boys came at me with a bat which I quickly snatched from him and swatted him on the butt. Of course then all the boys took off running. After I calmed the little boy down I walked him home to his parents.

It was then that I came to realize that I couldn't blame all Arabs for the actions of a misguided few. It wasn't long before I became friends with that family. After that one little incident I began to reexamine my life. I realized that in the instant that it took me to get to that little boy all I saw was a little boy being picked on and in trouble simply because he was a little different from the other boys. Not an Arab boy but just a little boy who needed help.

I realized that when it comes down to it we are all members of the human race. It doesn't matter the color of your skin or your nationality.

We're all just people trying to get through the day, trying to survive, trying to reach out to others so we don't feel so lonely. If bad things happen to us we have to learn to deal with it the best way we can and move on. The worse thing that one can do is giving up and quite trying to live which is what I had done.

I guess what I'm trying to say to you is that there is no angle. The best thing that Abe, Jacob and I can gain from all this is to see you start a new life and to start living again. Jacob didn't kill your father. The man in prison did. Jacob didn't kill your mother. The rogue policeman did. Did your father and mother get a raw deal? Yes they did. Did my husband and son get a raw deal? Yes they did. Did you and I get a raw deal? Yes we did, but we can do something about it. We can learn from what happened and try to make things better for others who may find themselves in a similar situation.

Abe and Jacob have had similar pain in their lives and maybe they sense that same pain in you. Their only angle is that they want to help you relieve that pain and have a less troublesome future. Good lord I've said enough. I didn't mean to tell my life story and lecture you."

Bobbi Ann got very quiet for a moment. It had been a long time since someone had talked to her like this. In fact she wasn't sure if anyone ever had. Maybe her Dad had in a small way once or twice.

Miriam had said a lot but most of what she said was true. Especially the part about being lonely. Bobbi Ann had felt alone for most of her young life. It was obvious that Miriam had her share of pain and heartache and over time had learned to deal with it and get past it. Bobbi Ann would have to do the same. There were some things that she would have to unlearn like that everyone was untrustworthy.

Maybe not everyone was playing an angle. It would take time, but she would have to learn who she could trust and who she couldn't. Deep down inside she felt that she could trust Miriam, Abe and Jacob. They had proven themselves to her by giving her this chance to change the direction of her life.

"No, no Miriam I'm glad that you told me what you did. I guess that I've been very selfish in believing that I'm the only one suffering in this world. You've given me a lot to think about, and I will. I appreciate it. Just promise me one thing."

"What's that?"

"That you'll be around when I need to talk to someone."

'Bobbi Ann, you know that I will. Anytime you need to talk let me know, okay."

"Okay."

"Now let's get busy. We have some chores to do before those guys get back for supper."

"Okay. I've just one question. How did you wind up here?"

"That my dear is a story for another day."

CHAPTER 16

PRELUDE TO THE RAID

Lisa felt so sorry for Teddy Sexton and what he must be going through. It's difficult enough just being a teen-ager in this day and age much less have a father who's running around the countryside executing people for who knows what reason. Lisa knew that the alleged crimes were committed out of her jurisdiction which meant that she would have to bring the sheriff's office on board.

Lisa wondered how that would play out. Sheriff Terry could be difficult at times when it came to cooperation. It was days like this that made Lisa wish for a brief moment that she would have chosen another profession like interior design or chef where you didn't have to deal directly with people problems. Lisa's great grandfather, grandfather, and father had been career law enforcement officers, and Lisa was the only grandchild that had followed in their footsteps. She never regretted her decision to enter law enforcement, but sometimes the demands of her job were disheartening. This was one of those times.

Lisa would have to confront Betty Sexton with the events that had transpired involving her son and husband which would be difficult. She and Betty were good friends and had participated in community activities together.

Betty had disliked Blair Logan from the beginning and had been increasingly disillusioned with the Sons and Daughters organization. She told Lisa in confidence that she thought her husband and Blair had a thing going but had no proof. Betty had almost filed for divorce but decided that she couldn't do that to Teddy who idolized his Dad. Maybe recent events would change her mind. Lisa did not for a moment believe that Betty had any knowledge of what Dan Sexton had been doing.

***

Sheriff Ray Terry did have some suspicions about Dan Sexton and his activities but nothing that would pass as concrete evidence. Ray Terry had been sheriff of Madison County for as long as anyone could remember, but he wasn't that old. When he first ran for office he was 27 years old. The previous sheriff was under indictment for corruption and didn't run for re-election. No one opposed Ray Terry. Twenty-three years later he was still running unopposed. Ray Terry had run a corruption free office and was considered to be fair minded among the general population. Even some of the local criminal element respected him.

Sheriff Terry had been impressed with Dan Sexton's performance as a Deputy Sheriff and even looked upon him as a possible successor. He felt that Dan's zealous nature in making arrested would temper with time and experience on the job. Sheriff Terry was disappointed with Dan Sexton after he started his own security firm. The Dan Sexton that he once knew no longer seemed to exist.

He didn't blame Dan for wanting to better himself and make a good living for his family, but Dan had become arrogant and distrustful of public law enforcement. At first Dan had come to Sheriff Terry often seeking his advice and opinion on security matters. Now he barely spoke to the Sheriff. Ray Terry sensed that the change in Dan's behavior began right after he signed on as security contractor for the Sons and Daughters organization.

It appeared as though Dan spent most of his time attempting to impress Blair Logan and Harvey Bacon than managing day to day security operations. Several of Dan's men had altercations with Sheriff Terry's deputies when arrested on charges of simple assault. Strangely the charges were dropped the next day after Dan paid a visit to the assault victims. None of the victims were willing to indicate what had been said in their meeting with Dan Sexton.

Rumors had been floating around for months about strange disappearances and freak fatal accidents throughout the county, but Sheriff Terry and his deputies could not nail down any specifics. The accidents appeared to be nothing more than freak accidents. The evidence would support no other finding.

Madison County had an abnormally high number of missing persons reports filed over the last six months, and the Sheriff and his deputies had been unable to locate about 35% of those reported as missing.

Sheriff Ray Terry knew from a lifetime of experience that one of these days the law of averages would bring forth some solid evidence of what was really going on. He would not be surprised to find Dan Sexton in the middle of it. He sincerely hoped not for Betty and Teddy's sake, but that was his gut feeling.

***

After he had rested Lisa had Teddy write down everything that he could remember. He wrote down everything about that terrible night and of the conversation that he heard about David Peterson's planned accident. Teddy was able to identify one of the execution victims. Ralph Jamison had been a very popular assistant basketball coach at the high school and had mysteriously disappeared about the same time that Teddy witnessed the executions.

Lisa placed a call to Sheriff Terry.

"Sheriff Terry this is Lisa Hamel. Are you available at the moment? I have an urgent matter that I need to discuss with you."

"Sure, Lisa," said Sheriff Terry. "I'm on my way to my office now. Meet you in about ten minutes."

"I'll be there."

"Fine, fine. See you then."

On the way to the Sheriff's office Lisa called Abe.

"We've just caught a break. Dan Sexton's son Teddy was an eye witness to his Dad's execution of some of the former Sons and Daughters members."

"Say what? Christ, how did that come about?"

"Well at first Teddy thought that he was having a reoccurring nightmare. He kept dreaming that he hid in the bed of his Dad's pick up to find out where he was going at all hours of the night. He observed his Dad and his security employees systematically executing former members including a missing High School Assistant Basketball Coach. He never told his parents what the nightmares were about.

This afternoon Teddy paid his Dad a surprise visit at his office and overheard his Dad on the phone with his associates plotting the demise of one David Peterson. After an agonizing couple of hours Teddy realized that his nightmares weren't nightmares at all and called me.

I have Teddy's signed statement witnessed by one of my staff, and Teddy has agreed to testify against his Dad. We have Teddy in protective custody. Teddy and I are on our way to the Sheriff's office since the crimes occurred in his jurisdiction."

"Damn.....that poor kid. How old is he?"

"Fifteen, but a very brave fifteen."

"I'd agree with that. Do you think that the Sheriff will cooperate?"

"I know Sheriff Terry pretty well, and he's strictly by the book.

Rumor is that Ray Terry is not very happy with the new Dan Sexton, Security Expert. Once he's had a chance to read Teddy's statement, I'm sure that he'll act."

"Well, he'd better act quickly before Dan Sexton finds out his son is missing. If Sexton goes to ground we may never find him. Jacob did a quick check with the FBI and found out that Dan Sexton was in Special Forces in the Army assigned to Delta Force. Those guys know how to hide."

"That's not good news. What have you and Jacob been up to?"

"As an officer of the court you don't want to know. Let's just say that we plan to drop in on some folks and leave it at that."

"I didn't hear a thing. Talk to you later. Just be damn careful this time, you hear!"

"I swear. One damn mistake. I'm flattered that you're worried about me, but Jacob's got my back."

"What makes you think that I'm worried about you? Maybe I just don't want to have to explain to my boss about your escapade if you fuck up."

"Thanks for the confidence builder....nice language."

"Comes with the territory. See you later, I hope."

"You will."

***

Blair Logan and Dan Sexton had been sleeping together for over a month. What began as casual sex had grown into a full blown torrid affair. Blair had never encountered anyone like Dan. He was the first male ever who had made her orgasm during sex, and she couldn't get enough of him. He was the first real man that she'd known.

Dan had actually rejected her advances in the beginning. His self-control was unbelievable. Then one evening when they were engaged in planning the details of the upcoming mission, he had reached over and pulled her to him and took her right there in the living room of her apartment. He never asked anything from her afterward, and that is when she knew that she could never control him. She had met her equal.

Early the next morning in the living quarters at The Barn after a night of love making Dan received a phone call on his secure line. Afterward he seemed totally stunned and disoriented for a moment. He had a look of shock on his face.

"What happened?" asked Blair.

"Nothing that I can't handle," snapped Dan.

"Excuse me to hell," responded Blair. "I'm concerned. You look like you just lost your best friend, damn it!"

"Yeah, yeah in a way I have," mumbled Dan.

Dan was angry. He was angry at himself. Previously, before he would travel to an execution site from home, he would check everything including the bed of his pick up before leaving. That night he was in a hurry and got sloppy, and it cost him big time. He wasn't angry at Teddy. There was no way that he could be angry with him. Dan had perked Teddy's curiosity for years with his tales of secret missions, so of course Teddy had to find out for himself what Dad was up to. Again in his office his secretary had stepped away to go to the bathroom and Teddy got close enough to hear a conversation he shouldn't have heard. Dan should have been more careful in choosing his words when the area wasn't secure.

Teddy was simply too young to fully understand what he saw and heard. He had no idea of what it takes to preserve liberty and freedom in these perilous times. His son knew next to nothing about traitorous behavior and what was required to deal with it. Maybe someday Teddy would understand but probably not now. Dan would simply have to disappear from his family and the community. As he had learned in Delta Force the mission is paramount.

"Dan, I need to know if what has happened will impact the operation?" queried Blair. "I'm seriously thinking in the light of recent events to delay the operation for a few months until things cool down."

"Are you nuts?" responded Dan. "It's too late to delay it. The operatives are primed and ready. If we stand down now they'll lose their edge. Some may even lose their nerve. Think of what it's taken to gets us to this point. If we wait someone is bound to break. As we discussed last night that someone could be Harvey. He's already asked me to keep tabs on you for Christ sake! We have to do it now!"

Blair had never seen Dan this animated about anything.

"Dan, what the hell has happened?"

"That was Eric Stiles on the phone. Eric is a Deputy Sheriff and part of my intelligence net. I trust him completely. The Sheriff has issued a warrant for my arrest and sent out an APB."

"For what!" yelled Blair.

"A source claims to have witnessed my execution of former members of the Sons and Daughters and overheard my phone conversation plotting the demise of David Peterson," replied Dan calmly.

"Can't we get to the source and eliminate them. I have absolutely nothing on Sheriff Terry but surely we can manufacture something on this so called source."

"The source is my son."

"Oh, Jesus Christ! Oh my God! What are we going to do? How did this happen?"

"It's not your problem. I'll handle it. I'll simply disappear and work in the background. If Special Forces taught me one thing it was how to hide in plain sight."

"You're right," said Blair. "We need to move forward. There can be no delay. I'll go to my apartment this morning and start packing some things. I should be back here in two days, and we can start the count down. I'll tell Harvey to meet us here day after tomorrow."

"I'll make sure that security is beefed up before I disappear. See you in two days."

***

Sheriff Terry couldn't believe what he was reading. He had to reread it several times. The law of averages had caught up with Dan Sexton.

Lisa had told Sheriff Terry everything that they knew up to this point and held nothing back. The Sheriff listened very carefully, but the kicker had been Teddy's statement.

"Who would have believed it? I would never have painted Dan as a fanatic. He's become a full blown raging fanatic. There've been all kinds of rumors floating around here about what goes on at those meetings in The Red Barn, but this beats all. I tried to warn Dan not to get involved with that bunch, but he wouldn't listen.

After you told me about the ledger code business and the deaths of those three folks, I knew that I wasn't far wrong in believing that something very sinister was in the works. I think that I might know where that burial ground is. At least Dan has raised a very brave young lad. It took a lot of guts for him to come forward. I'd like to be there with you when you talk to Betty. She's a strong woman, but this is really going to hit her hard."

"I know that it's going to be hard for Betty," responded Lisa.

"There is something else you need to know Sheriff. You may already know this, but Dan Sexton served in Special Forces in the Army assigned to a Delta Force Unit. If he gets wind of this, we may have a hard time tracking him down."

"Yeah, I knew about that , however since the only people who know about this statement are Teddy, you, me, Jacob Grant and this Abe Lincoln we should be alright. Where in hell did he get a name like that? His parents must have had a real sense of humor.

I've met Jacob Grant a few times, and I know our secrets are safe with him. That being the case Dan shouldn't suspect anything a head of time. However in case word gets out and he goes to ground, I have my own Special Forces tracker."

Sheriff Terry leaned over and hit his intercom button. "Miss Russell, would you ask Eric Stiles to come in here. Eric was in Delta Force as well and was a friend of Dan's before they had a parting of the ways."

Eric Stiles appeared at the door. He was a good two hundred and fifty pounds of solid muscle standing at six feet six inches with sandy hair and piercing ice blue eyes. He had a definite scar down his left cheek. His menacing looks probably evoked the fear of God into many a criminal.

"Eric come in here and take a look at this. Looks like our boy Dan has gotten himself into a heap of trouble."

***

Abe hung up with Lisa and immediately received another phone call from a number he had never seen before.

"Is this Abe Lincoln?"

"None other."

"Is that really your name?"

"'Fraid so."

"Amazing. This is Shelia MacMurphy. Obviously you don't know me. I was told to contact you by a Randy Lewis who was an informant for the FBI and working undercover as a member of the Sons and Daughters organization. Randy told me to get a hold of you if anything happened to him. I think that they've killed him."

"Who's they?"

"The Sons and Daughters Head of Security Dan Sexton did the killing."

"I see and how am I supposed to help you?"

"I was working as the Assistant to Maury Williams who was the Head of Communications for the Sons and Daughters, and I may have some information for you. Randy and I became involved, and I was helping him get information to the FBI. I think they killed Maury too."

"Dan Sexton?"

"No, Blair Logan and Harvey Bacon who are planning some kind of top secret operation probably did that deed. Maury was to meet them at Blair's apartment a few days ago, and he never came back to work. Harvey tried to tell me that he had resigned, but I know better. Randy told me no one resigns from the Sons and Daughters and lives to tell about it.

Anyway I have the combination to the storage vault where the secret operational plans are kept, however I've never seen them because they're in a separate small black metal box stored in a wall safe. I'm supposed to give you the combination to the storage vault and wall safe and tell you everything that I know about the organization. Randy said that I could trust you and that you would protect me."

"Where are you?"

"I'll come to you. I can't tell you where I'm hiding. I don't care if your name is Abe Lincoln, for all I know they may have you bugged. If they find me they'll kill me!"

"I can assure you that they don't have me bugged Shelia, but we'll play it your way. Tell you what. Do you know where the Wheaton Sports Complex is?"

"Of course I do. I grew up here."

"I'll meet you in the south end of the parking lot. Can you make it there from where you're at in thirty minutes?"

"Absolutely!"

"See you in thirty minutes from now."

"Okay!"

"Who the hell was that?" asked Jacob.

"We just caught another break. When it rains it pours," answered Abe. "Her name is Shelia MacMurphy, and she was the Assistant to Maury Williams. She is almost positive that Blair and Harvey killed Maury. Shelia claims to have the combination to the storage vault where the Sons and Daughters secret operational plans are stored in a little black box. I have a feeling that she can fill in a lot of missing blanks for us. I'm supposed to meet her in thirty minutes in the parking lot of the Sports Complex. Care to join me?"

"Wouldn't miss it for all the gold in Knox. You think that she's legit? This could be another set up. How the hell did she get our number?"

"Apparently the FBI gave our number to an operative by the name of Randy Lewis who had infiltrated into the Sons and Daughters organization. She was helping Randy get information for the FBI. She thinks that Dan Sexton found out about Randy and killed him."

"That Dan fellow sure has been busy. Are you sure that this isn't a trap like last time?"

"You and Lisa. I'll never live that down. That's why I'm taking you along to protect my backside. Think that you can handle that old timer?"

"I think this old timer still has a little juice left in his battery. I never got hit by any bat."

"Okay, okay!"

Abe and Jacob jumped into the rental and headed for the Sports Complex. It looked as though they were getting close to finding out what got Mari Denton killed.

"Shelia can give us the layout of the Red Barn for our unannounced visit tonight which will save us time in defeating any internal security," said Abe.

"Yeah, at least we'll know if they're any Dobermans lurking about. The polystyrene coated coveralls and the large beam red portable laser pointers should get us past the heat sensors and video camera, but if they're Dobermans about we need to know ahead of time," cautioned Jacob.

"You really got a thing about Dobermans don't you?"

"Well, when you've had one of those bastards snapping within an inch of your ass you kind of remember it. If a patrolman hadn't gotten off a lucky shot at the right time, we wouldn't be having this conversation right now. Damn I hate those animals."

"We're about to find out. There she is. Looks like she's alone."

Shelia was parked as far away from the Sports Complex building as she could get scanning the area with a pair of binoculars. She saw a black 2008 Honda Accord pull into the parking lot and park two rows in back of her.

A tall lanky looking gentleman got out of the Honda and ambled toward where she was parked. He had a rugged outdoor appearance about him. His psyche fit his name, however he was much better looking than the real Abe Lincoln.

Abe told Jacob to wait in the car and be on the lookout for any surprises. It appeared that the parking lot was deserted except for Shelia's car, but he had learned the hard way to practice caution. Abe approached the car as Shelia rolled down the driver's side window.

She was a blonde with sky blue eyes and a very pretty face with pouty lips. Shelia was slender and well proportioned. She was wearing a sweatshirt and jeans.

"So you're Abe Lincoln?" remarked Shelia. "You kind of look like him with your build and all but definitely better looking."

"I'll take that as a compliment. You must be Shelia. You have some identification?"

"I was going to ask you the same thing," replied Shelia. "Who's in the car with you?"

"That's Jacob Grant my associate. He's a retired detective and has been hired by the Wheaton Police as a consultant on this case. Here's my driver's license. If that isn't enough then we can call Lisa Hamel, Chief of Detectives for the Wheaton Police Department who will vouch for us."

"No that's fine. Here's my driver's license and that's all I have. The only people who can vouch for me want me dead. Sorry to be so suspicious, but I'm trying to stay alive."

"Don't blame you. The license is fine. You want to do this here or follow me back to our motel. We're kind of exposed out here. It'd be more comfortable at the motel, plus you may be better off in the long run under our protection."

"I agree. I'll follow you."

Abe jogged back to the Honda, and Shelia pulled her car around behind Abe's rental.

On the way back Jacob said, "Well, what do you think? She going to be helpful."

"I have a feeling that she's going to be very helpful."

After returning to the motel and getting Shelia settled in her own room under police protection arranged by Lisa, Shelia provided Abe and Jacob with a complete layout of the Red Barn and the combination to the storage vault and wall safe. Shelia would be moved later on that evening to a safe house.

Jacob cursed under his breathe when she told them about the two Dobermans who prowl at night inside the complex. Shelia gave Jacob her whistle to bring the dogs to heel.

She told them how the membership listings kept changing and that she was sure two of her friends had been killed because they wanted to leave the organization.

Shelia said it was apparent that Blair and Dan Sexton were having an affair and that they pretty much controlled everything that went on. Shelia gave Abe a rundown of how many security staff would be on duty late at night and that there best bet was to approach from the Southwest corner because there was only one security camera scanning that area and the heat sensor in that area didn't work half the time. Security staff was lax about the heat sensors going off anyway since they were usually set off by rabbits or a stray coyote. She gave them her access code to the building and warned them that Dan Sexton may have beefed up security in the last few days.

***

Dan Sexton was pissed. Shelia MacMurphy had not reported to work this morning which wasn't like her and no one seemed to know where she was. He called her cell phone and apartment and got her answering machine. He drove to her apartment complex and broke into her apartment. It was apparent that most of her clothes, valuables, cosmetics, and personal papers were missing. That could mean only one thing. She must have been helping Randy Lewis. Damn he tried to warn that wimp Harvey and Maury that she was a security risk, but was overruled by Blair.

Blair's big weakness was that she thought everyone could be controlled which was never the case. Dan immediately put out an alert to his security people to begin a kill on site search for Shelia MacMurphy. He would have Blair change the combination on the storage vault when she returned. Meanwhile Dan Sexton had to disappear until day after tomorrow.

***

The Sheriff's Department scoured the countryside looking for Dan Sexton to no avail. Sheriff Terry called Eric Stiles on the radio and told him to begin his search, since it looked like Dan Sexton had gone to ground.

The Sheriff was concerned about how the word had gotten to Sexton that he was a wanted man. The circle of knowledge was limited to essential law enforcement staff until the warrant was issued. He knew for sure that it wasn't Lisa, Abe or Jacob. It certainly couldn't have been Teddy. Someone in his office must have leaked the information.

Eric Stiles had an idea where Dan Sexton would be. He knew where he would go, if it were him. Eric knew that Dan would not flinch at committing an execution if it were a cause in which he believed.

In Iraq and Afghanistan it was part of their mission to infiltrate the enemy and assassinate their leaders. Dan really believed that their actions in those countries helped prevent another atrocity like 9/11.

To Dan the fight against criminals was no different than the cause which he supported while in their Delta Unit. After Dan came to Eric to explain that he had found another cause worth fighting for Dan joined the Sons and Daughters organization.

Eric just wasn't a joiner. After his indoctrination it became apparent to Dan that while they were fighting for freedom and liberty overseas the federal government was usurping those same values at home. In a way they had been fighting under false pretenses. It was obvious to Dan that it would take a second revolution to win their freedom back and limit the power of federal and state government.

Dan had married his high school sweetheart when he got back and they had started their family. At first Dan's wife attended some of the Sons and Daughters activities, but after a time her interest waned. She stopped going to the meetings. As he had always done once Dan committed to something he devoted his total energy to it. He had a new mission.

Eric never married, but he respected the institution. He knew that marriage would never work for him. He was selfish with his time and more comfortable as a loner. It's not that he didn't like women, he did. He had relationships with a number of women, but he just couldn't commit to one woman.

After Dan completed training with the organization Maury Williams took a special interest in Dan. He encouraged him to attend night school and get a degree in criminal justice. In fact the organization provided funds for Dan's tuition and books.

After Dan got his degree Maury put him in touch with a friend of the organization who owned a security company in Wichita. Soon afterward Dan resigned from the Sheriff's office and joined the security firm. After Dan had a couple of years' experience the organization arranged for the financing for Dan to start his own security company. It wasn't long until Dan received a lucrative contract to provide security for the Sons and Daughters organization.

Eric admitted that he felt somewhat jealous about Dan's move, however Eric was not as enthused about that organization. Frankly Eric was somewhat suspicious of Maury and his answers for everything attitude. He didn't trust Harvey at all, and he knew from the start that Blair Logan was a power hungry bitch. He'd seen women like her operate before.

Dan tried to get Eric to join his security company as a top lieutenant, but Eric decided to stay with the Sheriff's office. He told Dan that he could be his eyes and ears in the community and keep Dan informed about what law enforcement was doing. Dan agreed. As time went by Eric began to have serious doubts about what the Sons and Daughters organization was trying to accomplish. The targets that they had eliminated in Iraq and Afghanistan were evil and violent people who had killed indiscriminately. They had tried to silence anyone in the general populace who promoted freedom and liberty and were not in tune with their version of Islamic teachings.

The people that Dan and his staff had targeted for elimination were none of those things. They were simply former members of the organization who no longer agreed with the Sons and Daughters doctrine and decided to leave the organization's inner circle. The Sons and Daughters were taking on the characteristics of the Taliban and extremist radical religious groups in Iraq. Eric couldn't believe that Dan couldn't see that.

He and Dan argued for months. Finally they quit talking. Eric was deeply troubled about the killings that had taken place recently of Mari Denton, Martin Parrish, and Elaine Myers. Eric and Elaine had been dating for a couple of months prior to her untimely death. Eric took her death hard.

Eric had warned Dan about the warrant only because he felt obligated for the time that Dan had saved his ass overseas. But his loyalty ended there. After hearing from the Sheriff about the details of the investigation that was underway, it became apparent to him that Elaine's death was not a random hit and run. It was an execution carried out by Dan's organization.

Eric wasn't for certain about the nature of the Sons and Daughters secret operational plans, but he knew that there would be mass destruction involved. He knew that Dan had been screwing Blair and given his own background that really sickened him. Betty Sexton had always been kind to Eric and showed him respect. She didn't deserve that kind of treatment. Dan was out of control and had to be stopped.

Lisa decided to leave Teddy in protective custody for fear that Dan Sexton might have the house staked out.

Betty Sexton knew that something was amiss when the Sheriff's car pulled into her drive way. She had been expecting this day to come. Then Lisa Hamel's car pulled in beside the Sheriff.

When she saw the Sheriff getting out of the car she felt real fear. Something had happened to Teddy. That she could not bear. Her lips started to tremble and the tears began leaking from her eyes. Oh! Please God, No! Her legs felt weak and her heart began to race. Her legs felt like dead weights, and she barely made it to the front door.

"Is it Teddy?" said Betty in a voice shaky and barely audible.

"Teddy is alright Betty," responded Lisa as she place an arm around her. "It isn't Teddy."

"Oh, Thank God! That's such a relief. It's Dan, isn't it?" she said purposefully.

"Yes, it's Dan. Lisa gave Betty the whole story from start to finish and let her read Teddy's statement.

Tears welled up in Betty's eyes at the thought of what Teddy must have gone through over the past several hours. And yet she was so very proud of him.

"That's a very brave young man you have their Mrs. Sexton," injected the Sheriff. "I'm so sorry that we have to bring this kind of news to your door step."

Betty took a minute to compose then invited them into the living room to sit down.

"Thank you, Ray. Yes, I'm very proud of what Teddy did. One thing that his Daddy did teach him was to be honest and to always tell the truth. Dan told him over and over again that sometimes life requires you to do things that are very hard, but if it's right you must do them. Thank goodness that stuck with Teddy. Despite the fact that Dan has put my son through hell and apparently done things that are inexcusable he did try in his way to be a good father.

I had a strong feeling that this day was coming. Dan has been away from the house for most of the last two months. We've had very little conversation. He's been spending a great deal of his time at the Red Barn with Blair Logan. I'm not blind, so I guess that I wouldn't be too shocked if something was going on there as well.

Frankly, I've been close to filing for a divorce for over three months, but I just couldn't do that to Teddy. Now it appears that's not an issue. I know that you had to do what you did in issuing the warrant Ray, and I'll cooperate in any way that I can. Lisa, thank you for what you did for Teddy."

"Betty, I'm here for you any time you need me," replied Lisa.
"Could you stay for a few minutes after Ray leaves?" asked Betty.

"Sure, you know I will."

"Betty, we need a recent picture of Dan if you have it and any information that might help us to find him and then I'll be on my way," responded Sheriff Terry.

"Well, I do have a picture taken about six months ago. I'll go get it. It'll take just a second."

"Take your time, no rush."

After Betty left the room Sheriff Terry said, "She seems to be holding up given the circumstances. Always seemed like she had a lot of strength."

"Betty's pretty solid," said Lisa. "This type of thing would tear most women apart."

Betty walked back into the room.

"Here it is Ray. I hope it's what you need. As for Dan's whereabouts I haven't a clue if he's not at The Red Barn. Having been Delta I could imagine he could hide almost anywhere. If I hear anything I'll let you know, but I doubt that I will. He'd know better than to come back here. Where is Teddy?"

"He's in my protective custody at the moment, Betty," replied Lisa. "Since he's a material witness, we wanted to keep him safe until Dan was apprehended."
"Can I see him?"

"Sure, I can take you over there when you're ready. I think that he'd really like to see his Mom about now," responded Lisa.

"Well, I going to shove off," said Sheriff Terry. "I'll keep you posted Betty on our progress. There'll be a couple of deputies assigned to guard you and your house until we've got Dan. Sorry, but that's a necessity."

"I understand Ray. Like I said I'll cooperate in any way that I can. If you're going to guard us, I'd just as soon have my son home with me. Is that possible?"

"Don't see why not. Lisa may want to have a couple of her people on the property as well."

"Yes, I planned on that," replied Lisa. "It probably would be best to have Teddy at home. He's going to need all the support that you can give him."

"Okay, that's settled. See you all later. Hopefully we'll have Dan in custody within the next twenty four hours."

"Good bye Sheriff Terry, and thanks again for everything that you've done," replied Betty.

After Sheriff Terry left Betty gave a big sigh and collapsed on the couch.

"You know that I'd like to blame Blair Logan for all this, but I can't. I've found out over the past several years that the Dan Sexton I knew no longer exists.

I know that most men come home from a war or conflict a changed person. There are so many things that they can't talk about. But I think that Dan found out that he liked war, and when the war was over for him he found another one right here at home. He found a cause that gave him the excuse that he needed to continue his Special Forces activity.

I just couldn't bring myself to believe that he would do those things that Teddy saw him do. I should have had the strength to take Teddy and leave long before now. It sickens me with grief. I know that I shouldn't, but I feel responsible for all the evil that Dan has done."

"Betty, you can't control what another person is going to do. You did what you had to do to try and keep your family together for Teddy's sake. You can't live the rest of your life second guessing yourself. You'll drive yourself nuts. You've got a son to raise, and believe me he's going to need you more than ever to be strong for him," said Lisa.

"I already know what I want to do until this is over. I don't want Teddy to have to go back to school here and face the ugliness that he's sure to get from his school mates. Lord knows that he's been through enough turmoil already.
You know that the rumors will be flying when this breaks and how things get distorted. Young kids can be very cruel and judgmental.

I want to take Teddy to my sisters' house in Butte, Montana. She and her husband are overseas for several months, and I can house sit for her. I know that she won't mind at all. Teddy will be available anytime you need him to testify. I think that it would be best for the both of us."

"I see no problem with that," said Lisa. "I can run interference if we run into any legal issues, and I'm sure Sheriff Terry will be agreeable."

"I really don't know what I'd done without a friend like you. Can I go see my son now?"

"Sure, we'll take my car" replied Lisa. "It'll save you from having to drive or face the press. I know that they'll probably be camped out here when we get back. I'll make sure the patrolmen keep them in check."

CHAPTER 17

THE RAID

Abe and Jacob knew that they would have to infiltrate the Red Barn. After condensing the information that they had gathered from Teddy's statement and Shelia MacMurphy, Jacob had Lisa contact FBI Field Agent Bob Henderson. Henderson told them that he needed solid evidence that a violent act was about to be committed before he could call in a terrorist strike force. The FBI didn't want another Ruby Ridge or Waco.

Lisa said they could still use the search warrant issued by Sheriff Terry on Dan Sexton as a pretext for conducting a search of the Red Barn, but it would not allow them access to the storage vault and that little black box with the operational plans.

Abe figured that the only way they were going to get something solid was to go in and take it. They had figured out how to beat the heat sensors and video cameras, but for added insurance Jacob brought a couple of his retiree buddies on board. Their job was to create a diversion on the opposite side of the building to distract the security forces inside the facility.

"So, you ready to do this?" asked Jacob.

"Ready as I'll ever be," responded Abe. "We've got 20 seconds to cover 150 yards of open space. I hope your friends are ready to create a diversion on our go?"

"Hey, these guys may be retired but they ain't dead. They'll do what's expected and they'll deliver."

"Your word is good enough for me. Shelia gave us a floor plan. We can enter the South door using her pass code. Hopefully they haven't disabled her account. Using her information we shouldn't have any problem finding the storage vault.

Once inside the vault we need to find the wall safe with that black metal box and any other documents that'll convince the FBI to raid the place. If we can't get the box open, we take it with us."

"Right!' said Jacob. "If we encounter any security staff we neutralize them with the Taser gun, tie them up, and tape their mouths shut. We only use deadly force as the last option.

Once we're out of there we head straight for the motel where Agent Henderson is waiting. If he's convinced, he'll call in the strike force to raid the place."

"The key," said Abe "is getting our hands on those operational plans. A lot of lives could be lost without those plans."

"Don't forget the damn whistles to neutralize the dogs," remarked Jacob. "If one of those damn animals gets within 10 feet of me I'll tranquilize the son of a bitch."

"Alright Jacob, I've got the whistles. We better head out. By the time we get to the staging area and set up it's going to be dusk."

As they traveled along the route to the location, Jacob wondered aloud about how all this mess got started.

"Hard to say exactly," said Abe. "You've got a self-made millionaire with a lot of time on her hands and a genuine need to control everything around her, plus a real contempt for the general populace. She's schemed and plotted her way through life until its second nature to her. Humans are great imitators, so she probably learned at the foot of her parents, only she's been more successful and maybe lucky. She's intelligent, but her conscience IQ is non-existent.

In Maury you have a kid who was probably ignored or just tolerated growing up and felt that he couldn't measure up to dear old Dad, so he developed his own special skills in radicalism. The folks were probably too busy accumulating wealth that they didn't have time to clue him into any morality lessons. Maury probably had above average intelligence and a knack for articulation. He saw his opportunity for fame and adulation in the radical genre and took it. That was one arena in which he didn't have to compete with Daddy.

Finally we have Harvey Bacon. He was well indoctrinated into to right wing fringe conservative movement from childhood through puberty. He probably wasn't the most popular kid in school, but he made his mark academically.

He undoubtedly is the original prototype of today's nerd. Again his parents didn't have the time or inclination to instill in Harvey any semblance of a moral code, unless it was survival of the smartest.

We have three excellent sociopath types who have a very low or nonexistent Conscience IQ and the addition of an ex-Special Forces Delta Force type who has learned to suppress his conscience to fit the cause which makes for a very lethal combination. Mix those ingredients and add in a floundering right wing organization with a fuzzy ill-defined cause and you've created a real live monster with very sharp teeth.

These four predators have a cause to lead and control and the former soldier had a new mission in which to hone his black ops skills. History tells us that there's always a generous supply of malcontents and sheep handy to follow any new warped leadership. It's bad enough when they start killing off each other, but when they start targeting innocent lives, it's time to step in and say 'You're not playing that game in my country.'"

"I'd say that about covers it," remarked Jacob. "Just trying to get some clarification as to why we're breaking and entering and tangling with Dobermans."

"Now you know."

"I certainly do."

Abe and Jacob arrived at their location in a clump of Elm trees just south of their target without incident and kept an eye on the Red Barn until nightfall.

After scanning the area with a pair of high powered binoculars, they decided that Shelia was correct. The best approach would be from the Southwest corner.

"They're no sentries walking a post. That's good news," said Jacob. "Probably relying on the video cameras, dogs and heat sensors to warn them of trespassers. I have a hunch that they don't expect anyone to try to break into their precious facility overnight. Nevertheless we need to be careful."

"Agreed," remarked Abe. "Once inside you need to toot on that whistle to bring those dogs to heel, unless you want them snapping at your ass and bringing down the whole security force. We need to head straight for the second floor and the room that houses the storage vault. I've got Shelia's thumb print that will get us access to the room, providing they haven't removed her from the system by now.

If that's happened we'll know when we try the combination to get into the building. If we can't get in, we'll need to do things the hard way by forcing our way in. Hopefully, we won't need to do that cause someone liable to get hurt badly."

"Well, that ain't gonna be you or me ol' buddy. It's been a while since I've had me some real fun and kicked some ass. I'd like to get my hands on some of those bat welding bastards."

"I see that retirement hasn't mellowed you any. I wouldn't mind a little payback myself, but I'd just as soon slip in and out undetected. If they know that they're about to be had, they may panic and destroy the plans or worse implement those ops plans early in which case a lot of innocent folks could get killed."

"My blood gets to boiling when I think about all the folks that have died just to let this group of morons keep their dirty little secrets. I'll maintain my professionalism, but if one of those wacko's gets in my way, they're toast."

"It's good to know that you can maintain your professional decorum. Contact your buddies and tell them that we're going in ten minutes. That'll be at precisely 10:30 pm. You carrying?"

"I've got my Smith and Wesson M1911 9mm on my hip. You?"

"I've got my favorite toy, a Glock G21 .45."

"We are so ready!"

Abe and Jacob slipped on the heavy polystyrene coated coveralls. Both had a red portable laser pointer to disable the video camera.

All the heat sensor would detect was small splotches of heat which could easily be mistaken for a small animal, if they damn thing was even working.

They made their way to the predetermined staging area and waited for the disturbances on the other side of the building to begin.

Larry Ellison was the Security Section Head for the night shift. Ellison and his crew would work a double shift tonight, because Dan Sexton had placed them on high alert.

Larry was a twenty five year veteran in security work. Twenty of those years had been in the Army. Dan and Larry had served together on several occasions and had become good friends. When Larry retired from the Army five years ago, Dan immediately hired him. Larry knew pretty much everything there was to know about building and perimeter security. If he'd had a full crew, he would have posted guards outside the building.

Unfortunately, one of his folks was in the hospital, two were on funeral leave, one was on his honeymoon, and Dan had taken three staff to search the Wheaton area for Shelia MacMurphy. He had enough staff to monitor the heat sensors and cameras that surrounded the building, however no way did he have enough people to walk the perimeter in shifts for 12 hours.

Larry knew the shortcomings of heat sensors; therefore he would periodically take a random stroll outside the building as a precaution.

He'd just come back from strolling along the South and West side of the building. Larry thought the damn Dobermans were useless and had them penned up. They'd bark at anything and were annoying. The dogs were crazy Blair's idea. He had no idea what Dan saw in that woman, other than a piece of tail. She was totally nuts. Just goes to show what happens when you start thinking with your Johnson.

At 22:30 hours military time, staff reported a disturbance on the Northeast corner of the building. It looked as though two hunters had ventured into the open space and were obviously drunk. Both men were armed with rifles and were pointing them at the building as though they were getting ready for some target practice.

Bryce Miller and Fred Tatum were retired policemen who had worked intelligence for most of their careers and were experts at undercover work. They had known Jacob Grant when they had worked together on several cases.

Bryce and Fred knew from experience how far to take their act without creating suspicion. If they could distract the security crew for five minutes without putting themselves in jeopardy, they had done their job.

Two figures emerged from the Red Barn and walked slowly toward them. One was a tall slender gent with a shock of red hair and a physic that said that he worked out often.

His partner was short and stocky with a close crew cut and beady black eyes and built like a fire plug. Both wore grey and black security uniforms with weapons at the ready position.

"You two gents lost?" said red hair.

"Naw, we ain't lost. We just out here huntin' for wild turkey," said Bryce. "You lost Charlie?"

"Hell no, I ain't lost," said Fred aka 'Charlie'. "I jest gonna do some target practice on that red barn there."

"I'd think twice about that partner," said fire plug. "This is private property and you're trespassing. I'd suggest you take your whiskey and get on down the road before you get into real trouble. We could have shot you both on sight no questions asked, so consider this your one and only warning."

"Hey, man no need to get nasty," replied Bryce.

"Charlie can't hit the broad side of a barn anyways in his condition. We just tryin to have some fun. Can't find no wild turkey cept what's in the bottle. What you guys doin way out here anyways? This some kind of government operation?"

"What we're doing here is none of your business. So move along."

"Hey, I'm just tryin to be neighborly. You guys want a little snort?"

Bryce held the bottle out to them. Red Hair grabbed the bottle and flung it across the clearing and into the bushes.

"Now get the fuck out of here before you both have a serious hunting accident. Understand?" said red hair.

"Okay, okay we're goin. Come on Charlie, don't think these boys know how to have fun. Looks like they got the red ass."

"Shit, now we gotta have to go git another bottle," said Charlie.

"Don't you know where you are assholes. This is the US of A – Land of the Free. We can go anywhere we want. Fuckin paid for hire cops. Let's go git us another bottle Eddie."

Bryce and Fred stumbled off into the night having accomplished their mission.

While Bryce and Fred were putting on their act, Abe and Jacob slipped across the clearing and up to the building at the Southwest corner. Just as planned the guys monitoring the security cameras and heat sensors had been distracted by the comedy show at the Northeast corner of the building and completely missed the video camera going snowy for about fifteen seconds and the small splotches on the heat sensor.

If anyone reviewed the tape the fifteen seconds would be considered an acceptable anomaly and the small splotches would be considered to be nothing more than rabbits or squirrels.

"Well, the moment of truth," said Abe.

"Let's do this thing," replied Jacob.

Abe punched in the code for the door and it opened to their relief.

"Damnit, I wanted to hit someone," responded Jacob.

"Save it. You may get your chance yet," replied Abe.

Abe and Jacob discarded their coveralls outside the door, stuffed them in two garbage bags for quick retrieval and found the stairway just where Shelia said it would be. They slowly crept up the stairs to the second floor.

Larry Ellison approached Red Mason and Sandy Lindell as they reentered the compound.

"What the hell was that all about?" asked Larry.

"Just a couple of drunken hunters who got lost in the woods. Probably shoot each other as drunk as they are. I think the one guy was planning on shooting up the barn until we intervened."

"You sure that's all it was. You ask for any identification?"

"Naw. Come on Larry, this shit happens all the time. It's the price you pay for locating this place in a hunting area. We get hunters by here all the time. Many of them are soused."

"What were they hunting for?"

"The one guy said wild turkeys," replied Sandy.

"Well, at least they're in season. Just be careful we don't get any more visitors. Dan will be back tomorrow and want a full report. Better go to your station and write it up while it's still fresh in your mind. You know how Dan is about details."

"I know. I know. Don't worry we'll get it down verbatim," replied Red.

Abe opened the stairway door to the second floor and saw that the hall was empty. If confronted, they were to identify themselves as maintenance repairmen checking the central air system after hours. It wasn't uncommon for local workmen to conduct their business after normal hours. They were wearing the uniform similar to the local company who serviced the Sons and Daughters heating and air conditioning units.

Abe and Jacob walked briskly down the hallway to the room designated by Shelia as housing the storage vault. Abe couldn't believe that everything was working out so well. When they arrived at the room their luck changed.

Someone was in the room going through a desk. The name plate on the desk read Shelia MacMurphy.

"Great," whispered Jacob. "Looks like they're onto her."

"Looks that way," responded Abe. "At least we managed to get into the building. Hopefully they don't plan on changing the code to the storage vault until morning. Shall we go into our routine?"

"What's the story, checking the vents?"

"Right you are!"

"Do I get to use my toy?"

"Could be!"

As they entered the room, Abe said, "Sorry to interrupt but we're supposed to check the vents in here."

"No one told me that was on the schedule at this time of night? I'm goin to call the desk." replied Red.

"Must have forgot to tell you," responded Abe.

Jacob quickly walked up behind Red and zapped him with the Taser gun. Red stiffened, gyrated and then toppled over without a word.

Jacob proceeded to tie him up, tape his mouth, chloroformed him and deposit him in the supply closet. He'd be out of it for several hours.

"You enjoyed doing that didn't you?" asked Abe.

"Hey, man's gotta have some fun in his work."

Abe and Jacob looked around to make sure no one was watching. They found the storage vault entered the code and validated Shelia's thumb print to gain access. No one had changed the code or deleted her access. Since they had failed to ask Shelia about the procedure for exiting the vault, they left the door slightly ajar.

The storage vault was a rather large rectangular room with rows of metal cabinets spaced evenly apart in the center area and around the walls. Once inside they began a search for the wall safe and the black metal box containing the operational plans.

"I'm going to look for that wall safe," said Abe. "Take a look around and see if you can find any documents of an incriminating nature that might help our cause with the FBI."

"Hey, I'm the detective here with all the investigative experience," responded Jacob. "Shouldn't I be searching for the wall safe?"

"That's right. You are indeed the detective and as such better equipped than I to discern incriminating evidence."

"Discern?"

"Add it to your list of words to look up in your spare time."

"I didn't realize that working with you would be a literary experience," retorted Jacob.

"Absolutely!"

"Well, let me discern these documents over here in this pile."

Abe began searching around the free standing cabinets in the vault which yielded nothing. He started to turn away from the cabinets when he spotted a small recessed area of the wall hidden behind one of the cabinets. A small wall safe sat in the recessed area.

"Do you have that combination to the wall safe?" Abe asked Jacob.

"Indeed I do. That didn't take long."

Jacob dialed the combination to the safe.

"Walla, my friend. Nothing to it. My, my what have we here? I think that I discern a black metal box."

Jacob pulled the box out of the enclosure and placed it on a table.

"The box has a cipher lock. Looks like we're gonna have to take this baby with us and hope that they don't notice it's missing until we activate the strike force," said Abe.

"I've found a few documents that outline ideas on how to attack shopping malls and other public places, and some bills of lading for explosive devices and various bomb components as well as chemical elements for bombs. I think that should help our cause substantially," replied Jacob.

"I'd say that's an understatement. See I told you that you could discern incriminating stuff."

"Sure enough."

"Let's get the hell out of here while our luck holds," replied Abe.

As they moved toward the door the storage vault door clicked shut.

"Oh! Shit!" exclaimed Jacob. "I think we've been had."

"No kidding!"

Sandy Lindell couldn't figure out what happened to Red. He was dead certain that Red went into the Central Room. It was then that he noticed the storage vault door was slightly ajar. Funny cause Red didn't have access to the storage vault code. Only Dan, Blair, Harvey, Shelia, and Larry Ellison had access. Maybe Larry left it ajar. Without giving it the slightest thought he shut the door.

Damn, he thought what if Larry was still in there? I should've looked. He decided if Larry was still in there he'd call on the radio. A few minutes later Larry came walking into the break room where Sandy was drinking coffee.

"Where the hell is Red? I've tried to raise him on the radio several times, and he doesn't answer," said Larry.

"I dunno. I was wondering that myself. I saw him go into the Central Room, but he ain't there now. Last I saw he was going through Shelia's desk like you told him."

"Something strange is going on here," remarked Larry. "First we have two drunk hunters on the property and now Red disappears. Tell the staff to start searching the building top to bottom. He's got to be here somewhere. I've never known him to not answer a radio call."

"Will do. By the way I closed the storage vault door that you left ajar."

Larry Ellison did a perfect double take.

"Wait a minute! What did you say?"

"The storage vault door was slightly ajar, so I closed it. I figured you must of left it open."

"Why the fuck didn't you tell me that right away? Drunk hunters my ass. That was a diversion. I should have trusted my instincts."

Larry eased toward the storage vault door. He'd have to be extra cautious. Whoever was in there was probably armed. Maybe he should leave them in there and call Dan Sexton. On second thought not such a good idea. Dan would rake him over the coals and maybe replace him for his incompetence. It would be better for Larry to handle the situation and clean up his own mess.

"When I open this door be prepared to open fire if we're fired upon. For Christ sake don't fire unless they do. I don't want you shootin up the place unless we need to. Can you understand that simple order?"

"Yes sir, I can!"

"Good, now get ready."

Larry punched in the code and pressed his thumb against the screen. He heard the door lock click. He eased the door open and took a quick peak inside. He couldn't see anyone in his field of vision.

"Alright, we know you're in there. I suggest that you come on out here with your hands in the air. If we have to come in there, someone's gonna get hurt."

His admonishment was greeted with silence. Nothing moved or stirred.

"Okay. You've been warned. We'll do this the hard way."

Larry whispered to Sandy, "I'm going in, cover me. If something happens to me, slam this door shut and get help. You understand?"

"Yep, gotcha covered!" replied Sandy.

Larry drew his weapon and moved cautiously toward the door listening for any sound of movement. After hearing nothing he moved quickly through the door. As he turned to his left he was suddenly hit in the chest with a Taser gun and gyrated and slumped to the floor.

Sandy hesitated a few seconds too long, and before he could reach the door Abe appeared from inside the door and hit him with three spring loaded Taser prongs in his midsection. Sandy gyrated and fell forward flat on his face.

Abe dragged Sandy's body into the storage vault. He and Jacob tied both Larry and Sandy's hands and feet together, taped their mouths and chloroformed them. They pulled Red from the supply closet, chloroformed him again and carried him into the vault as well.

"Hopefully no one will think to look in here for these three jokers for a while," said Abe.

"Yeah, I suggest we take their radios and disable the phone in here in case they wake up and get loose," replied Jacob.

"Good idea. Then let's get the hell out of here before someone else shows up and starts shooting real bullets at us."

"I'm ready. Man, that's the most fun I've had in ages."

"You need to start getting out more," responded Abe.

Jacob closed the storage vault door. Abe grabbed the black metal box and they moved quickly down the hall, scampered down the stairs, and out the door without incident.

They slipped into their coveralls and quickly moved across the open clearing aiming their portable laser pointers at the video camera.

Meanwhile in the security control room, Lionel Sully remarked, "That's the second time tonight that video camera on the Southwest corner has had snow for several seconds. Better check it out. What's the heat sensor reading in that area?"

"I dunno," replied Matt Greenly. "It hasn't been working right all evening. It's been reported defective anyway. Someone needs to replace it."

"Okay, I'm going to check out the camera. See if you can raise Larry on the radio. I need to talk to him. Red and Sandy haven't reported in as scheduled."

"Will do," replied Matt.

Matt tried several times to raise Larry Ellison and got no response. That was highly unusual. Ellison was always quick to respond.

Matt was unsure about what to do next. Should he call Lionel? Maybe he should take some staff and search for Larry? Better call Lionel he thought. Let him decide, since he was next in command after Larry.

"Lionel, this is Matt, over?"

"What is it? I thought I told you to call Larry?" replied Lionel.

"Larry isn't answering. I called him three times and no response. You know Larry, he always answers."

"Shit! What the hell is gonna go wrong next? I'm not supposed to call Dan unless it's a dire emergency. Take two men and do a complete search of the facility, and I mean complete. If we don't find Larry, I'll call Dan. It'd be my luck to call Dan and have Larry show up before Dan gets here. Give me a couple of minutes to get back there, and I'll watch the monitors. Doesn't appear to be a damn thing wrong with this video camera that I can tell. There's something weird going on around here."

"You got that right," said Matt.

When Lionel got back to the control room he learned that Red and Sandy were missing as well. After a complete search of the facility, they could not find Larry, Red or Sandy.

The one place that they couldn't search was of course the storage vault, since no one had access. Lionel finally had to place his call to Dan and explain everything that had happened from the time the drunken hunters showed up to the present.

At night Dan Sexton had camped in a clearing about a mile and a half east of the Red Barn that was often used by hunters in the area. There was a small cave about 1000 feet from the clearing and barely detectable. Dan stored his security electronic gear and clothing there. About a 150 feet into the cave floor was a trap door covered with dirt and brush. The trap door led to a tunnel that ran into the basement area of the Red Barn. Only Blair, Harvey, Maury, and Dan knew of its existence. Dan heard his radio buzz and ran quickly to the cave.

After he answered Lionel explained the situation to Dan as best he could.

"Why the hell did you wait this long to call me?" demanded Dan. "Is Blair or Harvey there by chance?"

"No, sir!" replied Lionel. "Haven't seen them. We wanted to conduct a complete search of the facility before calling you. For Christ sake Dan, Larry told us not to contact you unless it was a dire emergency!"

"Well, I'd say it's a dire emergency when three of your key people are missing, especially Larry Ellison. It sounds to me like someone deliberately created a diversion in order to gain access to the building, probably with the help of that little bitch Shelia. I knew that I should have changed those codes before I left. I expect that we'll be having visitors by morning. Whoever got into the building got to Larry, Red and Sandy. Any idea if anyone was in the central room besides Red?"

"Not that we can tell, however one of the staff thought the room smelled funny."

"What do you mean smelled funny?"

"They thought it smelled like someone had taken some strong medicine."

"I have a strange feeling that our missing staff were drugged. My guess is that someone got into the storage vault with Shelia's help. Get a hold of Blair and Harvey and tell them to get their asses to the Barn ASAP. We've got some decisions to make rather quickly."

***

Jacob drove like a bat out of hell to get back to the motel. They needed to get that black box opened. Abe called ahead to make sure that Lisa, the Sheriff and FBI Agent Henderson were there. Abe and Jacob knew that it would be a race against time once Dan and Company found out that the black box was missing.

"Wonder what happen to the Dobermans?" asked Jacob. "I never heard a whimper."

"Yeah, kinda strange. Normally they usually whine a bit. Maybe Shelia was wrong. Could be there were never any Dobermans." replied Abe.

"Could be. At least we didn't have to shoot our way out of the place. Probably won't take them long to find our drugged friends."

"I suspect they've already called Dan Sexton where ever he is. It won't take him long to figure things out. We damn well need to get this box opened. That FBI strike team needs to be in action by dawn," responded Abe.

"The problem is that the more time we waste the more time these folks have to implement their plan. They may only get part of the plan implemented, but half a plan can cause a hell of a lot of damage," remarked Jacob.

"Well, the smart thing for them to do would be to destroy any evidence in the Barn, like burn it to the ground and clear out. They could lay low for a few months and start over again.

As far as Dan Sexton is concerned I doubt that we'll capture him alive under any circumstances.

The truth is that these groups never do the smart thing. They get caught up in their own rhetoric and drama," observed Abe.

"We damn well need to stop them now," declared Jacob.

***

12 Midnight

Harvey Bacon was close to unadulterated panic. Apparently all hell had broken loose since he last talked to Blair. His sources told him that David Peterson had disappeared without any report of a fatal accident. Dan Sexton's son, Teddy, had apparently witnessed his Dad executing former members and had overheard his Dad plotting the death of Peterson. There was an arrest warrant out for Dan and according to the call that he had just received security had been penetrated at The Barn. Three top security staff were missing. On top of all this he and Blair were being sought by law enforcement for questioning.

A couple of weeks ago Harvey would have never imagined these developments. They had definitely underestimated law enforcement and this Abe Lincoln fellow. Harvey was on his way by private helicopter to meet with Blair and Dan before dawn. Harvey wanted to destroy all the evidence and burn the damn Barn to the ground. There was no time to implement the plan if what Dan Sexton said was true about the Feds descending upon them at dawn.

Blair Logan was livid. Why the hell did those stupid fucking idiots pen the dogs up? Just like a bunch of little boys all they wanted to do was play with their electronic toys. There should have been guards outside the building with the dogs on a leash. That damn Larry Ellison and his twenty five years of security experience didn't mean shit. For Christ sake look what happened! Now they can't even find the son of a bitch and two of his men. If they find the bastard he ought to be shot. Better yet turn the dogs loose on him.

Blair was trying to calmly drive herself to The Barn. She certainly didn't need to get stopped for speeding under the current circumstances.

Blair kept checking her rear view mirror to be sure that no one was tailing her. She had purposefully pulled over to the shoulder of the road several times to allow traffic to pass her. She saw nothing suspicious.

She was amazed that Dan had sounded cool as a cucumber when she talked to him. That man had balls of steel. Nothing bothered him. Dan had restored her confidence in the plan. They would have to act quickly and drag Harvey kicking and screaming with them.

As far as Blair knew Harvey was the only one who knew the procedures to implement the plan. Harvey would cooperate or Dan would use his Special Forces training to convince Harvey to cooperate and that would be a sight to behold. Blair had to chuckle at the thought of Harvey stripped naked, hanging from a ceiling beam with electrodes connected to his nuts. He would be begging Dan to let him down in order to cooperate.

Blair was congratulating herself for removing the final operational plans from the black box before leaving the other night. Even though someone might have penetrated the storage vault they would not get their hands on the plans. That bitch Shelia had a lot to answer for. If they ever found her, Blair wanted just an hour with her. Shelia would wish that she had never heard of Blair Logan or the Sons and Daughters.

***

Lisa, Sheriff Terry, and FBI Agent Henderson had gathered in the motel room when Abe and Jacob arrived. Agent Henderson had brought Agent Bob Lattimore with him to the meeting. Lattimore was a fifteen year expert on opening locks of all kinds. His specialty was cipher locks.

While Lattimore began working on the cipher lock, the others began to discuss the material that Jacob had brought with him from the storage vault.

"What you have here would definitely indicate that something was being planned to include the use of explosives.

The big question is what?" asserted Agent Henderson. "We have no information regarding location or locations, time frame, or specific targets not to mention the sequence of events."

"Maybe that little black box will provide us with the answers to your questions," replied Jacob. "Based on what we do know you can't consider this group a benign organization. This is a very dangerous group of people who have the will and the resources to raise a great deal of havoc all over this country, unless we put a stop to it. If we hit now we may be able to stop them. If we wait another day it may well be too late."

"I don't disagree that the information so far does point to this group's potential for violence. What I need is something that tells me that the violence is imminent," responded Agent Henderson.

Bob Lattimore interrupted to tell them that he had figured out the code. It had taken him a little less than twenty minutes. It should have been obvious that the code would be 0611.

"The moment of truth has arrived," said Sheriff Terry.

Henderson opened the lid and everyone starred at a half page note on top scribbled in Blair Logan's handwriting with total disbelief.

The note read:

Harvey,

Don't be alarmed. I have taken the plans home for further review in case we have to revise our procedures in light of current developments.

Blair

"I'll be damned!" exclaimed Jacob. "We went through all that crap for nothing. Son of a bitch!"

***

Dan Sexton was the first to arrive at The Barn. He went directly into the storage vault. Lying side by side fast asleep were Larry, Red and Sandy like the Three Stooges all bound together with duct tape with their mouths taped shut. Dan smelled the distinct odor of chloroform and saw that the marks on them indicated that they had been hit with a Taser gun. He opened the wall safe and saw that the black box was missing which meant that the Feds had their operational plans by now.

Dan told Lionel to remove the tape and relocate Larry and company to another room until they woke up. He advised Lionel to brew some very strong coffee. Those three wouldn't be much use for the at least two hours after they woke up. When he returned to the control room Blair and Harvey had arrived.

"Here's the situation. It looks like Larry, Red and Sandy were tasered and the black box along with the operational plans were taken. We can assume that the Feds have the plans," exclaimed Dan in an angry tone.

"I can't believe that they got in and out of here without the sensors, video camera, or certainly the dogs detecting them. Obviously Larry and his folks were distracted by the phony drunk hunters.

If they got the plans, then the Feds will strike around dawn. We need to destroy the rest of the incriminating documents and be gone. I'll go to ground and assume another identity. After a few months we can regroup and figure out how to rebuild an organization."

"Well, Dan the good news is that they didn't get the plans. I took the plans home to review them the other night in case we needed to make revisions," replied Blair. "The bad news is that they took some documents that reflect our purchases of huge quantities of explosives and preliminary plans for creating havoc in shopping malls and other public places. I don't believe that Harvey and I can go back to business as usual either.

We're all going to have to go to ground as you put it no matter what we do. By the way our building security expert, Larry Ellison, had the dogs penned up and out of the picture.

The fact that he allowed his people to be fooled by the phony distraction is enough to warrant shooting him here and now for incompetence."

"I'll deal with him later. Right now we need to get busy and figure out if we can implement some of plans on short notice, then get the hell out of here before dawn.

While the Feds are dealing with firestorms in a few cities, we can make our way to a sanctuary I know about in Canada. We have enough funds in those secret offshore accounts to last us for quite a while. Once all the fury has died down we can reestablish ourselves elsewhere in the States and begin planning for Phase II of the operation."

Harvey decided that it was time to bring these two back from fantasy land.

"I don't think that we have time to implement anything. None of our people are in place and the trucks aren't near ready to be deployed. You're fooling yourselves if you think that we can pull this off in the next few hours. It's impossible. I say burn the place down and high tail it to Canada. We need to learn from the mistakes that Maury made. There simply isn't enough time."

"Well, Harvey I have to agree you're partially correct. Four of the five cities aren't near ready for the full scale attack, but one is", replied Dan.

"Our assets are ready in Kansas City. My recommendation is that we implement the full strike in Kansas City and hit the secondary targets in the other four cities. We can raise a lot of havoc in shopping malls and other public places."

"I agree with Dan. If we do nothing, we'll lose creditability with our membership and have failed in our mission," said Blair.

"The federal government will have prevailed again. I will not allow that to happen.

If we strike now it will weaken the government. The general public will know that we can strike anywhere at any time. The seed that we want to plant in every American mind is that it's not safe anywhere and their government cannot protect them.

I suggest that you think very carefully Harvey before you abandon the mission. Dan is replacing Maury in the hierarchy. Remember what happened to Maury?"

"How is it possible that our assets in Kansas City are ready much less anywhere else?" exclaimed Harvey. "You forget that I'm the only person who has knowledge and authorization to issue the implementation codes. If I don't issue the codes nothing happens. I have issued nothing, so Kansas City can't be ready to strike."

"Well, as much as I dislike deflating your ego Harvey, I'm afraid you forgot one important concept. Did you ever hear of redundancy? Maury and I discussed the issue on several occasions before his untimely death. He decided to give me the codes for safe keeping only to be used in case something untimely happened to you before we were ready to implement the operational plan. I have contacted our assets in Kansas City yesterday, and they assured me that they were ready for a full blown attack. As you can see no one in this organization is indispensable. I suggest you be ready to carry out your part of this mission or face the consequences."

Harvey was stunned. His Ace had just been trumped. That damn Maury had compromised him, after all that he had done for him. He could feel a huge ice cube in the pit of his stomach. None of them would get out of this thing alive. He felt Blair's cold stare on his back, and expected her to pull out her weapon and shoot him in the temple. After a few minutes nothing had happened.

"Alright, I know when I'm whipped. Count me in. Tell me what you want done, and I'll issue the procedures to the teams."

***

1:15 am

"Let's take a look and see what's in that black box," said Lisa. "There could be something that'll give us a clue as to their plans."

Abe, Jacob, Sheriff Terry, Lisa, Agent Henderson and Bob Lattimore gathered around the coffee table as Lisa emptied the contents of the black box on the table. Several of the documents pertained to the organizational structure of the Sons and Daughters and certain logistics matters; however a CD was buried within one of the documents.

The contents of the CD discussed the purchase, delivery, repainting and deployment of five GMC vehicles disguised as UPS vans and five Chevy Cobalts. A second document talked about the selection and training of teams to be deployed to five selected cities.

The teams were to be trained in the use of explosives and automatic weapons as well as fire team maneuvers.

The third document discussed the purpose of the mission which was to disrupt government operations in five selected cities and cause major damage and destruction in shopping malls and other public places in order to convince the American public that their government could no longer protect them. The attacks would continue on an escalated basis causing general panic and chaos.

The forth document discussed the aftermath. The Sons and Daughters organization would step in and establish home guard units of volunteers which would be composed of their own members. The attacks and violence would seize in those communities where the home guard set up and patrolled the area. After a period of time the home guard and the Sons and Daughters would gain public support because of their ability to control the violence. The organization would sponsor candidates for public office who after elected to Congress would follow the organization's agenda to drastically decrease the size and scope of the federal and state government. Once the organization gained sufficient control of Congress and State Governments, they would manage to downsize government and the mission would be accomplished.

Jacob summarized the information.

"Apparently, their theory behind this whole scheme is that the public feels powerless to control their government and will not take any action unless their personal lives are at stake. It's only when there is a major crisis that any real change is possible. The Sons and Daughters planned to manufacture and control the crisis and through that effort accomplish their mission which is to limit the power of government.

Unfortunately many people die in the process, but every great cause must have sacrifices according to this document. Whoever invented the idea of acceptable collateral damage ought to be shot. Didn't these people ever hear of a ballot box for Christ sake?

The sacrifice that they mention is to satisfy their own egos. I admit that they're partially right. It does take a major upheaval in this country to bring about any real change in government, but I draw the line when it comes to killing innocent civilians."

Mari Denton, Martin Parrish and Elaine Myers didn't deserve to die for this bullshit," stated Abe.

"My, my we do get passionate at times don't we," chided Lisa.

"I'm sorry, but I've never seen you this worked up before. It suits you well."

"There is a fifth document. It's an option paper that lists five cities as potential targets. The only thing missing is a timetable. The cities are: Austin, Texas; Kansas City, Missouri; Denver, Colorado; Philadelphia, Pennsylvania; and Seattle, Washington. If they follow the pattern of Oklahoma City, then they're probably planning to attack a federal building with explosives. Based on what's in the other documents they're planning some type of attack on shopping malls and other public places with automatic weapons and explosives using fire teams.

I need to alert the strike team immediately. I imagine that they know that we have the black box by now. Either they're going to cut and run or try to implement at least a portion of the plan. I'd sure like to know what part of the plan can be activated."

"I'm going to notify my deputies to cordon off the area around the Red Barn," said Sheriff Terry. "We can at least place road blocks on all the roads around that area. Lisa, can we get some of your folks to help?"

"No problem Sheriff. I'll make the call right now."

"Well, I've been discerning a couple of documents that I obtained from the storage vault that maybe of some value," remarked Jacob.

"That's a term by the way favored by my colleague. One document apparently penned by none other than the late Maury Williams is a hit list with the names of the people assigned to carry out each activity. Dan Sexton's responsibility was to install the explosives that killed Martin Parrish. Harvey Bacon was assigned to dispose of Mari Denton, and our own darling Blair Logan had the task of running down Elaine Myers. I can't believe the conceit of these people to keep such a list around.

The other document is a map of an escape tunnel running from the basement of the Red Barn to an encampment about a mile and a half away. I deduce that's the route that our principles will take once they've done what they're going to do. Unbelievably stupid to leave this kind of information around don't you think? You may want to reference this piece of information Sheriff when you set up your perimeter.

"Here's what I think is going to happen," continued Jacob. "Whatever they've been planning wasn't scheduled for implementation for a couple of weeks; hence they can't pull off a full scale attack in all five cities in the next few hours. My guess is that it would take them at a minimum three full days to go full scale operational. They know that we're coming after them probably at dawn. I expect that they'll opt for a possible launch on a federal building in one city that is closest which would be Kansas City. The fire teams are trained and ready and probably can go into action at a moment's notice. That will be the real danger in all five cities.

If I were you Agent Henderson, I'd get on the horn to the big boys and tell them to contact the Governors in each of those states that have cities targeted and tell them to call out the National Guard immediately. Law enforcement is going to be stretched thin and will need all the help they can get.

 I'd shut down every federal building and shopping mall possible and have patrols out covering any public function where large crowds may be gathering. These folks want to scare the shit out of the people by killing large numbers of folks. We can't let that happen."

"Well, I'm not sure that we can shut down the shopping malls unless the Governor is willing to implement Marshall Law which in some cases they may not. The Guard can sure as hell patrol them however," replied Henderson.

"Do they want the massive deaths of thousands of people on their heads, particularly after they've been warned of a potential threat?" remarked Jacob.

"All I can do is try. That's all I'm saying," retorted Henderson.

"Well, do what you can to scare the shit out of the Feds," offered Abe. "Play to their political sense which is the only sense most of them have. Tell them that their popularity may go in the shitter if the Sons and Daughters pull this thing off."

***

2:00 am

FBI Director Carlson was in a quandary. It was one of those damned if you do or damned if you don't situations. Carlson hated those situations with a passion. That son of bitch cowboy Henderson had the agency in another damn mess. The Director thought that reassigning Henderson to the sticks in Kansas City would keep him from getting the agency involved in any controversy. Leave it to Henderson to find trouble and to stumble into a domestic terrorist plot. It was bad enough that the Director was awoken from a sound sleep, but then to find out that all hell was about to break loose in five states made Carlson wish that he'd never taken this fuckin job.

He knew that his intelligence unit had fallen down on the job by not taking this Sons and Daughters organization seriously. For Christ sake the group had been running around the country buying up high grade explosives right under their God Damn noses! If he got through this debacle, he was damn sure going to shake up that unit and fire some folks.

The immediate question was what action to take. He knew that he had two choices.

He could pass all the information on to Homeland Security and let that asshole Foster deal with it, or he could call the President directly and tell him that he needed to federalize the Guard and declare a National Emergency in those five states.

He knew that Henderson had been right in his assessment of the situation, although there were legal issues that would have to be dealt with later. Henderson should have never let those two civilians break into that facility and take those documents without a search warrant, but then he hadn't known that those two were going to do that until after the fact. The fact was that they didn't have time for legal niceties. If Henderson's information was correct, thousands of their fellow citizens would be slaughtered before the day ended.

Before his transfer, Henderson had always provided accurate analysis and information on any assignment that he had undertaken. Bob Henderson's problem was the methods that he used in implementing a solution to a problem. He had a knack for short circuiting agency protocol.

His approach was to kick ass and take names later which didn't always endear him to his superiors, his law enforcement brethren, nor the legal staff not to mention any political leaders involved. In fact this President had heard Henderson's name mentioned once too often in a negative fashion by his political friends which had prompted the transfer.

Carlson wasn't about to pass this on to Homeland Security. Ronald Foster, the head of HS, would want to confirm every piece of information and would probably balk at the manner in which the information was gathered.

Then he would want to call a meeting of all the principle law enforcement agencies, both state and federal, to access the threat and determine the correct course of action which would most certainly lead to appointing a multi-agency task force. By that time thousands of innocent citizens would be dead and most probably several federal building would be bombed out shells not to mention the panic in the streets of the five cities.

Of course he would point the finger at Carlson and blame him and the FBI for the tardiness of his information and the failure of his intelligence unit to uncover the plot earlier and follow proper procedures.

Foster had been a politician all his adult life and had no clue what the term preserve and protect really meant. Sometimes one had to make quick critical and unpopular choices to preserve life. That was not in a politician's lexicon. All Foster's answers to problems were political in nature and rarely factored in real danger to the public. Foster's main concern was who came out on top in the eyes of the President.

Carlson would call the President and warn him of the imminent danger to those five cities and their citizens and advise him on a course of action to limit the destruction. It would be up to the President to act. If he wanted to call Foster that was his choice. Carlson called the Attorney General, his boss, and got immediate approval to call the President. The AG hated Foster.

If the President and Foster failed to act, they would be responsible for the deaths of all those folks not the FBI. The FBI had done its job. Carlson could live with that even though it would probably get him fired.

2:30 am

Eric Stiles received a phone call from Sheriff Terry instructing him to track down Dan Sexton. Eric had a fairly good idea where Dan would set up his camp. Eric did not relish the idea of tracking down his old friend and comrade in arms, but he knew that there was much more at stake here than old friendships. Dan was not the same person that he used to know. He had taken up a cause that threatened the very existence of the country that they had sworn to defend.

2:45 am

Agent Henderson reported that the Director had placed a call to the President and warned him of the imminent threat and advised him to mobilize the National Guard in those five states. Henderson said that the FBI Strike Force would be in place by 4:00 am.

Agent Henderson, Abe, Jacob, Lisa and Sheriff Terry headed to the assembly area to meet up with the strike force unit.

Sheriff Terry had set up road blocks on all roads leading out of the Red Barn area, but he doubted that would be the avenue of escape for Dave, Blair, and Harvey. He was counting on Eric to find the encampment at the end of the tunnel.

"What if the President doesn't act?" queried Lisa.

"Then we're going to have a bloody mess on our hands, and the President will be unlikely to serve a second term and he knows it. Unfortunately, that's probably the deciding factor that will compel him to act," replied Bob Henderson.

"Self-preservation always seems to be the bottom line with politicians," stated Jacob Grant. "We are digging ourselves a huge hole with this 'every person for themselves' routine.

People need to wake up and realize that we have to depend on each other if we're going to survive this threat of terrorism, both domestic and foreign."

"Sometimes I think that we're becoming a nation of self-indulgent fools," said Abe. "Everyone wants their fifteen minutes of fame from politicians to preachers to spoiled rich no talent brats to pimple headed kids wielding guns in schools to settle a score and even criminals for Christ sake. Everyone wants to feed the media machine. It's no wonder that Facebook and Twitter have become popular. It's another way to stroke your own ego. The truth is that it does usually take a major disaster like a depression; a major war or a terrorist attack to get people in touch with what's really important in this life. It's a sad commentary."

"What concerns me is how people will react if this group pulls off at least part of their plan," remarked Lisa. "Are we going to see wholesale panic and nothing but finger pointing from public officials and politicians? I hate to think what would have happened if the Sons and Daughters were able to implement their entire plan. Would the public have responded as the group anticipated? That's the scary part to me. I'd like to think that the general public and their elected leaders would rally against such violence, but I'm not certain that would be the case."

"That's a damn good question," replied Sheriff Terry. "There was a time when I would have had confidence in public reaction to such a crisis. Now I'm not so sure.

There is so much misinformation out there that it's unbelievable. Everything seems to be based on rumor and innuendo. Even the so-called respected media report rumor as fact. There was a time when news stories had to be checked out and substantiated. Not anymore. It all seems to be about ratings and audience share.

The only encouraging sign is that at least after Oklahoma City and 9/11 people did seem to come together and support the victims. Unfortunately, as you say it takes a major disaster. I guess that there is no real answer to your question Lisa until after the fact."

"I reckon that when this day is done we'll have your answer Lisa," remarked Jacob.

A few minutes later they arrived at the staging area for the strike force. Since Sheriff Terry had already issued the initial warrant for the arrest of Dan Sexton, he was designated the lead person for the raid. The FBI became involved based on the fact that Sexton was wanted for kidnapping folks and transporting them across state lines for the purpose of committing homicide.

***

3:30 am

Harvey Bacon sent coded messages to all fire teams to commence action at 9:35 am CST today on all predetermined targets. The explosives team in Kansas City was to park the UPS van next to the Richard Bolling Federal Building at 9:25 am and detonate the bomb at 9:30 am CST.
Dan Sexton instructed the Barn's Security Team to defend the Red Barn and delay the strike team entry as long as possible. He told them that he, Blair, and Harvey would be leaving shortly for an undisclosed destination and would contact them when possible.

What the security team didn't know was that they were being abandoned. Blair had completed the transfer of all the organization's monetary assets to a secret numbered account in the Caribbean and deleted all financial and incriminating information from the computer files. She had stowed away all essential sensitive documents in her briefcase.

Harvey Bacon couldn't believe that it had come to this. Shortly, he would become a wanted fugitive. He assumed that his wife of ten years would divorce him and probably sell their home; however he knew that she would not be lacking for financial resources since she had her own substantial inheritance.

Their marriage was a joke anyway, and he knew that she had several affairs in the past few years according to the detective that he had hired to follow her. Of course he hadn't been a virtuous husband either.

His only regret was that he would miss his son and the times that they spent together. Unfortunately, his son would suffer from his father's infamy.

Harvey wasn't sure how things would play out with Blair and Dan. He had a feeling that his usefulness to them was on thin ice. Once they were away from the area, he would slip away from them and go his own way. He had created a whole new identity and his own secret financial resources were stowed away in a Swiss Bank Account.

As they made their way toward the tunnel entrance Blair was almost giddy. Blair felt that she had finally found the man she'd been looking for in Dan Sexton. He was intelligent man of action. He knew how to survive in any environment. She was about to embark on a new life full of risks and adventure. Their attack on the federal government would become infamous and be the touchstone for future activity. Blair was on an adrenaline high. Dan had told her that once they were clear of the area they needed to get rid of Harvey. Blair said that she would take care of it.

Dan Sexton had his own plans. After Blair had provided him information on the off shore financial accounts, he would dispose of her. Dan had no emotional attachments to anyone, except his son Teddy. He knew that Blair Logan had used him to get what she wanted, and he had used her to get next to the financial accounts. Frankly, he despised her and her crude behavior, and it turned his stomach when they had sex.

Dan had always liked Betty because of her kindness and her gentle ways. Although he married her, as hard as he tried his emotional engine had been traumatized by his experiences in combat and dulled his senses. He simply couldn't give her the kind of love that she needed. He was grateful to her for giving him a son.

Dan was like Blair in that they used people like disposable tools to get what they wanted. Once they lost their usefulness they had no need for them. Teddy was different, because Teddy was a part of him. If Dan had ever loved anyone it was his son. He would set up a trust account for his son's education from the financial accounts under his control. Other than his son, Dan's only love was black ops.

He was planning on sending anonymous monthly checks to Betty as financial support, but he knew that she probably wouldn't accept them. He knew Betty well enough to know that she would probably move out of state and establish a new life for herself and her son.

Dan would keep track of them. After a few years had passed Dan would resurface in another country and establish himself as a hired assassin. That seemed to be the only trade that he was good at.

***

4:30 am

Like an eerie grey shadow a sole figure moved quietly through the wooded area in the pre-dawn morning fog and mist to the spot previously selected. Once there the figure assumed the firing position required for the task and settled in. The figure was an excellent shot and had never missed a target. The next hour was spent sighting in the weapon after factoring in the wind and terrain, slope and angle required for success. The figure knew that this would be a very satisfying kill.

***

5:00 am

Dan, Blair and Harvey jogged down the tunnel to the cave aware that in a few minutes freedom awaited them. Dan had parked the new Honda Ridgeline complete with Honda Satellite Navigational System about two hundred feet from the encampment area. The vehicle had been purchased in Lincoln, Nebraska under his new identity Caleb Purcell. Dan's men had carved a brush trail from the site to a point on Highway 61 thirty five miles away which would be well outside the twenty five mile perimeter set up by the Sheriff and the Strike Force. There would be no roadblock to confront them.

***

5:10 am

The Strike Force composed of FBI agents, several Sheriff's deputies who weren't on road block duty, and the Wheaton SWAT team was in place and ready.

The roadblocks were maintained for a twenty five mile radius by Sheriff's deputies and patrolmen from the Wheaton Police Force. Eric Stiles reported in that he had been unable to locate Dan's encampment as yet.

"Okay, Sheriff," said Agent Henderson. "We're ready when you are!"

"Tell your men to hold their fire until I give the word," replied Sheriff Terry. "I'm sure that they're aware of our presence. If not, they're damn idiots."

Sheriff Terry was concerned about the tunnel. If Dan, Blair and Harvey had already made their way to the tunnel, they could be long gone by the time he found the entrance. He was sure they had alerted their fire teams by now.

"Have you heard anything from your headquarters about mobilization, Agent Henderson?" asked Lisa Hamel.

"Not yet. The last I heard was the President had called a meeting of his top security advisors including the Homeland Security Director. If this gets tossed to him, we may have a real bloody mess on our hands."

5:15 am

President Lawrence David Morse was not in a good humor. His normally sunny and smiling disposition had been obliterated by the news of imminent danger to five American cities by a group of malcontent wackos. He had been awoken from a sound sleep by the FBI Director with the disturbing news.

If it weren't for the fact that he admired Director Carlson for his intelligence, accuracy and thoroughness, he might have just tossed the ball to Foster at Homeland Security and gone back to bed. The fact was that he really didn't like Ronald Foster. President Morse had appointed him to the Homeland Security post to appease party leaders. Larry Morse was no fool. He knew that Foster was nothing more than a political animal despite his prior experience on the National Security Council and as an advisor to two other Presidents. Foster was a kiss ass and Larry Morse couldn't stand kiss asses.

The Security Council meeting had just adjourned, and President Morse was not pleased with the advice proffered by Homeland Security. Director Foster kept insisting that the information provided by Director Carlson was sketchy and unconfirmed from his intelligence sources in the area. Foster's intelligence unit had reported that the Sons and Daughters were a benign organization without the capability or resources to pull off such an attack.

There was no solid evidence that the Sons and Daughters had actually acquired the explosives or arms necessary to carry out such an attack. What made Foster's arguments less credible was the fact that he kept insisting that the organization was located in Western Nebraska and not Kansas according to his intelligence sources. Foster wanted to form a multi-agency task force to assess the information further.

Director Carlson managed to silence Foster when he provided documented evidence that the Sons and Daughters were in fact chartered as a non-profit organization with headquarters in Wheaton, Kansas and had in fact purchased large quantities of explosives and arms not to mention vehicles under several different third parties. That information had been faxed an hour ago from Agent Henderson to Carlson. The Director didn't mention how the information had been acquired.

President Morse was convinced and was not about to let his administration go down the tubes under a hail of bullets and bombs that would leave thousands of their fellow citizens dead.

The President ordered his Chief of Staff to get the Governors of those five states on a conference call immediately in order for him to brief them on what was about to happen in the targeted cities.

He would request that the Governors air public announcements beginning immediately in those five cities warning citizens to stay at home and away from shopping malls, schools and public places and mobilize all law enforcement agencies. He had ordered the cabinet members who had agencies with federal offices in the Kansas City, Missouri area and the other four cities to contact their staffs and tell them under no circumstances should they go to work. They should consider it a day of paid leave.

The President told the Pentagon to immediately federalize and deploy the National Guard Units in those five states and ordered the Missouri and Kansas Units in the Kansas City area to cordon off all federal buildings in Kansas City, Missouri and detain any suspicious vehicles especially vans with UPS markings. Units in all the five states were to patrol all shopping malls, all schools and as many public facilities as feasible. Action was to commence at 0700 hours EST.

The President's Communications Director contacted the media outlets to let them know that the President would be making an urgent emergency announcement at 8:00 am EST from the Oval Office.

This President would act decisively for once.

***

5:30 am

Agent Henderson was elated.

"Well, for once they got it right," he said. "The President is federalizing the National Guard, notifying the five governors involved to mobilize their law enforcement agencies, and will be patrolling all federal buildings, shopping malls, schools and other public places in those five cities commencing at 7:00 am EST. They will warn everyone to stay home. All federal buildings will be closed in the five targeted cities, and public announcements will be broadcast declaring a national emergency. The President is scheduled to go on the air at 8:00 am EST with his announcement from the oval office which will be covered by all media outlets."

"Thank God," said Lisa. "For once we have some folks with some common sense."

"Your Director must have been very persuasive," remarked Abe.

"Yes, I believe he was," replied Henderson.

"We still need to get in there and stop those three folks from escaping," said Abe. "They've already killed enough innocent people."

"Time to go to work," said Sheriff Terry. "Get me the bull horn."

One of the FBI agents passed the bull horn to Sheriff Terry who then flipped the switch.

"This is Sheriff Ray Terry of Madison County. I have an active warrant for the arrest of Daniel J Sexton. There is a FBI Strike Force surrounding your facility that includes members of the FBI, Madison County Sheriff's office and the Wheaton Police Department SWAT team. All roads in and out of the area are blocked. I highly recommend that you throw down your weapons and come out the East door of the building with your hands high in the air. Otherwise we will be required to assault your building with deadly force. You have two minutes to comply starting now!"

Abe was impressed. He could understand why Sheriff Terry kept getting reelected. There was no question that he meant business.

Almost immediately Larry Ellison appeared in the East doorway.

"Dan Sexton is not here. This is a private property and an non-profit organization. We are under orders to defend this facility, and we intend to follow our orders. "

"So be it," replied Sheriff Terry in a guff voice. "You have sixty seconds starting now to throw down your weapons and come out or we open fire."

Ellison slammed the East door shut and twenty five security personnel opened up small arms fire in the direction of the sheriff.

Sheriff Terry quickly ducked behind the Strike Forces' Armored Command vehicle and called for the Strike Force to open fire using the rocket launchers.

The Strike Force had readied two FGM-148 Javelin Hand Held Rocket Launchers complete with conventional weapons grade missiles. Two missiles were launched at the Southeast corner and center of the building and quickly blew away one quarter of the Red Barn killing twelve security staff including Sandy Lindell, Red Mason and Lionel Sully.

Sheriff Terry quickly called for a seize fire as a white flag appeared from the gaping hole left in the building. What was left of the Security Staff started filing out of what used to be the East door with their hands in the air. No one was armed.

"Lisa, why don't you have your intelligence unit hit the storage vault and the computer system if it's still working and see if they can find any additional information including where the damn tunnel is," said Sheriff Terry.

Jacob pulled a bruised and bloody Larry Ellison aside and asked him about the tunnel, but Ellison had no knowledge of any tunnel connecting to the outside. In fact he looked extremely surprised when the question was posed to him.

Ellison had a sinking feeling that he and his men had been left to twist slowly in the wind.

Abe, Jacob, Agent Henderson, Sheriff Terry, and Lisa quickly descended the stairs to the basement and began searching for a false wall or trap door that would lead to a tunnel.

***

6:00 am

Blair Logan was the first to reach the ladder leading up to the trap door in the floor of the cave. Harvey and Dan quickly followed. Dan had purposefully brought up the rear in case someone from the Strike Force had stumbled onto the tunnel and was in hot pursuit of them. Dan had his AK-47 hanging loosely across his shoulder in case he had to use it.

Blair climbed the ladder and popped open the trap door and pulled herself onto the floor of the cave. Harvey came next and then Dan. Dan bolted the trap door in case they had been followed. He picked up Blair's briefcase.

Blair took a satisfying breath. "Freedom at last!" she exclaimed.

"We aren't home free yet," murmured Harvey.

"Harvey, quit being so negative," mocked Blair. "You're lucky you're getting out of this thing with your ass intact."

"I'll feel better when we're on that charter to Canada," retorted Harvey.

"Okay you two cut the squabbling," demanded Dan. "Let's get a move on it before those Feds find this tunnel."

Blair move to the entrance to the cave and began walking toward where the Honda was parked. She turned to say something to Harvey when a bright red spot appeared on her forehead right between the eyes. The back of her head and most of her hair blew backward.

"That bullet is from Elaine"......whispered the grey form laying prone a hundred yards away.

Harvey froze as fear began to creep up his spine. A red spot appeared on his left temple, and his head exploded like a pumpkin.

"That bullet is from Mari".......whispered the form again.

Dan knew instantaneously what was happening. That traitorous son of a bitch was his only thought. Dan's training had taught him to dive for cover. He hit the ground and scrambled behind a rather thick elm tree. He wasn't sure where the shooter was but his instincts told him that he was safe for the moment.

Dan smiled to himself. He had planned for all contingencies as he always did. There was no doubt in his mind that the Honda was rigged to blow the minute he turned the key. He had bought a second vehicle that was parked in the opposite direction of the Honda. It was an all-terrain vehicle.

He had packed it with all the essentials and covered it with brush. Redundancy was always necessary in any operation. Since he still had Blair's briefcase, he had access to the off shore financial accounts.

Dan stood very still for several minutes to see if he could detect any movement in the area. He doubted that he would hear anything. Dan moved very quickly to another tree on his left, then began circling away from the Honda. After about fifteen minutes of careful movement he located his vehicle and moved cautiously toward it. He slowly removed the brush. He then crawled under the vehicle to inspect for any planted bombs and found none. He moved around to the driver's side, opened the door and looked under the dash. Nothing. He popped the hood and quickly checked the engine. Again nothing.

He quickly closed the hood, jumped onto the driver's seat and cranked the engine. The vehicle started and idled smoothly. He allowed it to run for several seconds. When Dan was satisfied he hit the gas pedal and began to move away from the area.

The grey figure raised up and aimed his heat seeking missile right at the center of the cab..........."and this missile is from Martin Parrish"..............he whispered again.

The all-terrain vehicle and Dan Sexton glowed as a bright cloud of orange and disintegrated immediately into a thousand tiny pieces scattered across the floor of the forest.

After trees and rocks rattled and several small fires blazed as the nearby animals scurried away, the forest once again became silent. The lone grey figure moved quickly and silently away from the area. The figure went into the cave unbolted the trap door and quietly left.

***

6:35 am

Abe knew as he descended the stairs that the three fugitives had too much of a lead on them. They would probably be long gone from the area by the time Abe and the others found the tunnel entrance and made it to the encampment. His only hope was the roadblocks. If Eric had been able to find the encampment, then they might have had a chance.

He hated the thought that the folks that had ended the lives of Mari, Elaine, and Martin might never be caught. If they did manage to escape, Abe knew that he could not rest until he managed to find them. That's just the way Abe was. He would never give up until justice was served.

"Hey, over here," yelled Jacob. "Looks like I found a trap door that leads to somewhere. Get me some light over here."

Sheriff Terry, Abe, Agent Henderson and Lisa all converged on the West wall. Jacob pulled the trap door open, and Sheriff Terry shined his flashlight into the opening.

"Sure enough there's the ladder that goes down to a small room," said the Sheriff. "I think that we've found the tunnel."

The Sheriff went down the ladder first, followed by Abe, Lisa, Agent Henderson, and Jacob. The tunnel itself looked to be about seven feet from floor to ceiling and about six feet wide. It had been well constructed with ceiling beams and supports and was even lighted by a string of lights that ran along the left wall.

"I reckon that they've already made it to the end of the tunnel by now," remarked Sheriff Terry.

"I have a strong hunch that they're on the way to a confrontation with one of our roadblocks shortly. No need for all of us to go traipsing down this tunnel. One or two people ought to be enough."

"Why don't Jacob and I go," said Abe. "You, Lisa and Agent Henderson need to monitor the roadblocks and be ready to act if they hit one. When we figure out the location of the encampment will radio back and you can concentrate your resources in that direction."

"Sounds good to me," replied Sheriff Terry. "You men armed?"

"Definitely," said Jacob.

"Well, you'd better get goin then. Good Luck and don't take any unnecessary chances."

"Wouldn't think of it," replied Abe with a grin.

The Sheriff and Agent Henderson started up the ladder. Lisa came over to Abe and planted a big kiss smack on his mouth.

"Don't you dare go getting yourself killed. You're buying me dinner tonight," murmured Lisa.

She scurried up the ladder before Abe had a chance to reply.

"Don't you dare say a word Jacob Grant. Not a word."

"Me? I wasn't gonna say a thing," replied Jacob and smiled.

***

6:50 am

Abe and Jacob started off at a slow jog down the tunnel.

"What do think our chances are of catching up with those three assholes?" asked Jacob as he jogged along beside Abe.

"Not very good," replied Abe. "They've got too big of a head start. There's a slight chance that we might run into them at the encampment, but I doubt it. Could be they'll run into a roadblock and double back. If they have an all-terrain vehicle we may never catch them unless we get lucky."

"I don't like the idea of not catching them. Might have to come out of retirement and do a little tracking."

"I've had the same thoughts."

"Two trackers are better than one," replied Jacob.

"Absolutely," responded Abe.

It took about seventeen minutes to reach the end of the tunnel. They paused for a minute to catch their breath and collect their thoughts.

"Whoever goes up the ladder first stands a fifty/fifty chance of getting their head blown off," said Jacob.

"Naw, I'd say it was twenty/eighty," replied Abe. "What to flip a coin?"

"Since I'm the experienced detective in this partnership, it is best that I go first to discern what harm may lie before us."

"See I told you that word would come in handy someday. Lead on MacDuff, but when you pop the trap door I wouldn't linger at the opening. If you hear a click I'd duck back down here."

"My thoughts exactly," said Jacob. "I've had recent experience with firearms discharging in my direction. I'm well aware of the telltale sounds."

Jacob moved cautiously up the ladder, paused for a minute, then quickly gave the trap door and shove. He took a quick look around but saw or heard nothing alarming. He pulled himself out of the opening and flattened himself against the wall of the cave.

"Come on up, coast seems to be clear for the moment," he whispered to Abe.

Abe rapidly climbed the ladder, emerged from the opening and flattened himself against the wall opposite Jacob.

"Sure sounds quiet out there," said Abe. "I suspect they're long gone."

"Yeah, it's almost too quiet. I don't hear any birds chirpin or fury animals scurrying about," replied Jacob.

"Well, we're not going to find out anything standing here. I'll take the lead since I'm the professional woodsman."

"I've always believed in risk sharing. Go right ahead."

Abe edged his way forward to the cave entrance. The first thing that he spotted was the Honda Ridgeline parked about two hundred feet away. He abruptly halted and waved Jacob back. If the vehicle was still here it meant that Dan, Blair and Harvey must still be in the area.

But that made no sense. There was not one sign that anyone was nearby. He decided that he would make a run across the clearing to the tree line using a zig zag pattern to see if he drew any fire.

He whispered back to Jacob, "Their getaway vehicle is still parked outside the cave. I'm going to make a run for the tree line. Cover me. If I draw fire start shooting."

"Well make it fast and don't get yourself killed. You got a dinner date with a good looking dame, and she would never forgive you."

"I'll keep that in mind. Here goes nothing."

Abe raced across the clearing, but he only got half way when he tripped over something lying inert and went sprawling to the ground.

"Damnit! I didn't see that......well I'll be damned."

Lying across from him was what remained of Blair Logan minus the back of her head. It was apparent that some small critters had been giving her face a makeover. A few feet from her was the body of Harvey Bacon minus the right side of his head. He too had reentered the food chain. Dan Sexton was nowhere to be seen. Abe slowly got to his feet and walked to the tree line. No one shot at him. The woods were uncommonly quiet.

"Okay, Jacob come on out. It looks like we won't need to chase after Blair Logan and Harvey Bacon. Someone cancelled their travel plans rather abruptly."

Jacob saw what remained of Blair and Harvey and heaved a satisfied sigh of relief.

"Can't say they didn't get what they deserved. Better than a long drawn out trial with slick lawyers. They certainly won't be writing their memoirs from prison. How about Dan Sexton? You think he did this?"

"I can't tell for sure. But I doubt it. Not that he didn't plan something similar, but don't think he would have had the right angle to cause this damage. I'd say a very high powered rifle did this work from a distance judging from the wounds. Whoever did it was probably used hollow points."

"Well, I'd say that Dan Sexton probably planned for such a contingency and had a second vehicle stowed someplace nearby," remarked Jacob.

"Those Delta gents always try to stay two steps ahead of the game. When he saw Blair and Harvey take a hit, he probably figured the Honda was wired to blow."

"Why don't you check out the Honda," suggested Abe. "See if you can discover any faulty wiring. I want to comb the area to see if another vehicle was parked nearby."

"Alright. Give me the radio and I'll report what we found. I'd say we're about a mile and a half South and East of the Red Barn if I'm not mistaken."

"Sounds about right. I'll holler if I find something."

Abe headed off beyond the tree line. Jacob gave the Honda a quick once over but could find nothing that suggested a planted bomb. Looks like Dan outguessed himself. He called the Sheriff and reported what they had found and suspected had happened. The Sheriff said that he would send some men out to secure the area and notify roadblocks in that general vicinity to be on the alert.

Abe didn't have to journey far to see where the other vehicle had been parked and discover what remained of it and Dan Sexton. There wasn't much of Dan that hadn't disintegrated. There were a few pieces here and there, part of an arm and leg, and the remains of a skull. It was obvious that he'd been hit by something extremely powerful like maybe a missile.

Who in the hell would have a working missile out in these parts? It was hard telling in this day and age.

He walked back to where Jacob was standing beside the Honda and told him the news.

"Who in the hell would have a working missile? Must have been a hand held job. Whoever it was went three for three. They got all of them. Who do you suppose did it and why?"

"Hard to tell. We may never know. The way this thing was planned, I doubt they left any clues behind. They probably cleaned up the area including picking up the shell casings.
Could be someone in the Sons and Daughters organization who didn't like the way things were being run. It definitely had to be someone who knew the tunnel and this encampment area existed. I would bet that only Dan, Blair, Harvey, and Maury had that information; but things have a way of slipping out. If I had to guess, I'd say either Maury or Harvey told someone. Dan and Blair were pretty closed mouth about such details."

"Looks like I can go back into retirement. I wonder if they've rounded up the fire teams."

"Let's hope so. I'd hate to think that one shred of their plan got implemented."

CHAPTER 18

THE AFTERMATH

Lester Gordon couldn't believe that he'd received a phone call at 2:30 am MST with a pre-recorded message telling him to access his e-mail account. The coded email instructed him to prepare his fire teams for implementation of the operational plan commencing at 8:35 am MST that very morning. That meant that his teams would need to arrive at their designated locations in just two and a half hours to set their explosive charges and get ready for the assault. Lester wondered what had caused the timetable to be moved up so drastically. He was confident that his teams would be functional, but this was cutting it awfully close.

Lester had just moved to Denver, Colorado nine months ago and was still learning his way around the city. He would have to rely on Jeff Morton, his second in command, to get them quickly to their target. He called Jeff and told him the news. Jeff was dumbfounded to say the least. Lester told Jeff to get his ass in gear and get to his place within the hour. Lester then contacted all the other teams.

As he and Jeff traveled into the city, Lester began having some misgivings about what was happening. Traffic this early in the morning was extremely slow, and it shouldn't have been.

When he spotted a convoy of armed National Guard troops up ahead of them, Lester knew that things were not going as planned. Lester turned on the car radio to the all-news station and learned that the President of the United States was going to address the nation at 7:00 am CST on a matter of national urgency and would be declaring a national emergency. The National Guard in five states had been mobilized. It didn't take a genius to figure out the implications.

"Jeff, I would say that the time has come to abort the mission. We better contact the other teams immediately. They've mobilized the National Guard for Christ sake! I don't know about you, but I didn't sign on for any suicide mission. We can't confront that kind of fire power."

"Hey, me neither," replied Jeff. "I thought all this last minute stuff was kinda weird. We need to tell our folks to stand down."

"Yeah," said Lester. "I just heard a PA announcement telling folks to stay home and away from shopping malls and public places. They're even closing down the schools. Wonder why we haven't heard anything from Central Command?"

"Maybe there no longer is any Central Command."

"Right. Well, turn this baby around and head back to my place, while I contact the others. Maybe we'll hear something later."

And so it was in the other four cities. The fire teams had been assured that they would have the element of surprise and that there would be very little resistance in the beginning.

Apparently, that was no longer the case. None of the other teams were interested in confronting the National Guard in a fire fight. They were not religious fanatics.

In Kansas City, Missouri the UPS truck with the explosives was halted three miles from its target by alert Highway Patrol troopers and the passengers arrested on the spot. They gave up without a single shot being fired. The carefully crafted operational plan of the Sons and Daughters never got off the ground.

During the next couple of weeks most of the fire team members were rounded up and charged with conspiracy against the government and attempted homicide.

Several of the Security Guard staff including Larry Ellison were charged with homicide after their photos were identified by Teddy Sexton as having been at the scene where he witnessed the executions of former members. Ellison began singing like a bird. For all intense and purposes the Sons and Daughters organization seized to exist.

Agent Bob Henderson was transferred to the Secret Service and assigned to the protective detail for the President.

It was an assignment that he coveted. Director Carlson was cited for exemplary performance of his duties by the President and the Congress and appointed the new head of Homeland Security, as Ronald Foster was asked to resign from the government.

Although he was disappointed that they hadn't been able to apprehend Dan Sexton, Blair Logan, and Harvey Bacon, Sheriff Terry was grateful that the whole plot had been thwarted. Abe had been right. There were absolutely no clues to follow in the deaths of Blair, Harvey and Dan Sexton. Sexton had been positively identified through DNA samples as the victim in the explosion of the all-terrain vehicle. Pieces of the missile fired were identified as Army surplus.

All the documents in Blair Logan's briefcase pertaining to financial accounts and related matters had been shredded in the explosion. The FBI and the IRS were attempting to piece together information on those matters.

Sheriff Terry informed his staff that he would not run for reelection. He felt that it was time to step down and enjoy family life for a change. His wife was elated.

Eric Stiles resigned from the Sheriff's Department and moved out of state. No one knows where he went.

No family members or friends came forward to claim the remains of Blair Logan, Harvey Bacon or Dan Sexton. They were buried without ceremony at State expense.

Harvey Bacon's family sold their home and quickly moved out of state. Blair Logan's businesses were sold and the estate was claimed by the State. There were no living heirs or a will.

Betty and Teddy Sexton moved to Butte, Montana to be with her sister. Betty decided that it was the only way for them to start a new life. Eventually she married a local rancher who formally adopted Teddy. Teddy went on to study Criminology and graduated with honors. Eventually he was accepted into the FBI Academy.

The Board of Directors of the 4th National Bank asked David Peterson to resign. Peterson divorced his wife and moved to Boca Raton, Florida.

Abe Lincoln and Lisa Hamel had their dinner date and much more. The much more lasted a couple of weeks. Finally, Abe had to get back to his Lodge, and Lisa had to go back to work.

After a final debriefing from the FBI Jacob Grant gathered his belongings and headed back to the Lodge for a meeting with Miriam and Bobbi Ann Henry.

***

Bobbi Ann was unsure as to what her status would be when Abe and Jacob returned. She knew that Miriam would have some say in the matter. When she heard that Jacob was on his way back to The Lodge she was a little apprehensive about her fate. She knew that he could still turn her over to the Sheriff. Deep down inside she didn't think that he would. If he was going to do that he would have done it already.

Bobbi Ann Henry knew what she wanted to do. She had grown fond of Miriam and her life at The Lodge. She enjoyed the give and take with the guests and the easy going atmosphere. If Abe would agree to take her on as a permanent employee, Bobbi would apply for a student loan and enroll in a local Community College. If not, she would find a job similar to the work that she had been doing and pursue her education.

For the first time in her life she was seriously thinking about her future. Miriam had played a major part in helping Bobbi gain some self-confidence and self-esteem. Miriam had demonstrated to her that not everyone was playing an angle and some people can be trusted. For once in her young life she didn't feel used. She felt valued.

When she had applied herself, Bobbi had done well in school. Bobbi knew that if she was going to make a decent life for herself, she needed an education. She wasn't sure what her major would be, but she was considering teaching, nursing, or social work.

Bobbi had a strong desire to help others who had gone or were going through ordeals like hers and felt that she could draw on her past experiences to provide guidance to those who were troubled. She had come to realize that what she had tried to do to Jacob Grant was horrific.

Jacob Grant arrived at The Lodge in the early afternoon. After unpacking he huddled with Miriam in the den. Jacob spent about a half an hour recapping the events of the past few days.

"Sounds to me that you were lucky the young boy and the young lady came forward with information to expose the organization," said Miriam. "Although I realize the government is far from perfect, there are certainly more civilized ways to improve it without killing a bunch of innocent folks. I really feel sorry for the young man. It must have been very hard for him to do what he did."

"He showed a great deal of courage, that young man," replied Jacob. "It's ironic that his actions were based on what his father had taught him and drilled into him. Despite how painful it must have been, he did his duty. Not many kids his age could have done that. By the way how is our young lady doing?"

"Frankly, she's been a Godsend. She's a real worker that one, and she gets along great with our guests. Bobbi Ann has been no trouble at all.

I've sent her to town a couple of times as sort of a test, and she always comes back on time and in good spirits. I'd like to keep her on permanent, if Abe would let me."

"What does Bobbi Ann want?" asked Jacob.

"I think that she'd like to stay on, but why ask me. Why don't you go ask her?" replied Miriam.

Jacob called Bobbi Ann into the den. When she walked into the room, she seemed like a whole different person. There was a spring in her step and her whole manner seemed to display a confidence that wasn't there before.

"Miriam tells me that you've been a real help around here. In fact she'd like to keep you on permanent," said Jacob. "How would you feel about that?"

"Are you serious?" responded Bobbi Ann. "I mean after all that has happened. I mean I was a perfectly horrible person and wouldn't blame you if you wanted me gone."

"You're damn right I'm serious Bobbi Ann. What's past is past. I'm talking about right now. I'm talking about your future young lady. I know you're not going to want to stay here forever, but I can't think of a better place to restart your life."

"Mr. Grant I would like nothing better than to work here on a permanent basis. I've done a lot of thinking in the past few weeks, and I want to go back to school and get a degree. It's the only way that I can think of to repay my debt for what has happened. I really want to be able to support myself with a good job and to be of help to others who may be going through what I did."

"You can call me Jacob, Bobbi Ann. No more of this Mr. Grant crap. I'm going to call Abe right now and tell him that Miriam would like to hire you permanent, if you're sure that's what you want to do. I think that for once you're on the right track."

"I'm sure that's what I want Mr. Grant...Jacob. Maybe I have been a help to Miriam, but she's been a bigger help to me."

Jacob smiled. "I figured she would be."

Jacob called Abe and Abe immediately agreed to hire Bobbi Ann permanently. When Jacob and Miriam told her the news, Bobbi Ann gave Miriam a great big hug and walked over and kissed Jacob on the cheek. Jacob actually blushed.

CHAPTER 19

EPILOGUE

The last few decades have created the gap generations. The generations that read by bullet statements, listen to sound bites, and get the news through video clips. It is generations of young people that absorb information that is at best fragmented and at worst distorted.

The attention span of this generation has been atrophied by too much television, abbreviated blogs and twitter and their inability to learn patience and sustain thought longer than a sound bite. We haven't taught them the real values like loyalty and trust and commitment...and that the race doesn't always go to the swift but sometimes to the steady and sure. We've taught them that the only true goal in life is winning...and that place and show are disgraceful.

Mari was a victim of the gap generations. The weapon and the bullet that took her life were not the cause of her death. It was the mindless, thoughtless act of someone who needed to make a statement...a bullet point with an exclamation. She got in the crosshairs of someone's diabolical plot.

Lisa accompanied Abe to the cemetery to visit the grave site for Mari Denton. Abe placed a dozen red roses beside her headstone.

Her radio station had picked up the tab for her funeral and headstone. On the headstone were engraved the words:

Mari Beth Denton

January 29, 1980 – March 21, 2010

"We lost a star in the making and heaven gained an angel"

Abe had come full circle. He had discovered her cold still body in the early amber morning on that lonely road, and now in good conscience he could pay his final respects. What had killed her was not a disease of the body, but a disease of the soul called arrogant greed. It was the kind of greed that seeks power for the sake of power and that seeks to dominate and control others. It is an arrogance that says I know the truth and you do not and that makes you less than me. The carrier of that disease can be either secular or religious, but in all cases it is fanatical and fatal to all who claim it or suffer by it.

"It's sad to think about all the struggles that she went through in her life," said Lisa. "Then when she was about to claim her destiny her life was cut short. It's very unfair and fragile sometimes, this thing that we call life."

"Life can be very unfair, but at least she didn't wind up as a cold case in some police file" replied Abe. "If it hadn't been for Mari Beth Denton's death many more people could have died and who knows how successful Blair, Maury, and Harvey would have been. Maybe her destiny was to expose the evil that killed her. Justice sometimes works in strange ways."

"It's fortunate that you were the person who discovered her body. Not many people would have had the persistence or take the time to uncover the truth behind her death. She was lucky to have you as her champion."

"Well, if you remember correctly her champion almost got his brains handed to him. If it hadn't been for Jacob and you and Agent Henderson not to mention that brave youngster Teddy and Shelia we would have never discovered the truth. What happened to Mari, Martin, and Elaine was a terrible tragedy for sure, but what could have happened would have been so much worse in the long run and on a larger scale. Some have the nerve to call it collateral damage."

"What does collateral damage mean anyway?" questioned Lisa.

"It sounds so impersonal. They were real people who struggle to live a somewhat normal life, yet the term makes them sound almost not relevant. I hate that term. My strong belief is that every life counts and has relevance."

"That's probably why you do what you do, Lisa. It's one of the things that attracted me to you."

"Is that the only way in which we're attracted to each other?" queried Lisa coyly.

"Well, I can probably think of a few other traits, not all of them physical of course."

"Well, it's a relief to know that you don't think of me as merely a sex object."

"If I'd have thought that, I wouldn't have stayed two extra weeks."

"That's encouraging. Does that mean you'll be back this way again?"

"Damn, you're a pushy woman."

"You wouldn't have me any other way."

"That's true."

Abe pause before Mari's grave for a moment and said: "Well, Mari you can rest in peace. I feel like I'm a better person for having known you."

Abe and Lisa slowly walked back to the car hand in hand.
"Can I ask you a personal question?"

"Sure Lisa, what is it?"

"How do you deal with all the guff you seem to get with your name?"

"Simple. I ignore it. It never defines me. I just do what I do."

Abe and Lisa had a candlelight dinner that night complete with a fine merlot and a brandy later. Then they made sweet passionate love until the wee hours of the morning.

The next morning Abe had his usual breakfast of scrambled eggs, toast, and piping hot coffee. He kissed Lisa good-bye and headed for The Lodge.

After catching up on Lodge business with a briefing by Miriam, he enthusiastically welcomed Bobbi Ann on as a permanent employee. Then he and Jacob adjourned to the den.

"You know what you're going to do now?" queried Abe. "You know that you're more than welcome to stay on here. We've got plenty of room, and I think that Bobbi Ann would like you to stick around for a while."

"I hadn't really thought about it," replied Jacob. "It probably would do me good to sell the house. Everything there reminds me of the time that Beth and I had together. Not that I want to forget her. I never will, but I think that she would want me to move on with my life. I can't do that staying there for sure. As for Bobbi Ann, I'll always be around if she wants some advice from this old coot. Of course she'll probably get a lot better advice from Miriam.

Now if you have another little project in mind that requires the skill of a discerning detective I'm always available. After all you do need someone to watch your back."

"Well, I don't have anything brewing at the moment, but you never know when something might develop. Of course I can always use an experienced hunting and fishing guide. Interested?"

"I might be. I might be at that," replied Jacob.

"Then it's settled. You can move the rest of your stuff in here."

"You know, it still puzzles me as to who did the hit on Blair, Harvey, and Dan," stated Jacob. "It was obviously a professional job. Had to be to take down Dan."

"No doubt about that," said Abe. "If I'd have to guess, I'd say it could have been someone on Dan's staff who knew his habits, or maybe even Eric Stiles. You know that he resigned from the Sheriff's Department and has totally disappeared. He was Delta Force and a member of Dan's unit."

"I didn't know that," replied Jacob. "I'd say Eric's a good bet then. I had heard a rumor that he was dating Elaine Myers prior to her death. Understand that he took it pretty hard."

Later that evening alone in his study, Abe was going through his accumulated mail when he came across an envelope with no return address postmarked Denver, Colorado. It was formally addressed to Abraham Lincoln and stamped with the word Confidential in red ink.

Abe tore open the envelope and began reading the typed message:

"Justice has been served. The organization is dead, but the principles are still valid. TJ had it right. This was the preamble. The Second American Revolution has begun."

Below the inscription appeared these words with relevant sections highlighted.

"We hold these truths to be self-evident, that all men are created equal, that they are endowed by their Creator with certain unalienable rights, that among these are life, liberty and the pursuit of happiness. <u>Prudence, indeed, will dictate that governments long established should not be changed for light and transient causes;</u> and accordingly all experience hath shown that mankind are more disposed to suffer, while evils are sufferable, than to right themselves by abolishing the forms to which they are accustomed.

<u>*That to secure these rights, governments are instituted among men, deriving their just powers from the consent of the governed.*</u>

That whenever any form of government becomes destructive to these ends, it is the right of the people to alter or to abolish it, and to institute new government, laying its foundation on such principles and organizing its powers in such form, as to them shall seem most likely to affect their safety and happiness.

But when a long train of abuses and usurpations, pursuing invariably the same object evinces a design to reduce them under absolute despotism, it is their right, it is their duty, to throw off such government, and to provide new guards for their future security.

TJ would have been Thomas Jefferson and the words were culled from the Declaration of Independence.

A cold shiver went up Abe Lincoln's spine.

ACKNOWLEDGEMENT

A special note of thanks to Vicki L Jennings for the excellent job she performed in editing the text. Her efforts improved the quality of the storyline immensely.